DROWNED WEDNESDAY

A thin film of frothy water was slowly spreading across the floor, like the leading wash of a wave across the sand. It ran almost to the bed, then ebbed back.

"I can hear something," said Leaf. "Kind of like a train."

Arthur heard it too. A distant thunder that got louder and louder.

"That's not a train! Grab hold of the bed!"

Leaf grabbed the rail at the end of the bed as Arthur gripped the headboard. Both turned to look at the far wall just as it disappeared, replaced by a thundering grey-blue wave that crashed down upon them. Tons of sea water smashed everything else in the room to bits, but the bed itself was carried away by the wave.

Dazed, drenched and desperate, Arthur and Leaf hung on.

Also by Garth Nix

For a full list of titles and more information, go to:
www.garthnix.co.uk

DROWNED WEDNESDAY

GARTH NIX

ILLUSTRATED BY TIM STEVENS

HarperCollins *Children's Books*

First published in the USA by Scholastic Inc 2005
First published in Great Britain by HarperCollins*Children'sBooks* 2005
HarperCollins*Children'sBooks* is a division of HarperCollins*Publishers* Ltd
77–85 Fulham Palace Road, Hammersmith, London, W6 8JB

www.harpercollinschildrensbooks.co.uk

www.garthnix.co.uk

This production 2013

ISBN-13 978 0 00 793260 3

Printed and bound in Great Britain by
Clays Ltd, St Ives plc

To Anna, Thomas and Edward, and to
all my friends and family.

PROLOGUE

A three-masted square-rigger with iridescent green sails that shone by day or night, the *Flying Mantis* was a fast and lucky ship. She sailed the Border Sea of the House, which meant she could also sail any ocean, sea, lake, river or other navigable stretch of liquid on any of the millions of worlds of the Secondary Realms.

On this voyage, the *Flying Mantis* was cleaving through the deep blue waters of the Border Sea, heading for Port Wednesday. Her holds were stuffed with goods bought beyond the House and illnesses salvaged from the Border Sea's grasping waters. There were valuables under her hatches: tea and wine and coffee and spices, treats for the

Denizens of the House. But her strongroom held the real treasure: coughs and sniffles and ugly rashes and strange stuttering diseases, all fixed into pills, snuff or whalebone charms.

With such rich cargo, the crew was nervous and the lookouts red-eyed and anxious. The Border Sea was no longer safe, not since the unfortunate transformation of Lady Wednesday several thousand years before and the consequent flooding of the Sea's old shore. Wednesday's Noon and Dusk had been missing ever since, along with many of Wednesday's other servants, who used to police the Border Sea.

Now the waters swarmed with unlicensed salvagers and traders, some of whom would happily turn to a bit of casual piracy. To make matters worse, there were full-time pirates around as well. Human ones, who had somehow got through the Line of Storms and into the Border Sea from some earthly ocean.

These pirates were still mortal (unlike the Denizens) but they had managed to learn some House sorcery and were foolish enough to dabble in the use of Nothing. This made them dangerous, and if they had the numbers, their human ferocity and reckless use of Nothing-fuelled magic would usually defeat their more cautious Denizen foes.

The *Flying Mantis* had lookouts in the fighting tops of each of its three masts, one in the forepeak, and several on the quarterdeck. It was their task to watch for pirates, strange weather and the worst of all things – the emergence of Drowned Wednesday, as Lady Wednesday was now known.

Most of the ships that now sailed the Border Sea had incompetent lookouts and inferior crews. After the Deluge, when the Border Sea swept over nine-tenths of Wednesday's shore-based wharves, warehouses, counting rooms and offices, more than a thousand of the higher rooms had been rapidly converted into ships. All these ships were crewed by former stevedores, clerks, rackers, counters, tally-hands, sweepers and managers. Though they'd had several thousand years of practice, these Denizens were still poor sailors.

But not the crew of the *Flying Mantis*. She was one of Wednesday's original forty-nine ships, commissioned and built to the Architect's design. Her crew members were nautical Denizens, themselves made expressly to sail the Border Sea and beyond. Her Captain was none other than Heraclius Swell, 15,287th in precedence within the House.

So when the mizzentop lookout shouted, "Something big... err... not that big... closing off the port bow... underwater!" both Captain and crew reacted as well-trained professionals of long experience.

"All hands!" roared the mate who had the watch. "Beat to quarters!"

His cry was taken up by the lookouts and the sailors on deck, followed only seconds later by the sharp rattle of a drum as the ship's boy abandoned his boot polish and the Captain's boots to take up his sticks.

Denizens burst out from below decks. Some leapt to the rigging to climb aloft, ready to work the sails. Some stood by the armoury to receive their crossbows and cutlasses. Others raced to load and run out the guns, though the *Flying Mantis* only had eight working cannons of its usual complement of sixteen. Guns and gunpowder that worked in the House were very hard to come by, and always contained dangerous specks of Nothing. Since the toppling of Grim Tuesday fourteen months before, powder was in very short supply. Some said it was no longer being made, and some said it was being stockpiled for war by the mysterious Lord Arthur, who now ruled both the Lower House and the Far Reaches.

Captain Swell climbed on to the quarterdeck as the cannons rumbled out on the main deck, their red wooden wheels squealing in complaint. He was a very tall Denizen, even in stockinged feet, who always wore the full dress coat of an admiral from a small country on a small world in a remote corner of the Secondary Realms. It was turquoise blue, nipped in very tightly at the waist, and had enormous quantities of gold braid on the shoulders and cuffs. Consequently Captain Swell shone even more brightly than the green sails of his ship.

"What occurs, Mister Pannikin?" Swell asked his First Mate, a Denizen as tall as he was, but considerably less handsome. At some time Pannikin had lost all his hair and one ear to a Nothing-laced explosion, and his bare skull was ridged with scars. He sometimes wore a purple woollen cap, but the crew claimed that made him look even worse.

"Mysterious submersible approaching the port bow," reported Pannikin, handing his spyglass to the Captain. "About forty feet long by my reckoning, and coursing very fast. Maybe fifty knots."

"I see," said the Captain, who had clapped the telescope to his eye. "I think it must be... yes. Milady has sent us a messenger. Stand the men down, Mister Pannikin, and prepare a side-party to welcome our illustrious visitor. Oh, and tell Albert to bring me my boots."

Mister Pannikin roared orders as Captain Swell refocused his telescope on the shape in the water. Through the powerful lens, he could clearly see a dull golden cigar-shape surging under the water towards the ship. For a second it was unclear what propelled it so quickly. Then its huge yellow-gold wings suddenly exploded ahead and pushed back, sending the creature rocketing forward, the water behind it exploding into froth.

"She'll broach any moment," muttered one of the

crewmen to his mate at the wheel behind the Captain. "Mark my words."

He was right. The creature's wings broke the surface and gathered air instead of water. With a great flexing leap and a swirl of sea, the monster catapulted itself up higher than the *Flying Mantis*'s maintop. Shedding water like rain, it circled the ship, slowly descending towards the quarterdeck.

At first it looked like a golden winged shark, all sleek motion and a fearsome, toothy maw. But as it circled, it shrank. Its cigar-shaped body bulged and changed, and the golden sheen ebbed away before other advancing colours. It became roughly human-shaped, though still with golden wings.

Then, as its wings stopped flapping and it stepped the final foot down to the deck, it assumed the shape of a very beautiful woman, though even the ship's boy knew she was really a Denizen of high rank. She wore a riding habit of peach velvet with ruby buttons, and sharkskin riding boots complete with gilt spurs. Her straw-coloured hair was restrained by a hairnet of silver wire, and she tapped her thigh nervously with a riding crop made from the elongated tail of an albino alligator.

"Captain Swell."

"Wednesday's Dawn," replied the Captain, bending his head as he pushed one stockinged foot forward. Albert, arriving a little too late, slid along the deck and hastily tried to put the proffered foot into the boot he held.

"Not now!" hissed Pannikin, dragging the lad back by the scruff of his neck.

The Captain and Wednesday's Dawn ignored the boy and the First Mate. They turned together to the rail and looked out at the ocean, continuing to talk while hardly looking at each other.

"I trust you have had a profitable voyage to date, Captain?"

"Well enough, Miss Dawn. May I inquire as to the happy chance that has led you to grace my vessel with your presence?"

"You may indeed, Captain. I am here upon the express command of our mistress, bearing an urgent dispatch, which I am pleased to deliver."

Dawn reached into her sleeve, which was tight enough to hold no possibility of storage, and pulled out a large thick envelope of buff paper, sealed with a knob of blue sealing wax half an inch thick.

Captain Swell took the envelope slowly, broke the seal with deliberation, and unfolded it to read the letter written on the inside. The crew was quiet as he read, the only sounds the slap of the sea against the hull, the creak of the timbers, the momentary flap of a sail, and the faint whistle of the wind in the rigging.

Everyone knew what the letter must be. Orders from Drowned Wednesday. That meant trouble, particularly as they had been spared direct orders from Wednesday for several thousand years. They were almost certainly no longer going home to Port Wednesday and the few days' liberty they usually received while their precious cargo was sold.

Captain Swell finished the letter, shook the envelope, and picked up the two additional documents that fell out of it like doves from a conjurer's hat.

"We are instructed to sail to a landlocked part of the Secondary Realms," the Captain said to Wednesday's Dawn, the hint of a question in his voice.

"Our mistress will ensure the Sea extends there for the time it takes for your passenger to embark," replied Dawn.

"We must cross the Line of Storms both ways," added the Captain. "With a mortal passenger."

"You must," agreed Dawn. She tapped one of the documents with her riding crop. "That is a Permission that will allow a mortal to pass the Line."

"This mortal is to be treated as a personal guest of milady?"

"He is."

"This passenger's name will be required for my manifest."

"Unnecessary," Dawn snapped. She looked the Captain

directly in the eyes. "He is a confidential guest. You have a description, a location and specific sailing instructions drawn up personally by me. I suggest you get on with it. Unless of course you wish to challenge these orders? I could arrange an audience with Lady Wednesday if you choose."

The crew members all held their breath. If the Captain chose to see Drowned Wednesday, they'd all have to go as well, and not one of them was ready for that fate.

Captain Swell hesitated for a moment. Then he slowly saluted.

"As ever, I am at Milady Wednesday's command. Good day, Miss Dawn."

"Good day to you, Captain." Dawn's wings stirred at her back, sending a sudden breeze around the quarterdeck. "Good luck."

"We'll need it," whispered the helmsman to his mate as Dawn stepped up to the rail and launched herself in a long arcing dive that ended several hundred yards away in the sea, as she transformed back into a golden winged shark.

"Mister Pannikin!" roared the Captain, though the First Mate was only a few feet away. "Stand by to make sail!"

He glanced down at the complex sailing instructions that Dawn had given him, noting the known landmarks of the Border Sea they must sight, and the auguries and incantations required to sail the ship to the required place and time in the Secondary Realms. As was the case with all of Drowned Wednesday's regular merchant marine, the Captain was himself a Sorcerer-Navigator, as were his officers.

"Mmm... Bethesda Hospital... room 206... two minutes past the hour of seven in the evening. On Wednesday, of course," muttered the Captain, reading aloud to himself. "House time, as per line four, corresponds with the date and year in local reckoning in the boxed corner, and where... odd name for a town... never heard of that country... what will these mortals think of next... and the world..."

He flipped the parchment over.

"Hmmph. I might have known!"

The Captain looked up and across at his running, climbing, swinging, rolling, swaying, sail-unfurling and rope-hauling crew. They all stopped as one and looked at him.

"We sail to Earth!" shouted Captain Swell.

CHAPTER ONE

"What time is it?" Arthur asked after the nurse had left, wheeling away the drip he didn't need any more. His adopted mother was standing in the way of the clock. Emily had told him she'd only pop in for a minute and wouldn't sit down, but she'd already been there fifteen minutes. Arthur knew that meant she was worried about him, even though he was already off the oxygen and his broken leg, though sore, was quite bearable.

"Four-thirty. Five minutes since you asked me last time," Emily replied. "Why are you so concerned about the time? And what's wrong with your own watch?"

"It's going backwards," said Arthur, careful not to

answer Emily's other question. He couldn't tell her the real reason he kept asking the time. She wouldn't – or couldn't – believe the real reasons.

She'd think he was mad if he told her about the House, that strange building which contained vast areas and was the epicentre of the Universe as well. Even if he could take her to the House, she wouldn't be able to see it.

Arthur knew he would be going back to the House sooner rather than later. That morning he'd found an invitation under the pillow of his hospital bed, signed Lady Wednesday. *Transportation has been arranged*, it had read. Arthur couldn't help feeling it was much more sinister than the simple word '*transportation*' suggested. Perhaps he was going to be taken, as a prisoner. Or transported like a parcel...

He'd been expecting something to happen all day. He couldn't believe it was already half past four on Wednesday afternoon and there was still no sign of weird creatures or strange events. Lady Wednesday only had dominion over her namesake day in the Secondary Realms, so whatever she planned to do to him had to happen before midnight. Seven and a half hours away...

Every time a nurse or a visitor came through the door, Arthur jumped, expecting it to be some dangerous servant of Wednesday's. As the hours ticked by, he'd become more and more nervous.

The suspense was worse than the pain in his broken leg. The bone was set and wrapped in one of the new ultra-tech casts, a leg sheath that looked like the armour of a space marine, extending from knee to ankle. It was super strong, super lightweight, and had what the doctor called "nanonic healing enhancers" – whatever they were. Regardless of their name, they worked, and had already reduced the swelling. The cast was so advanced it would literally fall off his leg and turn into dust when its work was done.

His asthma was also under control, at least for the moment, though Arthur was annoyed that it had come back in the first place. He'd thought it had been almost completely cured as a side effect of wielding the First Key.

Then Dame Primus had used the Second Key to remove all the effects of the First Key upon him, reversing both his botched attempt to heal his broken leg and the Key's beneficial effect on his asthma. But Arthur had to admit it was better to have a treatable broken leg and his familiar, manageable asthma, than to have a magically twisted-up, inoperable leg and no asthma.

I'm lucky to have survived at all, Arthur thought. He shivered as he remembered the descent into Grim Tuesday's Pit.

"You're trembling," said Emily. "Are you cold? Or is it the pain?"

"No, I'm fine," said Arthur hastily. "My leg's sore but it's OK, really. How's Dad?"

Emily looked at him carefully. Arthur could see her evaluating whether he was fit enough to be told the bad news. It was bound to be bad news. Arthur had defeated Grim Tuesday, but not before the Trustee's minions had managed to interfere with the Penhaligon family finances... as well as causing minor economic upheaval for the world at large.

"Bob has been sorting things out all afternoon," Emily said at last. "I expect there'll be a lot more sorting to do. Right now it looks like we'll keep the house, but we'll have to rent it out and move somewhere smaller for a year or so. Bob will also have to go back on tour with the band. It's just one of those things. At least we didn't have all our money in those two banks that failed yesterday. A lot of people will be hurt by that."

"What about those signs about the shopping mall being built across the street?"

"They were gone by the time I got home last night, though Bob said he saw them too," said Emily. "It's quite strange. When I asked Mrs Haskell in number ten about it, she said that some fast-talking estate agent had made them to agree to sell their house. They signed a contract and everything. But fortunately there was a loophole and they've managed to get out of it. They didn't really want to sell. So I guess there'll be no shopping mall, even if the other neighbours who sold don't change their minds. The Haskell place is right in the middle, and of course, we won't be selling either."

"And Michaeli's course? Has the university still got no money?"

"That's a bit more complicated. It seems they had a lot of money with one of the failed banks, which has been lost. But it's possible the government will step in and ensure no courses are cancelled. If Michaeli's degree is discontinued, she'll have to go somewhere else. She was accepted by three... no, four other places. She'll be OK."

"But she'll have to leave home."

Arthur left another sentence unsaid.

And it's my fault. I should have been quicker to deal with the Grotesques...

"Well, I don't think she'll be too concerned about that. How we'll pay for it is a different matter. But you don't need to worry about all of this, Arthur. You always want to take too much on. It's not your responsibility. Just concentrate on getting better. Your father and I will make sure everything will be—"

Emily was cut off by a sudden alert from the hospital pager she always wore. It jangled a few times, then a line of text ran around the rim. Emily frowned as she read the scrolling message.

"I have to go, Arthur."

"It's OK, Mum, you go," said Arthur. He was used to Emily having to deal with gigantic medical emergencies. She was one of the most important medical researchers in the country. The sudden attack and then abrupt cessation of the Sleepy Plague had given her a great deal of extra work.

Emily gave her son a hurried kiss on the cheek and a good luck rap of her knuckles on the foot of the bed. Then she was gone.

Arthur wondered if he'd ever be able to tell her that the Sleepy Plague had come from Mister Monday's Fetchers, and had been cured by the Nightsweeper, a magical intervention he'd brought back from the House. Though he had brought back the cure, he still felt responsible for the plague in the first place.

He looked at his watch. It was still going backwards.

A knock on the door made him sit up again. He was as ready as he could be. He had the Atlas in his pyjama pocket, and he'd twisted numerous strands of dental floss together so he could hang the Captain's medallion around his neck. His dressing gown was on the chair next to the bed, along with his Immaterial Boots, which had disguised themselves as slippers. He could only tell what they really were because they felt slightly electric and tingly when he picked them up.

The knock was repeated. Arthur didn't answer. He knew that Fetchers – the creatures who had pursued him on Monday – couldn't cross a threshold without permission. So he wasn't going to say a word – just in case.

He lay there silently, watching the door. It slowly opened a crack. Arthur reached across to the bedside table and picked up a paper packet of salt he'd kept from his lunch, ready to tear it open and throw it if a Fetcher peered around.

But it wasn't a dog-faced, bowler-hatted creature. It was Leaf, his friend from school, who had helped save him from a Scoucher the day before, and who had been injured herself.

"Arthur?"

"Leaf! Come in!"

Leaf closed the door behind her. She was wearing her normal clothes: boots, jeans and a T-shirt with an obscure band logo. But her right arm was bound from elbow to wrist in white bandages.

"How's your arm?"

"Sore. But not too bad. The doctor couldn't figure out what made the cuts. I told him I never saw what the guy hit me with."

"I suppose he wouldn't believe the true story," said Arthur, thinking about the shape-changing Scoucher and its long, razor-tendrilled arms.

"What *is* the true story?" asked Leaf. She sat down on the visitor's chair and looked intently at Arthur, making him uncomfortable. "I mean, all I know is that last week you were involved in some weird stuff with dog-faced guys, and it got even weirder this week, when you suddenly appeared in my living room on Monday with a kind of history girl who had... wings. You ran up the bedroom stairs and vanished. Then yesterday, you came racing into my yard with a monster chasing after you, which could easily have killed me, only it got... destroyed... by one of my dad's old silver medals. Then you had to run off again. Then today I hear you're in the next ward with a broken leg. What's going on?"

Arthur opened his mouth, then hesitated. It would be a great relief to tell Leaf everything. At least she could see the Denizens of the House, when no one else could. Perhaps, as she'd claimed, it was because her great-grandmother had possessed second sight. But telling Leaf everything might also put her in danger.

"Come on, Arthur! I need to know," urged Leaf. "What if one of those Scoucher things comes back to finish me off? Or something else. Like one of those dog-faces. I've got a couple of Dad's medals for the Scouchers, but what do I do about the dog-faces?"

"Fetchers," Arthur said slowly. He held up the paper

sachet. "The dog-faces are called Fetchers. Throw salt on them."

"That's a good start," said Leaf. "Fetchers. Where do they come from? What do they want?"

"They're servants," Arthur explained. He started to talk faster and faster. It was such a relief to tell somebody about what had happened. "Creatures made from Nothing. The ones you saw were in the service of Mister Monday. He is... was one of the seven Trustees of the House—"

"Hang on!" Leaf interrupted. "Slow down. Start at the beginning."

Arthur took a deep breath, as deep as his lungs allowed, and started at the beginning. He told Leaf about his encounter with Mister Monday and Sneezer. About Monday's Noon pursuing him through the school library with his flaming sword. He told her how he got into the House the first time, and how he met Suzy Turquoise Blue and the First Part of the Will, and the three of them together had ultimately defeated Mister Monday. How he'd brought back the Nightsweeper to cure the Sleepy Plague, and how he'd thought he would be left alone till he grew up, only to have that hope dashed by Grim Tuesday's Grotesques, whose appearance had led to his return to the House, his descent into the Pit, and his eventual triumph over Grim Tuesday.

Leaf occasionally asked a question, but most of the time

she just sat there, taking in everything Arthur had to say. Finally, he showed her the cardboard invitation from Lady Wednesday. She took it and read it several times.

"I wish I had adventures like you do," Leaf said as she traced her finger over the writing on the invitation.

"They didn't feel like adventures," said Arthur. "I was too scared most of the time to actually enjoy anything or get excited about it. Weren't you scared by the Scoucher?"

"Sure," Leaf said, with a glance at her bandaged arm. "But we survived, didn't we? That makes it an adventure. If you get killed it's a tragedy."

"I could do without any more adventures for a while." Arthur thought Leaf would agree with him if she'd had the same experiences. They sounded much more exciting and safer just as stories. "I really just want to be left alone!"

"They're not going to leave you alone, though." Leaf held up Wednesday's invitation, then flipped it over to Arthur, who put it back in his pocket. "Are they?"

"No," Arthur agreed, resignation all through his voice. "The Morrow Days aren't going to leave me alone."

"So what are you going to do to them?" said Leaf.

"What do you mean?"

"Well, since they won't leave you alone, you'd better get in first. You know, attack is the best form of defence."

"I suppose..." said Arthur. "You mean I shouldn't wait for whatever Wednesday is going to do, but go back into the House now?"

"Yeah, why not? Get together with your friend Suzy, and the Will, and work out some plan to deal with Wednesday before she deals with you."

"It's a good idea," admitted Arthur. "The only thing is, I don't know how to get back into the House. I can't open the Atlas because I've used up all the power I had from holding on to the Keys. And in case you haven't noticed, I do have a broken leg. Though I suppose..."

"What?"

"I could phone Dame Primus if I had my phone box, because it'll probably be reconnected now that Grim Tuesday's bills have been paid."

"Where's the phone box? What's it look like?"

"It's at home," said Arthur. "In my bedroom. It's just a velvet-lined wooden box about this big." He held his hands apart.

"Maybe I could get it for you," said Leaf. "If they ever let me out of this hospital. If it isn't one thing, it's another. Quarantine this, quarantine that..."

"Maybe," said Arthur. "Or maybe I could... what's that smell?"

Leaf sniffed the air and looked around. As she looked, the pages of the calendar on the wall started to flutter.

"I don't know. I think the air-conditioning just came on. Feel the breeze."

Arthur held up his hands to feel the air. There was a definite rush of cold coming from somewhere, and a kind of salty odour, like when they stayed at the beach and the surf was big...

"It smells kind of damp," said Leaf.

Arthur struggled up to a sitting position, reached over and grabbed his slippers and dressing gown, and hurriedly put them on.

"Leaf!" he cried. "Get out! That's not the air-conditioning!"

"Sure isn't," Leaf agreed. The wind was getting stronger every second. "Something weird's going on."

"Yes, it is... get out while you can!"

"I want to see what happens." Leaf backed up to the bed and leaned against it. "Hey! There's water coming in under the wall!"

Sure enough, a thin film of frothy water was slowly spreading across the floor, like the leading wash of a wave across the sand. It ran almost to the bed, then ebbed back.

"I can hear something," said Leaf. "Kind of like a train."

Arthur heard it too. A distant thunder that got louder and louder.

"That's not a train! Grab hold of the bed!"

Leaf grabbed the rail at the end of the bed as Arthur

gripped the headboard. Both turned to look at the far wall just as it disappeared, replaced by a thundering grey-blue wave that crashed down upon them. Tons of sea water smashed everything else in the room to bits, but the bed itself was carried away by the wave.

Dazed, drenched and desperate, Arthur and Leaf hung on.

CHAPTER TWO

The hospital room vanished in an instant, replaced by the savage fury of a storm at sea. The bed, submerged to within an inch of the mattress-top, had become a makeshift raft. Picked up by the first great wave, the raft rode the crest for a few seconds, then fell off the back, sliding down and down into the trough behind.

Leaf cried out something, two words lost in the thunder of the waves and the howl of the wind. Arthur couldn't hear her, and he could barely see her through the spray that made it difficult to tell where the sea ended and the air began.

He felt her grip, though, as she clawed herself fully on

to the bed and grabbed his foot. Both of them would have been washed off then, if Arthur hadn't managed to get his arms wedged through the bars of the headboard.

Fear lent her strength, and Leaf managed to crawl up to the headboard railings. She leaned over Arthur and screamed, "What do we do now?"

She didn't sound like she was enjoying this adventure.

"Hold on!" Arthur shouted, looking past her at the towering, office-block-high wall of water that was falling towards them. If it broke over the bed, they would be smashed down and pushed deep into the sea, never to surface.

The crest of the wave curled high above them, blotting out the dim, grey light of the sky. Arthur and Leaf stared up, not breathing, eyes fixed on the curving water.

The wave didn't break. The bed rode up the face of the wave like a fisherman's float. As it neared the top, it tipped up almost vertically and started to roll over, until Arthur and Leaf threw their weight against the curl.

They were just in time. The bed didn't roll. It levelled out as they made it to the crest of the second wave. They balanced there for a few seconds, then the bed started its downward slide once more. Down into another sickeningly deep trough in front of another giant, blue-black, white-topped cliff of moving water.

But the third wave was different.

There was a ship surfing down it. A hundred-and-sixty-foot-long, three-masted sailing ship with sails that glowed a spectral green.

"A ship!" yelled Leaf, hope in her voice. That hope rapidly fled as the bed continued to run down into the trough at alarming speed, and the ship surfed down the opposite side even faster still.

"It's going to hit us! We have to jump!"

"No!" shouted Arthur. If they left their makeshift raft he felt sure they'd drown. "Wait!"

A few seconds later, waiting seemed like a very bad decision. The ship didn't waver in its course, a great wooden missile coming at them so fast that it would run right over them and the crew probably wouldn't even notice.

Arthur shut his eyes when it got within the last twenty yards. The last thing he saw was the ship's bow plunging down into the sea, then rising up again in a great spray of froth and spray, the bowsprit like a spear rising from the water.

Arthur opened his eyes when he didn't feel the shocking impact of a ship ramming them. The ship had turned just enough at the last instant to meet the bed in the very bottom of the trough between the waves. Both had lost speed, so that the bed would be right next to the ship for a matter of seconds. It was an act of tremendous seamanship by the Captain and crew, particularly in the middle of such a mighty swell.

Through the blowing spray, Arthur saw two looped ropes like lassos come down. One loop fell over Leaf. The other, clearly aimed for Arthur, fell over the left bedpost instead. He scrambled for it and started to lift it off. But before he got it clear, both ropes went taut. Leaf went up like a rocket, up towards the ship.

The other rope tipped the bed over.

Arthur lost his grip and tumbled into the sea. He went down several feet, his breath knocked out of him. Through the veil of water and spray, he saw Leaf and the bed spinning up to the ship's rail high above. The bed went up several yards, then the rope came free and it fell back down.

He kicked as best he could with one immobilised leg, and struck out with his arms, desperate to get back to the surface and the ship. But by the time his head broke free of the sea and he got a half-breath of spray-soaked air, the vessel was already at least fifty yards away, surfing diagonally up the wave ahead, moving faster than the swell. New sails unfurled and billowed out as he watched, accelerating its passage.

The bed was much closer, perhaps only ten yards away. It was his only chance now. Arthur started to swim furiously towards it. He could feel his lungs tightening, an asthma attack closing in on him. He would only be able to swim for a few minutes at most. Panicked, he threw all his energy into getting back to the bed, as it started its rise up the front of the following wave.

He just made it, grabbing a trailing blanket that had twisted through the bars at the end of the bed. Arthur frantically pulled himself along that, hoping it wouldn't come loose.

After a struggle that used up all his remaining strength, he managed to haul himself up on to the mattress and once again wedge his arms through the bars.

He shivered there, feeling his breath getting more restricted as his asthma got worse. That meant that wherever he was, it wasn't the House. This sea was somewhere in the Secondary Realms.

Wherever it is, I'm probably going to die here, Arthur thought, his mind numbed by cold, shock and lack of breath.

But he wasn't going to go easily. He freed his right hand and pressed it against his chest. Perhaps there was some shred of remnant power from the First Key in his hand, or even of the Second Key.

"Breathe," whispered Arthur. "Free up. Let me breathe."

At the same time, he tried to stop the panic that was coursing through his body. Over and over, inside his head, he told himself to be calm. Slow down. Take it easy.

Whether it was some remaining power in his hand or his efforts to stay calm, Arthur found that while he still couldn't breathe properly, it didn't get any worse. He started to take stock of his situation.

I'm kind of OK on the bed, he thought. *It floats. Even wet blankets will help me stay warm.*

He looked up at the wave the bed was riding up. Maybe he'd got a bit used to these enormous waves or just couldn't get any more terrified, but it did seem a bit smaller and less curling at the top than the first few. It still scared him, but it felt like less of a threat.

He thought about what else he might have. He was wearing hospital pyjamas and a dressing gown, which weren't much good for anything. The cast on his leg looked like it might be disintegrating already, and he could feel a dull, throbbing ache deep in the bone. His Immaterial Boots kept his feet warm, but he couldn't think of anything else they could be used for. Other than that, he had—

The Atlas! And the Mariner's whalebone disc!

Arthur's hand flashed to his pyjama pocket and then to the multiple strands of floss he'd woven into a string for the whalebone disc. The Atlas was still in his pocket. The Captain's medallion, as he'd come to think of it, was still around his neck.

But what use were they?

Arthur wedged his good leg through the bars and

curled up as much as he could into a ball. Then he gingerly let go with his hands and got out the Atlas, keeping it close to his chest to make sure that it couldn't get washed away. But as he'd half-expected, it wouldn't open. He slowly put it back in his pocket.

The Captain's whalebone disc, on the other hand, might work. Tom Shelvocke was the Mariner after all, son of the Old One and the Architect (by adoption), a man who had sailed thousands of seas on many different worlds. He'd told Suzy Turquoise Blue to warn Arthur to keep it by him. Perhaps it might summon help or even communicate with the Captain.

Arthur pulled the disc out from under his pyjama top and looked at the constellation of stars on one side, and then at the Viking ship on the other. They both looked like simple carvings, but Arthur thought there had to be some kind of magic contained in them. Because it seemed more likely to be of immediate help, Arthur concentrated on the ship side and tried to will a message to the Captain.

Please help me, I'm adrift on a bed in the middle of a storm at sea, he thought over and over again, even whispering the words aloud, as if the charm could hear him.

"Please help me, I'm adrift on a hospital bed in the middle of a storm at sea. Please help me, I'm adrift on a hospital bed in the middle of a storm at sea. Please help me, I'm adrift on a hospital bed in the middle of a storm at sea..."

It became a chant. Just saying the words made Arthur feel a little better.

He kept up the chant for several minutes, but had to give up as his lungs closed down and he could only just get enough breath to stay semiconscious. He lay next to the headboard, curled up as much as he could with one leg straight and the other thrust through the bars. He was completely sodden, and the sea continually sloshed over him, so he had to keep his head up to get a breath.

But the waves were definitely getting smaller and the wind less ferocious. Arthur didn't get a bucketful of spray in his eyes and mouth whenever he turned to face the wind.

If I can keep breathing, there's some hope, Arthur thought.

That thought had hardly crossed his mind when he felt an electric thrill pass through his whole body, and his stomach flip-flopped as if he'd dropped a thousand feet in an aircraft. All the water around him suddenly looked crisper, clearer and a more vivid blue. The sky turned a charming shade of eggshell blue and looked closer than it had before.

Best of all, Arthur's lungs were suddenly clear. He could breathe without difficulty.

He was in the House. Arthur could feel it through his whole body. Even the ache in his broken leg subsided to little more than an occasional twinge.

Hang on, he thought. *That was too easy. Wasn't it?*

This thought was interrupted by what sounded like an explosion, far too close for comfort. For a moment Arthur thought he was being shot at by a full broadside of cannons from a ship like the one that had taken Leaf. Then it came again and Arthur recognised it as thunder.

As the bed reached the top of another wave, he saw the lightning – lightning that stretched in a line all the way across the horizon. Vicious forks of white-hot plasma that ran in near-continuous streams between sea and sky, constant thunder echoing every flash and bolt.

The bed was being taken straight towards the lightning storm. Every wave that it rode up carried it forward. There was no way to turn it, stop it or avoid the collision.

To make matters as bad as they could possibly be, the bed was made of metal. It had to be the biggest lightning conductor for miles. And any lightning that hit would go through Arthur on its way to connect with the steel frame.

For a few seconds, Arthur's mind was paralysed by fear. There seemed to be nothing he could do. Absolutely nothing, except get fried by a thousand bolts of lightning all coming down at once.

He fought back the fear. He tried to think. There had to be something. Perhaps he could swim away... but there was no way he was strong enough to swim against the direction of the swell. It would be better to die instantly by lightning than to drown.

Arthur looked at the line of lightning again. Even in only a few minutes he'd got much closer, so close he had to shield his eyes from the blinding bolts.

But wait, thought Arthur. *The ship that took Leaf went in this direction. It must have gone through the lightning storm. I just have to get through. Maybe Lady Wednesday's invitation will protect me...*

Arthur checked his pocket. But there was only the Atlas.

Where could the invitation be?

The pillows were long gone, lost overboard, but the sheets were partially tucked in. Arthur dived under the drenched linen, his hands desperately groping into every corner as he tried to find the square of cardboard that might just save him.

The bed rose up the face of a wave, but did not reach the crest. Instead, bed, wave and boy rushed towards the blinding, deafening barrier of thunder and lightning that was the Line of Storms. The defensive inner boundary of the Border Sea, which no mortal could cross without permission.

The penalty for trying was a sudden, incendiary death.

CHAPTER THREE

Arthur never saw the lightning or heard the water boiling where the bolts struck, the noise lost in the constant boom of thunder. He was under the sheet, a soggy piece of cardboard clutched in one trembling hand. He didn't even know if it was the invitation from Drowned Wednesday, his medical chart from the end of the bed, or a brochure about the hospital telephones.

But since he was still alive a minute after the blinding glow beyond the sheets faded, he guessed it must be the invitation in his hand.

Arthur slowly pulled his head out from under the sheet. As he blinked up at the clear blue sky, he instinctively took another deep breath. A long, clear, unrestricted breath.

As the bed moved in the mysterious current, the swell it was riding subsided to a mere ten or twelve feet, with a much longer interval between waves. The wind dropped and there was no blowing spray. It also felt much warmer, though Arthur couldn't see a sun. He couldn't see any clouds or lightning either, which was a plus. Just a brilliant blue sky that was so even and perfect that he supposed it must be a painted ceiling, like in the other parts of the House.

Arthur took several more deep breaths, revelling in the rush of oxygen through his body. Then he took stock of his situation once more. The one thing he had learned about the House was that you couldn't take anything for granted. This warm, rolling sea might turn into something else at any moment.

Arthur tucked the Captain's disc back under his pyjama top and slid Lady Wednesday's sodden and barely legible invitation next to the Atlas in his pocket. Then he braced his cast against the headboard, stood up and looked around.

There was nothing to see, except the sea. The bed rode too low in the water. Even standing up, Arthur's view was blocked by the next wave. What he could see was much closer and immediately obvious.

The bed was sinking. Even in this calmer ocean, the

mattress was now totally submerged, losing its buoyancy as it absorbed more and more water, the steel frame dragging it down.

It wasn't going to sink in the next five minutes, but it was going to sink.

Arthur sighed and sat back down, water splashing almost up to his waist. He looked at the cast on his leg and wondered if he should take it off. It was very lightweight and it hadn't dragged him down before, but that had been a truly panic-driven swim and it would be hard to swim any real distance with it on. But if he took it off, his leg might snap apart again or hurt so much that he couldn't swim anyway.

He decided to leave the cast on and got out the Captain's disc again. This time he just held it in his hand and tried to visualise the ship with the glowing green sails coming back to pick him up.

He hoped that was a good thing to visualise. At the back of his mind was a nagging worry that Leaf hadn't been actually rescued but had gone from one trouble to another. What would the Denizens do to her? They would have been after him, not her. He hoped that since Lady Wednesday had sent him an invitation instead of an attack squad, she might be at least kind of friendly. But maybe that was just a sneaky plan to get him where she wanted. In which case, Drowned Wednesday might take out her bad feelings on Leaf...

If Leaf survived that line of lightning, Arthur thought guiltily. *Surely that ship would have had some protection...*

The bed gurgled under his feet and sank a bit more, reminding Arthur of his immediate problem.

"A ship!" he called out. "I need a ship! Or a boat! A better raft! Anything!"

His voice sounded alone and empty, lost amid the waves. He was answered only by the sloshing of the sea under, through and around the mattress.

"Land would do," said Arthur. He said this directly to the Captain's disc, but once again it didn't appear to do anything. It was just a carving of a boat on a piece of whalebone.

No land came in sight. Though he still couldn't see any sun, it got warmer and then positively hot. Even the sea water now constantly washing over Arthur didn't cool him down. It was tepid and very salty, as he found when he tasted some on the end of his finger. He was getting very thirsty, and had started to remember all kinds of terrible stories about people dying of thirst at sea. Or going crazy from thirst first and hurling themselves into the water or attacking their friends and trying to drink their blood...

Arthur shook his head several times. It looked like he was already starting to go crazy, thinking of stuff like that. Particularly since he knew he couldn't die of thirst in the

House. He might feel like he was, and of course he could still go crazy...

Better to think of something positive to do. Like send a signal or catch a fish. If there were any fish in this strange sea within the House. Of course, if there were fish, there might also be sharks. A shark would have no trouble pulling him off the bed. It hardly qualified as a raft any more, it had sunk down so far.

Arthur shook his head again to try and clear away the negative thoughts.

Stop thinking about sharks! he told himself.

Just at that moment, he saw something in the water not far away. A dark, mostly submerged shape. A shadow largely under the surface.

Arthur yelped and tried to stand up against the headboard, hopping as his immobilised leg got caught under a fold of sheet. This violent action changed the balance of the bed, and one corner went down several feet, releasing a huge air bubble.

This downward progress halted for a few seconds as air bubbles continued to pop to the surface, then the bed sank like the *Titanic*, one end briefly sticking straight up before it subsided beneath the waves. Arthur let go of it just in time and pushed himself away. He thrashed out a rough backstroke for a few yards to make sure he wouldn't be sucked down, then trod water with one leg and his arms circling, as he frantically looked around for the dark shadow again.

There it was, only a few yards away! Arthur braced himself for the shock of a shark's attack, his body rigid. His head sank under the water as he stopped moving, then broke free again as he instinctively struggled to swim again.

The dark shape didn't attack. It didn't even move. Arthur stared at it and saw that it wasn't a shark. He swam closer to confirm that it was, in fact, a dark green ball about six feet in diameter. It had an irregular surface rather like matted weeds and was floating quite deep, so that only a curve fourteen inches or so high rode above the sea.

Arthur splashed over to it. On closer inspection, it was clearly a buoy or some floating marker, totally covered in green weeds. Arthur reached out to touch it. A huge strand of green weeds came away in his hand, revealing a bright red surface beneath.

Arthur touched that. It felt slightly sticky, and some of the red stuff came away on his hand. It was like chewing gum, impossible to get off. Arthur crossly wiped his hands but that only smeared it across his fingers, and his head dipped under. His broken leg wasn't weighed down that much by the cast, but he couldn't bend his knee and he couldn't tread water well enough just with one leg to really try and clean his hands, since he had to make swimming motions as well.

Arthur started to clear the weeds away with one hand. While doing that, he noticed that the buoy didn't move far with the swell. Each time one of the bigger waves came past, it swept Arthur five or six yards away and he had to swim back. The buoy didn't move anywhere near as much.

It had to be fixed to something. Arthur duck-dived down and, sure enough, a barnacle-encrusted chain led down from the buoy, down through the sunlit water and into the dark depths.

He resumed cleaning the weeds away with new enthusiasm and so got a lot more of the sticky stuff on his hands. It was tar, or something like tar, though it didn't smell.

The buoy has to mark something, Arthur thought. *It must be used by someone, who'll come past. I might even be able to climb up on it.*

When the buoy was almost clean it rode much higher in the water. Arthur had hoped he might find some handles on it, or projections he could hold on to, because he was getting very tired. But there weren't any. The only part of the buoy that was of any interest was a small brass ring right near the top. Arthur could only just reach it.

The ring was about the size of the top joint of Arthur's little finger, far too small for him to hold on. It also felt a bit loose. Arthur gave it a pull, hoping that it might come out and he could somehow make the hole bigger to create a handhold.

It came out with a very loud popping sound, followed immediately afterwards by a ten-foot-high shower of sparks and a loud ticking noise as if a large and noisy clock had started up deep within the ball.

Arthur started frantically backstroking away from it, his body almost reacting faster than his brain, which had rapidly processed the fact that this floating ball was some sort of floating bomb – a mine – and it was going to explode.

A few seconds later, with Arthur only ten yards away, the buoy did explode. But it was not the lethal blast Arthur feared. There was a bright flash, and a rush of air above Arthur's head, but no deadly rain of fragments.

Smoke poured out of the ball, dark black smoke that coiled up into the air in a very orderly fashion, quite unlike any smoke Arthur had seen before. It started to whip about like a snake, dancing all over the place. Eventually its "head" connected with its "tail" to form a giant smoke ring that hovered ten feet above the buoy, which was still intact, though its upper half had broken open into multiple segments like a lotus.

The smoke ring slowly closed in on itself to become an inky cloud that spun about for a minute or so, then it abruptly burst apart, turning into eight jet-black seabirds that shrieked "Thief!" above Arthur's head before they each flew off in a different direction, covering the eight points of the compass rose.

Arthur was too tired to worry about what the seabirds were doing, or who they might be alerting. All he cared about was the fact that now the top half of the buoy was open, he could pull himself up on it and have a rest.

Arthur had only just enough energy to drag himself over and into the buoy. It was full of water, but he could sit in it quite comfortably and rest. That was all he wanted to do for a while. Rest.

But after only twenty minutes, according to his still-backwards but otherwise reliable and waterproof watch, Arthur found that he had rested enough. Though there was still no visible sun, it felt like one was beating down on him. He was really hot, and he was sure he was getting sunburned and that his tongue had started to swell from lack of water. He wished he'd managed to keep a sheet from the bed to use as a sunshade. He took his dressing gown off and made that into a makeshift turban, but it didn't really help.

At that point, Arthur started to hope that whoever the birds were supposed to alert would show up. Even if they thought he was a thief. That implied there was something to steal here, which didn't seem to be the case. The buoy was just a big, empty, floating ball with the top hemisphere opened up. There was nothing inside it except Arthur.

Another baking, uncomfortable hour passed. Arthur's broken leg began to ache again, probably because the painkillers he'd had in the hospital were wearing off. The high-tech cast didn't seem to be operational any more and Arthur could see distinct holes in it now.

Arthur picked at one of the holes and grimaced. The cast was falling apart. He was definitely sunburned as well, the backs of his hands turning pink, as if trying to match the bright red stain on his palms. According to Arthur's watch it was nine o'clock at night, but there was no change in the light. Without being able to see any sun, he couldn't tell whether night was approaching. He wasn't even sure there would be a night. There was in the Lower House, but that didn't mean anything. There might not be any relief from the constant heat.

He wondered if he should try and swim somewhere, but dismissed the idea as quickly as it came up. He was lucky to have found this buoy. Or perhaps it wasn't luck, it was the Mariner's disc that had led him here. In any case, Arthur couldn't swim for more than half an hour at the most, and there wasn't much chance of finding land in that time. Better to sit here and hope that the smoky seabirds brought someone.

Two hours later, Arthur felt a much cooler breeze waft across the back of his neck. He opened his puffy eyes to see a shadow passing across the sky. A veil of darkness advanced in a line across the horizon. Stars, or suitable facsimiles of them, began to twinkle as the light faded before the approaching line of night.

The wind and the lapping sea grew cold. Arthur turned his turban back into a dressing gown, shivered and hunched up into a tighter ball. Clearly he was going to be sunburned during the day and then frozen at night. Either one would kill him, so not dying of hunger and thirst was no great bonus.

As he had that thought, Arthur saw another star. A fallen star, quite close to the sea, and moving towards him. It took another moment for his heat-addled brain to recognise that it was in fact a light.

A light fixed to the bowsprit of a ship.

CHAPTER FOUR

The fallen star grew closer and the ship became more visible, though it was still little more than a dark outline in the fading light. A rather rotund outline, for this ship looked to be very broad, wallowing its way through the waves. It had only two masts, rather than the three of the ship that had picked up Leaf, and its square-rigged sails were definitely not of the luminous variety.

Arthur didn't care. He stood up gingerly, his muscles cramping from weariness and confinement in the buoy, and waved frantically.

"Help! I'm over here! Help!"

There was no answering shout from the ship. It rolled

and plunged towards him, but he could see some of the sails being furled, and there were Denizens rushing about on the deck. Somebody was shouting orders and others were repeating or questioning them. All in all, it didn't appear very organised.

Particularly as the ship sailed right past him. Arthur couldn't believe it. He shouted himself hoarse and almost fell out of the buoy from jumping up and down. But the ship kept on its way, till Arthur could only see the glow of the single lantern that hung from its stern rail.

Arthur watched till the light disappeared into the darkness, then he sat down, totally defeated. He rested his head in his hands and fought back a sob.

I am not going to cry, he told himself. *I will work something out. I am the Master of the Lower House and the Far Reaches. I am not going to die in a buoy in some rotten sea!*

Arthur took a deep breath and lifted his head up.

There will be another ship. There must be another ship.

Arthur was clutching at this hope when he saw the light again, followed by another.

Two lights!

They were a hundred feet apart and perhaps two hundred yards away. It took Arthur only a second to understand that he was looking at the bow and stern lights of the ship. He'd lost sight of the stern light as the vessel turned, but now it was heaved-to, broadside on to him.

A few moments later, he heard the slap of oars in the water and Denizens chanting as they rowed a small boat towards him. Arthur couldn't make out the words till they were quite close and the light of a bull's-eye lantern flickered across the water, searching for Arthur and the buoy.

> *"Flotsam floats when all is sunk.*
> *Jetsam thrown isn't just junk.*
> *Coughs and colds and bright red sores*
> *Waiting for us, so bend yer oars!"*

The yellow beam of light swept over Arthur, then backtracked to shine directly in his face. Arthur raised his arm to shield his eyes. The light wasn't bright enough to blind, but it made it hard to see the boat and its crew. There were at least a dozen Denizens aboard, most of them rowing.

"Back oars!" came a shout from the darkness. "Yarko was right! There *is* a Nithling on that buoy! Make ready your crossbows!"

"I'm not a Nithling!" shouted Arthur. "I'm... I'm a distressed sailor!"

"A what?"

"A distressed sailor," replied Arthur. He had read that somewhere. Sailors were supposed to help one another.

"What ship? And what are you doing on that treasure marker?"

"Uh, my ship was the *Steely Bed*. It sank. I swam here."

There was a muttering aboard the boat. Arthur couldn't clearly hear all the words, but he heard "claim", "ours", "stick 'im and sink 'im" and the sound of someone being knocked on the head and grunting in pain. He hoped it was the Denizen who said "stick 'im", since he was fairly sure he was the "'im" being referred to.

"Give way," shouted the Denizen in charge. The oars dipped into the sea again and the boat moved forward. As it came alongside the buoy, Arthur got his first real look at the crew, with the Denizen holding the bull's-eye lantern opening its shutters to spread the light around.

They were not a good-looking bunch. There were eight men and five women. They might have started with the usual handsome features of Denizens, but the great majority of them had eye patches, livid scars across their faces and an illustrated catalogue of tattoos, ranging from ships to storms to skulls and snakes, up and down their forearms, on cheeks and foreheads and bared midriffs. They wore many different styles of clothing, all in bright colours, the single common feature being a wide leather belt that supported a cutlass and knife. Half of them also had red knitted caps, and the leader, a broad-shouldered male Denizen with scarlet sunbursts tattooed on his cheeks, wore a leather Napoleon hat that looked a little too small for him.

He smiled at Arthur, revealing a mouth with most of its teeth missing. Of the remaining four or five, three were capped in gold.

Pirates, Arthur figured.

But there was something strangely non-aggressive about them too. Something that reminded Arthur of people playing dress-up. Surely real pirates would just kill him without a second thought, not sit quietly looking at him. And one of them was drawing a picture of the scene with a charcoal stick in a sketchbook.

"The *Steelibed*," said the leader. "Can't say I've heard of her. When did she sink? Carrying any cargo?"

"Maybe a day ago," said Arthur cautiously. "Not much cargo. Um, cotton and stuff."

"And stuff," repeated the leader, with a wink at Arthur. "Well, with a treasure marker in front of us, we'll not bother with 'cotton and stuff' if there's anything below. The question is, are you claiming salvage?"

"Uh, I don't know," said Arthur cautiously. "Maybe. I might."

"Well, if you're not sure, then it don't matter!" declared the leader, with a laugh that was echoed by the crew.

"We'll just have a look below and if there's anything left, we'll have it up. Then we'll be on our way and you can get on with your own business."

"Hold on!" cried Arthur. "Take me with you!"

"Lizard, take a line and have a glance under the buoy," said the leader to one of the crew, a small woman who had blue scales tattooed all over her face. At least Arthur *hoped* they were tattoos and not actual scales. She undid her belt, kicked off her boots and quickly dived over the side with a rope held between her teeth.

"Please, I need to get to land," said Arthur. "Somewhere I can make a phone call."

"Ain't no phone calls in the Border Sea," said one of the Denizens. "Exchange got flooded and they never built a new one on the high ground."

"Shut yer trap, One-Ear," instructed the leader. He turned back to Arthur. "You want to come aboard the *Moth* as a passenger, then?"

"That's your ship?" asked Arthur. "The *Moth*?"

"Aye, the *Moth*," replied a Denizen who had a shark's toothy mouth tattooed around his own. "What's wrong with that? Moths can be extremely frightening. If you get trapped in a cupboard with a whole passel of moths—"

"I didn't mean anything bad about the name," said Arthur. He thought quickly. "It's just I was surprised to be picked up by such a famous ship."

"What?" asked one of the other Denizens. "The *Moth*?"

"Yes. Such a famous ship and its crew of... uh... such renowned pirates!"

Arthur's speech was met by a sudden silence. Then the crew of the boat erupted, falling over themselves as they tried to run out the oars again. All of them shouted at once:

"Pirates! Where?! What pirates?! Back to the ship!"

"Hold hard!" roared the leader. He waded in among the crew, slapping them openhanded across the backs of their heads till they subsided on to the slats. Then he turned to Arthur.

"I ain't never heard anything so insulting. Us! Pirates! We're Salvagers and proud of it. We don't take anything that hasn't been thrown away first or sunk and come up. Or treasures left in the open sea."

"Sorry," said Arthur. "It was just the eye patches and the clothes and the tattoos and everything... I was confused. But I really would like to be a passenger."

"Just because we're only Salvagers doesn't mean we can't dress nice and wear an eye patch if we want," muttered Shark-Mouth. "Or two eye patches, come to that."

"Can't wear two, you idiot," said another Denizen.

"Can so," replied the first. "Get some of that one-way leather from the doctor—"

"Shut up!" roared the leader. He turned back to Arthur

and said, "I'm not saying you can be a passenger, right? I'm only the Second Mate of the *Moth*. Sunscorch is my name. But we'll take you back to the ship. The Captain can decide your fate."

"Thanks!" said Arthur. "My name's Arth—"

He stopped halfway through. Better to keep his name to himself, he thought.

"Arth? Well, get aboard, Arth."

Two of the closer Denizens held the boat against the buoy and another one helped Arthur across.

"Gettin' yer leg ready to cut off, are yer?" asked the helping Denizen with a grin. He slapped Arthur's cast and waved his own leg, showing off a wooden peg that started below the knee. "They grow back too quick, though, I'm telling yer."

Arthur grimaced at the sight and quickly suppressed a flash of fear that his leg might have to be cut off. And his wouldn't grow back, unlike a Denizen's.

"I've had this one chopped a dozen times," continued the peg-legged crew member. "Why, I remember—"

He stopped in midsentence and recoiled, staring at Arthur's red-stained hands.

"He's got the Red Hand!"

"Feverfew's mark!"

"We're all doomed!"

"Quiet!" roared Sunscorch. He peered down at Arthur.

"It's only red tar or something from the buoy," said Arthur. "It'll wash off."

"From the buoy," whispered Sunscorch. "This here buoy?"

"Yes."

"There wasn't any smoke, was there?"

"Yes."

"What about birds? That smoke didn't turn into cormorants, did it? Smoky black cormorants that screamed out something that might have been 'Death' or 'Dismemberment' or anything like that?"

"There were birds," admitted Arthur. "They screamed out 'Thief' and flew away. I thought they must have brought you here."

Sunscorch took off his hat and wiped his bald head with a surprisingly neatly folded white handkerchief that he took out of a pocket.

"Not us," he whispered. "Lookout saw the open buoy and the Captain thought it worth a glance. That there treasure marker must be one of Feverfew's. The birds will have flown to find him, and his ship."

"*Shiver*," intoned the crew. "The ship of bone."

As they spoke, the Denizen with the lantern shuttered it right down to the merest glimmer and everybody else looked out at the sea all around.

Sunscorch ran his tongue over his remaining teeth and

kept wiping his head. His crew watched him intently, till he put away his handkerchief and clapped his hat back on.

"Listen up," he whispered. "Seeing as we're probably dead or headed for the slave-chain anyway, we might as well see what's below. Lizard? Where's Lizard?"

"Here," came a whisper from the water. "There's a chest all right, a big one, sitting pretty as you please atop a spire of rock, ten fathom down."

"The chain?"

"Screwed to the rock, not to the chest."

"Let's be having that chest, then," whispered Sunscorch. "Bones, you and Bottle back oars. Everyone else, hands on the line. You, too, Arth."

Arthur joined the others to grab hold of the rope. At Sunscorch's hoarsely whispered commands, they all hauled together.

"Heave away! Hold on! Heave cheerily! Hold on! Heave away! Hold! One more!"

At the last command, a dripping chest as long as Arthur was tall and as high as his waist scraped over the gunwale and was manhandled into the boat. As soon as it was settled, there was a mad dash to the oars. With Sunscorch whispering more commands and the rowers very gently dipping their oars, the boat moved ahead and then turned towards the lights of the *Moth*.

"Hope we get back to the ship in time so as we can all

die together," whispered the Denizen on the oar next to Arthur. "It'd be better that way."

"What makes you so sure we're going to die?" asked Arthur. "Don't be so pessimistic."

"Feverfew never leaves any survivors," whispered another Denizen. "He slaves 'em or kills 'em. Either way they're gone for good. He's got strange powers. A Sorcerer of Nothing."

"He'll torture *you* first, though," added one of the women, with a grin that showed her teeth were filed to points. "You touched the buoy. You've got the Red Hand that shows you tried to steal from Feverfew."

"Quiet!" instructed Sunscorch. "Row quiet and listen!"

Arthur cupped a hand to his ear and leaned over the side. But all he could hear was the harsh breathing of the Denizens and the soft, regular swoosh and tinkle of the oars dipping in and out of the water.

"What are we listening for?" Arthur asked after a while.

"Anything we don't want to hear," said Sunscorch, as he looked back over the stern. Without turning around, he added, "Shutter that lantern, Yeo."

"It is shuttered," replied Yeo. "One of the moons is rising. Feverfew will see us miles away."

"No point being quiet, then," said Sunscorch.

Arthur looked where the mate pointed. Sure enough, a slim, blue-tinged moon was rising up on the horizon. It wasn't very big and it didn't look all that far away – a few tens of miles, not hundreds of thousands – but it was bright.

The blue moon rose quickly and rather jerkily, as if it was on a clockwork track that needed oiling. By its light Arthur could easily see the *Moth*, wallowing nearby. But he could also see something else, far away on the horizon. Something that glinted in the moonlight. A reflection from a telescope lens, atop a thin dark smudge that must be a mast.

Sunscorch saw it too.

"Row, you dogs!" roared the Second Mate. "Row for your miserable lives!"

CHAPTER FIVE

Their arrival aboard the *Moth* resembled a panicked evacuation more than an orderly boarding. The boat was abandoned as most of the Denizens clawed their way up the side ladder or the untidy mess of netting that hung along the *Moth*'s yellow-painted hull, all of them shouting unhelpful things like "Feverfew!" and *"Shiver!"* and "We're doomed!"

Sunscorch managed to drag several Denizens back and get them to take the line from the chest. But even he wasn't able to get the crew to do anything about retrieving the boat. As it began to drift away, he jumped to the ship's side himself, reaching back to help Arthur get hold of the netting.

"Never lost salvage nor a passenger," he muttered. "No thanks to the scum of the sea I have to sail with. Mister Concort! Mister Concort! There's a boat adrift!

"Concort's the First Mate," he confided to Arthur as they climbed the side. "Amiable, but hen-witted. Like most of this lot he was with the *Moth* when it was a counting house. Chief Clerk. You'd think after several thousand years at sea he'd have learned... but I'm misspeaking meself. Up you go!"

Arthur was pushed up and over the rail. He fell on to the deck, unable to get his bad leg in place in time. Before he could get up himself, Sunscorch gripped him under each elbow and yanked him upright, shouting at the same time.

"Ichabod! Ichabod! Take our passenger to the Captain! And get him a blanket!"

A thin, non-tattooed Denizen neatly dressed in a blue waistcoat and an almost white shirt stepped out of the throng of panicking sailors and bowed slightly to Arthur. He was thinner than most of the other Denizens and moved very precisely, as if he was following some mysterious dance pattern in his head.

"Please step this way," he said, doing an about-turn that was almost a pirouette and would have looked more in keeping on a stage than on the shifting deck of a ship.

Arthur obediently followed the Denizen, who was

presumably Ichabod. Behind him, Sunscorch was yelling and slapping the backs of heads.

"Port watch aloft! Prepare to make sail! Starboard watch to the guns and boarding stations!"

"Very noisy, these sailors," said Ichabod. "Mind your head."

The Denizen ducked as he stepped through a narrow doorway. Though Arthur was considerably shorter, he had to bend his head down too. They were in a short, dark, narrow corridor with a very low ceiling.

"Aren't you a sailor?" asked Arthur.

"I'm the Captain's Steward," replied Ichabod severely. "I was his gentleman's gentleman when we were ashore."

"His what?"

"What is sometimes called a valet," replied Ichabod as he opened the door at the other end, only a few yards away. The Denizen stepped through, with Arthur at his heels.

The room beyond the door was not what Arthur expected. It was far too big to be inside the ship, for a start: a huge, whitewashed space at least eighty feet long and sixty feet wide, with a decorated plaster ceiling twenty feet above, complete with a fifty-candle chandelier of cut crystal in the middle.

There was a mahogany desk right in the middle of the room with a green-shaded gas lantern on it, and a long row of glass-topped display cases all along one wall, each illuminated by its own gently hissing gaslight. In the far corner, there was a curtained four-poster bed with a blanket box at its foot, a standing screen painted with a nautical scene, and a large oak-panelled wardrobe with mirrored doors.

It was also absolutely quiet and completely stable. All the noise of the crew and the sea had vanished as soon as the door was shut behind Arthur, as had the constant roll and sway of the deck.

"How—"

Ichabod knew what Arthur was asking before the boy even got the question out.

"This is one of the original rooms. When the Deluge came and we had to turn the counting house into a ship, this room refused to transform to something more useful, like a gun deck. Eventually Dr Scamandros managed to connect it to the aft passageway, but it isn't really in the ship."

"Where is it, then?"

"We're not entirely sure. Probably not where it used to be, since the old counting house site is well submerged. The Captain thinks that this room must have been personally supervised by the Architect and retained some of Her virtue. It lies within the House, that's for sure, not out in the Realms."

"You're not worried that it might get cut off from the

ship?" asked Arthur as they walked over to the bed. The curtains were drawn and Arthur could hear snoring behind them. Not horrendous "I can't bear to hear it" snoring, but occasional drawn-out snorts and wheezes.

"Not at all," said Ichabod. "The ship is still mostly the counting house, albeit long-transformed and changed. This room is of the counting house, so it will always be connected somehow. If the passageway falls off, some other way will open."

"Through the wardrobe maybe," said Arthur.

Ichabod looked at him sternly, his eyebrows contracting to almost meet above his nose.

"I doubt that, young mortal. That is where I keep the Captain's clothes. It is not a thoroughfare of any kind."

"Sorry," said Arthur. "I was only..."

His voice trailed off as Ichabod's eyebrows did not return to a more friendly position. There was a frosty silence for a few seconds, then the Denizen twitched his nose as if something had irritated his nostrils, and bent down to open the blanket box.

"Here is a blanket," he said unnecessarily, handing it to Arthur. "I suggest you wrap yourself in it. It may stop that shivering. Unless of course it is merely an affectation."

"Oh, thanks," said Arthur. He hadn't realised he was shivering, but now that Ichabod mentioned it, he realised he was very cold, and little tremors were running up and down his arms and legs. The heavy blanket was very welcome. "I am cold. I might even have a cold."

"Really?" asked Ichabod, suddenly interested. "We must tell Dr Scamandros. But first I suppose I should wake the Captain."

"I'm already awake," said a voice behind the curtain. A quiet, calm voice. "We have a visitor, I see. Anything else to report, Ichabod?"

"Mister Sunscorch is of the opinion that we are being pursued by the awful pirate Feverfew, on account of stealing one of his treasure chests."

"Ah," said the voice. "Is Mister Sunscorch doing... um... things with the sails and so on? So we can, ah, flee?"

"Yes, sir," said Ichabod. "May I present the potential passenger Mister Sunscorch took aboard from Feverfew's buoy? He is a boy and, I believe I am correct in assuming, a true mortal. Not one of the Piper's children."

"Yes," said Arthur.

"First things first, Ichabod," came the reply. "Second-best boots, third-best coat and my, ah, sword. The proper one with the, err, sharpened blade."

"The sharpened blade? Is that wise, sir?"

"Yes, yes. If, ah, Feverfew catches us... now, mortal boy, what is your name?"

"My name is – look ou—!" said Arthur as Ichabod walked straight into the wardrobe mirror. But the Denizen didn't hit it. He went right through, like a diver into a pool of still water, the silvered glass rippling as he passed.

"Lookow?" asked the Captain.

"Sorry, I got distracted," said Arthur. "My name is Arth."

"Lookow sounds better than Arth," said the Captain. "Pity. Names can be a terrible burden. Take mine, for example. It's Catapillow. Captain Catapillow, at your service."

"Caterpillar?" asked Arthur, not sure he'd heard it right through the bed's curtains.

"No! Cat-ah-pillow. See what I mean? Suitable name for the manager of a counting house, but hardly the stuff of nautical legend."

"Why don't you change it?"

"Officers not allowed to," came the muffled reply. "Name was issued by the Architect. Inscribed in the Register of Precedence. That's why I'm Captain. Most senior aboard, 38,598th in precedence within the House. Prefer not to be, but no choice in the matter. Mister Sunscorch is, um, the only professional sailor aboard. Boots?"

"Here they are, sir," said Ichabod, inserting boots, coat and sword between the curtains. Arthur hadn't seen him come back through the mirrored door of the wardrobe, but there he was.

There was a muffled curse from the bed and the curtains billowed out. Then the boots thrust out under them, half on Captain Catapillow's feet. Ichabod helped him ease them on all the way, and Catapillow slid out of the bed and stood up and bowed to Arthur.

He was tall, but not as tall as Dame Primus or Monday's Noon. He was also not particularly handsome, though not exactly ugly either. He didn't have any tattoos, or at least none visible. He just looked very plain and ordinary, with a rather vacant face under a short white wig with a kind of ponytail at the back tied with a blue ribbon. His blue coat was quite faded and he only had one gold epaulette, on his left shoulder.

"Now, young Arth," Catapillow said as he tried to buckle on his sword-belt and failed. He stood still while Ichabod fixed it up. "You want to be a passenger aboard a ship that will shortly be sunk and everyone on it put to, umm, the sword or made slaves by the pirate Feverfew?"

"No," said Arthur. "I mean I want to be a passenger, but surely we can escape? I saw that ship, the pirate one, but it was a long way away. We must have a good lead."

"A stern chase is a long chase," muttered Catapillow. "But they'll, you know, probably catch us in the end. I suppose we should go and, er, have a look. Mister Sunscorch might have some – what-do-you-call-'em – ideas. Or Dr Scamandros. Just when I was going to examine some new additions to my collection. I suppose it will be Feverfew's collection soon and he won't appreciate it."

Arthur started to ask about the Captain's collection. He could tell from Catapillow's fond gaze that it was housed in the display cabinets along the wall. But before he could get the words out, Ichabod trod on his foot and coughed meaningfully.

"What's that?" asked Catapillow, looking back at the boy.

"The Captain's needed on deck!" said Ichabod in a loud, firm voice.

"Yes! Yes!" said Catapillow. "Let's see where that vile, um, vile ship of Feverfew's has got to. We can talk about your passage fee later, Arth. Follow me!"

He led the way back to the door. As soon as it opened, Arthur heard the deep roar of the sea, the groan of the ship's timbers, and the continuing shouts of the crew and Sunscorch.

He had to shut his eyes as he left the room and stepped into the corridor because the floor of the ship was rocking but the room's wasn't, creating a very sick-making feeling at the back of his eyes. But it passed as soon as he was in the ship proper again, though the ship was pitching up and down so much he had to use a hand to steady himself every few paces.

It was bright out on the main deck. The moon was high above them, its light cool and strong. Arthur could even have read by it, he thought, and he noticed that it was strong enough to cast shadows.

He hugged his blanket tighter around his shoulders as he felt the wind. It had grown colder still, and stronger. Looking up at the masts, all the sails were full. The *Moth* was heeled over quite steeply to starboard and was plunging ahead at quite a rate.

Unfortunately, when he looked over his shoulder, Arthur saw that the pirate ship was sailing even faster. It was much smaller than the *Moth*, and narrower too, with only two masts and triangular sails rather than the square ones on the merchant vessel.

"The ship looks white in the moonlight," said Arthur. "And are those sails brown?"

"They're the colour of dried blood," said Ichabod. "A shade called 'vintage sanguinolent' by tailors. The hull is supposedly made from a single piece of bone, that of a legendary monster from the Secondary Realms. Feverfew himself is said to be a pirate from the Realms, once mortal, who mastered the darker depths of House Sorcery and is now half-Nithling, half—"

"That will... that will do, thank you, Ichabod," said Catapillow nervously. "Come with me."

He led the way up to the quarterdeck, where two

Denizens wrestled with the wheel, and Sunscorch shouted orders at the Denizens aloft and on the deck, trimming sails and yards. There were two other Denizens there as well. One stood next to Sunscorch, nodding sagely at every order but saying nothing. He looked rather like Captain Catapillow, with a bland face and similar clothes, so was clearly an officer. *Probably the First Mate*, Arthur thought. *The one who used to be the Chief Clerk in the counting house.*

The other Denizen was completely different. He was crouched on the deck next to the wheel. A strange, small figure not much taller than Arthur, he was almost completely lost inside a voluminous yellow greatcoat with rolled-up cuffs. He was bald and his face and head were completely covered in small, colourful tattoos that Arthur realised after a moment were animated, moving and shifting around. Tattoos of ships and sea creatures, birds and clouds, maps and moons and stars and suns and planets.

"Mister Concort, who is First Mate," whispered Ichabod, pointing to the Denizen next to Sunscorch. "And Dr Scamandros, our most accomplished sorcerer and navigator. He's casting the haruspices to see where we might be able to go. No one must interrupt, take note. Dreadful things would happen."

At that moment, a gust of wind hit the *Moth* hard and she heeled over even further. As everyone on the quarterdeck scrambled to keep their footing, Arthur stumbled against Captain Catapillow, and both of them ended up sliding across the deck and into the rail.

Arthur almost went over, into the dark sea that was surprisingly close below. He managed to save himself and, at the last second, his blanket, but at the cost of a jolt to his broken leg that sent a savage, stabbing pain up his side and into his head.

As the ship righted itself in response to Sunscorch's shouted commands, Arthur noticed that almost everybody else had ended up on the starboard rail, apart from the two helmsmen clinging to the wheel, Sunscorch next to them, and Dr Scamandros to the side. He was still crouched where he'd been, as if he were glued to the deck. All the things he was studying were also still there, which seemed impossible. Several maps were laid out on the deck, with a pair of gilt-bronze dividers on top, a ruler and the skull of a small animal that had been converted into a cup to hold a dozen or so pencils.

There were also lots of small pieces of coloured cardboard strewn apparently at random next to the map. Dr Scamandros was studying them and whistling through his front teeth. After a few seconds, he gathered them up into his cupped hands and threw them down again. To Arthur's surprise, they joined together as they fell, and he realised they were jigsaw pieces. When they hit the deck, nearly all of them had joined, but two or three pieces remained separate. The jigsaw was incomplete.

Dr Scamandros stopped whistling and the wind, as if in response, eased a little. The Denizen gathered the jigsaw pieces together again and put them in a cardboard box that had a picture of a sheep on it, which he then put inside his yellow greatcoat. After this was done, he stood up. This was obviously the point at which he could be interrupted, because Catapillow and Concort rushed over to him.

"What are the signs, Doctor?" asked Catapillow. "Is there a course out of here?"

"No," said Scamandros. His voice was very high and pure, and reminded Arthur strangely of a trumpet. "There is some power interfering with both the goat and sheep auguries. I dare not try the ox in such circumstances. Without guidance, I can find no true course."

"Is it Feverfew?" asked Sunscorch. "Even so far away?"

"No," said Scamandros. He had caught sight of Arthur for the first time and his dark eyes were staring straight at the boy. "It is much closer. Who is that?"

"Arth," said Sunscorch. "A mortal boy. We picked him up with Feverfew's treasure."

"He holds an object of great power," said Dr Scamandros, excitement in his voice. He rummaged inside his coat and pulled out a pair of glasses with gold wire rims and thick smoked-quartz lenses, which he slipped on to his forehead, not over his eyes. "Bring him here."

Arthur stepped forward of his own accord and staggered across the deck. Sunscorch caught him and held him, loosely enough for the grip to be either a friend helping out or a guard about to secure a prisoner.

"What is in your pocket, boy?" asked Dr Scamandros. "It is interfering with my augury and, thus, my navigation of this ship."

"It's... it's a book," said Arthur. "It won't be of any use to you."

"I'll be the judge of that!" Scamandros exclaimed. He reached forward to Arthur's pocket and Sunscorch tightened his grip on the boy's arms. "What have we—"

As he touched the top of the Atlas, there was a loud report, like a pistol shot. Scamandros's hand came back so quickly Arthur didn't even see it, and then the navigator was hopping around the deck with his fingers thrust into his armpit, screeching, "Ow! Ow! Ow! Throw him overboard!"

Sunscorch hesitated, then picked up Arthur in a bear hug and tottered to the starboard rail, crashing into it with considerable force.

"Sorry, lad," he said as he lifted Arthur up and prepared to heave him into the waiting sea. "We need the doctor."

CHAPTER SIX

"No!" screamed Arthur. Then, as Sunscorch continued to lift him up, "I'm a friend of the Mariner! Captain Tom Shelvocke!"

Sunscorch lowered Arthur to the deck.

"Prove it," he said coldly. "If you're lying, I'll carve you a set of gills before I throw you over."

Arthur reached with a shivering hand into his pyjama top and pulled out his makeshift floss-chain. For a dreadful moment he thought the disc was gone, then it slid free and hung on his chest.

"What are you waiting for, Sunscorch?" yelled Dr Scamandros angrily. "Throw him overboard!"

Sunscorch looked closely at the disc, flipped it with his finger and looked at the other side. Then he sighed and let go of Arthur. Just then, the ship rolled to port and back again, almost sending Arthur over the side anyway.

"Do as the doctor says, Mister Sunscorch!" called Catapillow. "We must have a course to get away!"

"I can't, Captain!" shouted Sunscorch. "The boy has the mark of the Mariner. If he asks for aid, as sailors we must give it."

"I *am* asking," said Arthur hastily. "I don't want to be thrown overboard. I only want to send a message to the Lower House. Or the Far Reaches."

"He has the what? The who?" asked Catapillow.

Sunscorch sighed again and helped Arthur along the sloping deck to the group gathered around the wheel. Dr Scamandros still had his hand under his arm. He scowled at Arthur.

"No seaman will go against the Mariner," said Sunscorch. "The boy has the Mariner's medal, so you'll have to figure something else out, Doc. He ain't going over the side."

"The Mariner," said Scamandros. "A figure of reverence for the nautically inclined. One of the Old One's sons, I believe?"

"Yes," said Arthur, though the question hadn't been asked of him. "And the Architect's."

"Perhaps I was a little hasty," Scamandros continued. "I thought perhaps you had something in your pocket we wouldn't want aboard. But any friend of the Mariner... please do accept my apology."

"Sure," said Arthur. "No problem."

"Well, ah, welcome aboard," said the Captain. "We're delighted to have you here. Though I fear that our voyage is, um, about to be cut short."

Everyone looked back over the stern. The *Shiver* had closed in and was now less than a mile away.

"She'll be firing her bowchasers soon," said Sunscorch. "If they've any powder. They've the weather gauge too. We'll have to fight it out."

"Oh," said Concort. He swallowed and frowned at the same time. "That doesn't sound very good."

"Can you get us a better wind, Doctor?" asked Sunscorch. "Untie one of your knots?"

"No," replied Scamandros. "Feverfew is already working the wind and his workings are stronger. There is no escape within the Border Sea."

"And is there, er, no plausible course out to the Realms?" Catapillow pulled his sword partly out of its scabbard as he spoke, and almost cut his nervous fingers on the exposed blade.

"There is one possibility that I may have overlooked due to extreme pain in my hand," said Scamandros. "I cannot cast the haruspices because of magical interference. But the young have natural ability, so this boy may be able to. Can you read portents of the future in the strewn intestines of animals, young sir?"

"No," said Arthur with a grimace of revulsion. "That sounds disgusting!"

"They don't use actual intestines any more," whispered Ichabod. "Just magical jigsaw puzzles of intestines."

"Indeed, the art has grown more orderly and less troublesome for the laundry," said Scamandros, who clearly had very superior hearing. "Though personally I believe it is best to be trained the old way, before coming to the puzzles. So you are not a haruspex or seer?"

"No..."

"Then you shall cast the pieces and I will read them." Scamandros took a large box out from under his coat – bigger than the one he'd put away before – and handed it to Arthur. There was a picture of an ox on the box, the back half cross-sectioned to show its innards. "Quickly now. Take the box and empty the pieces into your hands."

As Arthur opened the box, something shrieked overhead. It sounded like a cross between a train whistle and a terrified parrot. Sunscorch looked up, then muttered, "They've got powder! That's a ranging shot!" and started to shout more commands to the helmsman and crew. The *Moth* lumbered and rolled to port as the wheel spun and the crew hauled on lines to trim the yards, the horizontal spars on the mast that the sails were attached to.

Arthur knelt down on the deck and put his hands in the box. Though all he could see were pieces of coloured cardboard, he recoiled as he touched them.

"Ugh! They feel like raw mince or... or worse!"

"Ignore that!" instructed Scamandros. "Pick them up and cast them on the deck! Quickly now!"

Arthur shuddered and hesitated. Then he heard the whistling again and a huge plume of water exploded just behind the *Moth*, showering them all with freezing water.

"Over and under," said Sunscorch grimly. "They'll have the range inside a minute."

Arthur took a deep breath and plunged his hands into the box. Picking up the pieces was like picking up handfuls of dead worms. But he got them all, raised them up and threw them at Scamandros's feet.

As before, the jigsaw came together as it fell. But this time all the pieces joined to make a perfect rectangle. The colours ran and shimmered like spilled paint, then formed into lines and patterns. In a few seconds, a picture appeared. A picture of a rocky island, a mound of tumbled yellow stones, surrounded by a sea of curious colour, more violet than blue.

Scamandros looked at the picture, muttering to

himself, then he rolled up the chart at his feet and immediately unrolled it again, revealing a completely different map.

"Forlorn Island, Sea of Yazer, on the planet we call Gerain," said Scamandros. "That'll do!"

"Err, Mister Concort..." said Catapillow.

"Ah, Mister Sunscorch..." said Concort.

"Prepare to Cross the Line!" roared Sunscorch. "Idlers take a hold!"

Catapillow and Concort rushed to the rail and gripped it. Sunscorch joined the two Denizens on the wheel. Scamandros picked up the jigsaw, which didn't fall apart, and stood by them.

"Grab hold of a rope or the rail," Ichabod instructed Arthur. "When the doctor shouts, look down and close your eyes. And whatever you do, don't let go!"

Arthur did as he was told, taking a firm grip on the portside rail. He looked back at Dr Scamandros, who was holding the jigsaw and muttering to himself, with occasional instructions to Sunscorch.

"Port five, steady," he said. "Starboard ten and back again amidships, hold her as she goes, port five, port five, starboard ten..."

The *Moth* rolled and tilted first to one side and then the other, but didn't seem to change its actual direction very much for all the turning of the wheel this way and that.

But Dr Scamandros kept ordering small changes of direction.

Arthur heard a muffled bang come from behind them and looked astern, just in time to see the flash of the *Shiver*'s bowchasers, followed by that same whistling screech. This time, it didn't end in a waterspout or a pass overhead. Just as Dr Scamandros shouted something unintelligible and threw the jigsaw in the air, Arthur heard a terrible splintering, crashing noise that momentarily blotted out all other sounds.

But he didn't look. He closed his eyes and bent down as instructed, hoping that whatever the cannonball had hit wasn't going to fall down on his head.

There was a moment of silence after the terrible sound of some major part of the ship breaking, immediately followed by a flash so bright Arthur's eyes were filled with white light, even through shut eyelids. That flash was accompanied by a crash of thunder that shook the whole ship and stirred a vibration so strong it made Arthur's limbs and stomach ache.

Arthur knew what was happening at once. His hand went to the invitation card in his pocket and he hunkered down as low as he could, still clutching his pocket.

They were about to pass through the Line of Storms again!

The thunder was so deafening that its echoes lingered

in Arthur's ears and head, so even when it ceased it took him awhile before he stopped trembling and his hearing started to return. The after-image of the lightning remained in patches, and dark spots danced around his eyes.

Arthur opened his eyes to a scene of destruction and wonder. One of the huge horizontal spars from the *Moth*'s mainmast had been struck by the cannonball and broken off. Half of it was sprawled over the deck and half was in the water, a tangled mass of timber, ropes and canvas.

Arthur only glanced at that. His attention was drawn ahead of the ship. There, extending upward from the sea into the sky, was a huge gilt picture frame, easily four hundred feet long and three hundred feet high. It bordered an enormous, brightly glowing version of the jigsaw picture Arthur had made, with the yellow stone island and the violet sea. But this didn't look like a picture. The sea was in motion, there were purple-tinged clouds drifting above the island, and birds or birdlike things were flying around. Arthur could still see the jigsaw piece outlines – much narrower and more wriggly pieces than in a normal jigsaw – but the lines were very faint.

"Starboard Watch! Cut away that yard! Quickly now!"

The *Moth* rolled as Sunscorch spoke, sending its sails flapping, to make a sound like sarcastic applause.

"Helm! Hold her steady!" shouted Sunscorch.

The *Moth* was trying to sail straight for the framed

image, Arthur saw. He understood it was not an image. It was a doorway to another world, out in the Secondary Realms.

"Did we lose 'em?" asked Sunscorch to the doctor.

Scamandros looked astern, lowering his smoked glasses over his eyes to stare at the now surprisingly distant Line of Storms.

"I'm not... no!"

Arthur looked back, too, blinking at the still-bright flashes of lightning, though they were now several miles away. At first he couldn't spot anything, then he saw the silhouette of the *Shiver*'s dark sails. She had dropped back but would soon catch up again, particularly with the *Moth* slowed by the broken spar over the side, which acted like a large and clumsy sea anchor.

"They'll try and follow us through the portal," said Sunscorch.

"Um, is there anything... some manoeuvre or other?" asked Catapillow anxiously.

"Get that spar cut away!" roared Sunscorch. Arthur winced. Clearly Sunscorch got louder the more anxious he was.

Dr Scamandros looked ahead at the vast gilt-framed doorway to the violet-hued sea. It was several hundred yards away. He looked back at the pursuing ship, took out a pencil and made some calculations on the cuff of his big yellow coat.

"At our current speed Feverfew will board us short of the portal," he said. "Even if they don't take down a mast or hole us below the waterline."

"He won't fire again," said Sunscorch. "Don't need to, does he? We're slow enough now. Anything more might damage the loot."

This confident assessment was immediately undermined by the report of a cannon astern, resulting in another plume of water, this time well short.

"Then again, he might sink us for sport," added Sunscorch. He looked down at the main deck where the Denizens were hacking ineffectually with axes at the fallen yard. "Cut away! Don't slap at it! Cut! Doctor, if there's anything you can do, do it. No seamanship can save us now! I'm for an axe!"

"Carry on!" Catapillow called out as Sunscorch leapt down the companionway to the waist of the ship.

Arthur looked at the rapidly gaining pirate vessel, then at the living picture in its vast gilt frame. Even without calculating anything, it was clear the *Shiver* would catch them before they could get to the transfer portal. It was too far away...

Arthur suddenly had an idea.

"I don't know any sorcery or anything," Arthur said. "But that big painting is like a transfer plate you step on, isn't it?"

Scamandros nodded distractedly.

"So if we can't get to it in time, can it somehow be moved to us?"

Scamandros frowned, then cocked his head as if struck by Arthur's suggestion. Arthur noticed that all the small tattoos on the doctor's face were showing scenes of trouble. Storms at sea. Sunken ships. Exploding suns. Imploding planets.

Just as the doctor opened his mouth to speak, the *Shiver* fired again.

"Interesting. Yes, it is theoretically possible to—"

Whatever Scamandros was going to say was lost as a cannonball struck the *Moth's* side just behind and below the wheel, smashing the heavy timber into a spray of deadly foot-long splinters that went whistling across the quarterdeck.

CHAPTER SEVEN

The next thing Arthur knew, he was lying on the deck, right up against the rail, with his good leg hanging overboard. He could hear screaming all around him, and shouting. For a moment he thought he'd suffered a sudden asthma attack and had passed out from lack of air. But his breathing was fine, or so his mind reported before it suddenly switched back to the current situation. The splinters flying through the air—

Arthur pulled his leg in, sat up and stared around him. He was vaguely aware that his broken leg hurt, but that was nothing new. There was blood on his dressing gown, but it was bright blue. A pain in his left hand made him lift it up. There was blood there too – red blood, but not much of it. Arthur focused on his middle finger, and pulled out a needle-shaped splinter that had sliced across a knuckle and was still hanging there.

"Will you look at that?! Ruined!" said a voice next to Arthur. The boy slowly turned to look. There was a large hole on the far side of the deck. The planking was gouged all around and there was blue blood splattered all over the place, amid shattered wood and splinters.

Ichabod was pointing at his waistcoat. A splinter as long as Arthur's forearm was sticking out of the Denizen's stomach. Blue blood was trickling out of the wound and into his waistcoat pocket.

"Doesn't it hurt?" asked Arthur. He was in shock and part of his mind was telling him to check himself over again. He knew the Denizens could recover even from a beheading, but that didn't help. It also didn't apply to him. A wound like Ichabod's would kill him for sure.

"It certainly does hurt," replied Ichabod with a grimace. "But just look at my favourite waistcoat!"

Arthur looked along his own arms and legs. They were fine. He gingerly felt his stomach and head. They seemed fine too. Only his finger had been touched.

The Denizens around the wheel had not been so lucky. Arthur could hardly bear to look at them, they were so pierced by splinters. At least the blue blood didn't look so serious as real human blood would. And they were still standing and complaining about their bad luck.

"Seriously wounded to the Captain's quarters!" instructed Dr Scamandros. He didn't appear to be injured, but blue fluid dripped from the sleeve of his yellow greatcoat. "You too, mortal! You could be killed up here! Get below at once. Ichabod, take charge of our valuable passenger!"

Arthur struggled to his feet and hesitantly walked to the gangway, Ichabod at his side.

"Are you going to do something, Doctor?" asked Captain Catapillow plaintively, as he stared down at the spot where his foot and one of his third-best boots used to be. "I think that cannonball was coated in Nothing."

"You'd feel a lot worse if it was, Captain," said Dr Scamandros. "As I was saying, it is *theoretically* possible to accelerate the transfer by bringing the portal to the traveller, rather than the other way around. It is of course exceedingly difficult and dangerous."

Everyone looked at the pirate vessel astern. It fired again, a great gout of water exploding out of the sea a little ahead and to the port side of the *Moth*.

"What could happen that would be worse than eternal slavery or a slow and torturous death by Nothing-based sorceries at the hands of Feverfew?" asked Concort. He didn't sound like he really wanted to know.

"If I fail, we shall transfer not into that Secondary Realm, but into the Void of Nothing, and be immediately expunged from existence."

"My collection too?" asked Captain Catapillow.

"The ship and everything on it or connected with it," said Scamandros. "Including all your stamps, sir. So what are your orders?"

Arthur hesitated on the steps, waiting to hear Catapillow's commands. Surely there was some other way? Perhaps he could escape via the Infinite Stair... no... not in his current state. He probably didn't have the power any more...

"I can't have the collection fall into Feverfew's hands," said Captain Catapillow in a small voice. "All or... or Nothing!"

Arthur saw Scamandros open his yellow greatcoat. The inside was lined with dozens of pockets and loops for magical implements and apparatus. Scamandros selected two lengths of bronze rod with curved-back hooks set near their pointed ends. Though they were in miniature under his coat, only a few inches long, they expanded as he dragged them out, till they were at least a yard in length.

"Fire irons," said Ichabod. "Matching set. Very nice. Come along!"

Arthur started to follow Ichabod down the port-side ladder to the waist, where Sunscorch and the crew had finally succeeded in cutting away the last of the broken yard and its accompanying debris. But Arthur stopped on the companionway to look back. He saw Scamandros reaching out with a fire iron in each hand, the bronze rods continuing to extend till they became shafts of curdled sunlight that reached up into the sky and to each side of the ship.

Only a few seconds later, the transformed fire irons reached all the way to the vast gilt-framed portal to the Secondary Realm. The hooks on the end were now easily thirty feet long. The irons wavered outside the edges of the frame, then Scamandros brought them in and seated them. As sun bronze met magical gilt, there was a horrendous metallic noise, like an angle grinder suddenly cutting into steel, magnified a hundred times.

Everyone on the ship stared up at the portal and the doctor's two levers. Ichabod didn't protest or try to make Arthur go below. Like everyone else, he wanted to see what would happen next.

Scamandros shouted something, a word that passed through Arthur like a hot wire, causing him to cry out and clap his hands to his ears. The doctor shouted again and Arthur, suddenly stripped of strength, fell down the ladder on to the deck, taking a surprised Ichabod with him.

Then Scamandros yanked the fire irons back towards himself. This action was magnified all along their sun-curdled length. With the squeal of ten thousand fingers on a giant blackboard, the entire vast doorway to Forlorn Island shuddered towards the *Moth*.

At first, it looked like all was going well. The portal rapidly grew closer and the *Moth* continued to sail straight at it.

Then, when it was only yards away, the portal began to totter and shake, and the top edge started to lean forward. Behind it, in place of the normal sky, was a dark mass that glittered like some volcanic stone.

The Void of Nothing.

"Faster!" shouted Scamandros, fear in his voice. "Make the ship go *faster!*"

Denizens who had been frozen in awe sprang into action, goaded again by the now unbelievably loud voice of Sunscorch. Yards were trimmed, ropes hauled, sails hoisted where sails were hardly ever seen.

"Faster!" screamed Scamandros. The portal was falling towards them now, and instead of dragging it with the fire irons, the doctor was trying to hold it up. Darkness rippled behind it. "We must get through before it drops!"

The portal fell further and the bowsprit of the *Moth* pierced its shining jigsaw-crazed surface. Then the bow passed through and the rest of the ship followed. The light changed to a softer, golden tone and the breeze around Arthur became instantly warm.

As the sternpost of the *Moth* passed the portal, Scamandros fell to the deck, his fire irons clattering at his side, no longer anything more than lengths of bronze. The portal, its work done, collapsed in on itself. The threat of Nothing was gone.

But there were other troubles for the *Moth*.

"Splashdown! Brace!" roared Sunscorch. "Take hold!"

Arthur instantly shuffled back and wound his arms through the port-side ladder. He knew from the volume of Sunscorch's order that this was serious.

The *Moth* had come through the portal all right, but because of the angle of entry, they had not come through at the same level. The ship had entered this new world thirty feet above the water.

Now it was crashing down into the sea.

Before the echo of Sunscorch's shout had gone, the ship tilted precipitously forward. Arthur saw Ichabod slide past, till the Denizen managed to grab hold of a grating. Other Denizens tumbled along further down the deck and some fell or jumped from the rigging, though as far as Arthur could tell they went into the violet sea.

Then the ship struck. Arthur's legs went up in the air but he managed to keep hold of the ladder. His good foot kicked desperately for a hold as he tried to avoid sliding down the deck to the bow, which went completely under-water. For a dreadful second it looked to Arthur like the whole ship was going to nosedive straight into the deeps. But though the forward twenty feet or so were completely covered in foaming water, the *Moth* somehow came back up with a violent rolling action that spilled more Denizens into the sea.

Arthur was covered in spray, but he kept his grip. Gradually, the *Moth*'s roll slowed. Ichabod got up, dusted himself off with a *tsk*-ing noise and walked back to Arthur. The splinter that had been in his stomach was gone, but the waistcoat was still sodden with blue blood.

"Come down below," said Ichabod. "I've stopped bleeding but I have to help the doctor if there's anyone really seriously wounded."

"Is it safe to stand up?" asked Arthur. He didn't want to even guess what *really seriously wounded* might mean.

Ichabod looked around.

"I trust that is the case," he replied. "We have made it clear through the Transfer Portal. The sea here is quite placid, at least at present."

Arthur climbed wearily to his feet, grimacing as pain shot through his leg. When that subsided a little, he looked around. Sunscorch was giving orders, but not very loudly. Denizens were climbing back up the rigging and the ones that hadn't fallen off were already inching their way out across the yards, getting ready to furl the sails.

It all looked surprisingly calm, until a Denizen stuck his

head out of a forward hatch and shouted, "Mister Sunscorch! She's cracked a dozen strakes or more! There's four foot of water in the well!"

Arthur looked at Ichabod.

"I believe that means we are sinking," Ichabod said calmly. "Doubtless we shall hear more in a moment. Allow me to remove some flecks of wood from your coat."

Without waiting for permission, Ichabod started to remove tiny pieces of wood from Arthur's shoulders, reminding the boy how easily they could have been larger splinters that would have killed him.

He had to get out of the way as Sunscorch ran back to the quarterdeck, jumping halfway up the steps. There was a confused milling about going on around the wheel. As far as Arthur could tell, Dr Scamandros was barely conscious, but he had all the maps. They needed the maps to work out what to do before the ship sank, which was going to happen within the next thirty minutes at the rate they were taking in water through the cracked hull.

Though Captain Catapillow and First Mate Concort were both there, once again it was Sunscorch who really took charge.

"I'm guessing you'll want us to beach her dead ahead on Counter-Crab Beach, Captain?" Sunscorch asked, quite calmly. He pointed at Forlorn Island, which was only a mile or so away. "I've been here before, more than once. Good deep sand, quite steep. Once we're aground we can warp her about and careen her."

"Um, yes, very good, carry on, Mister Sunscorch," said Catapillow. "I'm just going to... ah... see to the situation belowdecks. Counter-Crab Beach, eh? Excellent. Excellent. Mister Concort, I believe we may leave the ship to Mister Sunscorch."

"Pardon?" asked Concort. The back of his coat was peppered with many holes, some of them stained with his own blue blood. "Aye, aye, sir."

They both left the quarterdeck, trooping down past Arthur and Ichabod. Neither looked at the boy and they seemed in a hurry to get back to the Captain's cabin. Catapillow was muttering something about humidity, gum Arabic and perforated edges.

"Exciting times," said Ichabod. "We don't normally have these sorts of goings-on going on. Not for a hundred years or more, we haven't. Come on."

"Can't we stay on deck?" asked Arthur as they walked away. He was still feeling very shaky after the shock of the cannon blast and, as he had expected, was already having a little trouble breathing now they had left the House. He also had little inclination to see the "really seriously wounded" and had a strong inclination to stay out in the open air. If he went below he thought he might throw up from reaction to shock. He needed fresh air and distraction.

"I suppose we might," said Ichabod. "The Captain and Mister Concort will be checking over the collection. They won't notice anything else. And Dr Scamandros will call if he needs me. We shall ask permission to join Mister Sunscorch on the quarterdeck."

Ichabod called up, and after a moment Sunscorch nodded and waved them both up. The original two helmsmen had gone below to have their wounds treated, accompanied by Dr Scamandros. They had been replaced by two of the Denizens who had brought Arthur in from the buoy.

"A fine bit of sailing and no mistake," said Sunscorch as Arthur rejoined him. The Denizen seemed very cheerful. "There's not many as can say they showed the *Shiver* a clean pair of heels."

"But aren't we sinking?" asked Arthur.

"We're taking water, that's certain," said Sunscorch. "But we'll be on the beach afore she drowns. And just as well, for there's at least a week's worth of repairs to be done."

"A week!" Arthur protested. He coughed as he spoke, sudden anxiety making his chest tight. A week out in this Secondary Realm might mean a week lost in his own world. He still didn't understand how time worked between the House and the Secondary Realms, but it couldn't be good to be out here for so long. What if he lost a week at home? His parents would freak out. So would Leaf's. Plus, he didn't have any asthma medication, so he might not even survive a week. What if his broken leg got worse?

"I can't spend a week on some deserted island!"

"You'll have to, 'less you're a better swimmer than you look," replied Sunscorch. "There's precious little on this world. Lots of islands, some things you might call fish and fowl, and a bit of useful timber, that's all. A safe haven from both Feverfew's pirates and any nosy parkers from the House."

"Nosy parkers?"

"Officials. Inspectors. Quaestors. Auditors. You know."

"Officials? Why would we be hiding from them?" asked Arthur. Not that he wanted to meet any himself. Too many of them served the Trustees who were his enemies.

"We're in the Secondary Realms without a licence," explained Ichabod. "It's the Original Law and there's fierce penalties to be here without permission. Not that there's much chance of trouble, not since Lady Wednesday's mind went adrift and she ate up half her officials and drowned—"

"Avast that!" interrupted Sunscorch. "We are still in Her Ladyship's service!"

"True! True! Mister Sunscorch, I beg your pardon."

"In any case, we have good reason to be here, which might prove sufficient excuse," said Sunscorch, after a moment. Though he spoke to Arthur, his gaze continued to roam over the masts and rigging, the ship and the crew. "As soon as we're able, we'll be back to the Border Sea and our business of salvage. Now we must shorten sail. We're riding deep and the sand is soft, but we've still too much way on."

Immediately Sunscorch raised his volume enormously, bellowing out some incomprehensible orders involving clewgarnets, buntlines, leechlines and slablines. These were all met with sudden activity by the crew.

"Now, all we need to do is get her safely lodged before teatime," said Sunscorch cheerfully, without looking away from the rapidly closing beach. "Try as I might, I can never get them to give up their afternoon tea. Once made clerks, always clerks, no matter how much salt they taste."

The ship slowed as sails were furled, and even Arthur could tell she was lower in the water and more sluggish to answer the helm. But they were only a few hundred yards from the beach, a wide crescent of sparkling sand that looked much like an earthly beach, save that the sand was a very light blue.

"We'll make it," said Sunscorch. But as he spoke, a bell rang from somewhere deep inside the ship. The peal quickly repeated several times. In answer to it, the crew left their posts, abandoned lines and slid down from the rigging. The Denizens who'd fallen overboard stopped treading water and started to swim for the ship, showing near-Olympic speeds without Olympic-standard grace or style. Even the helmsmen made as if to join the throng milling about a grating on the main deck of the ship, till they were physically restrained by Sunscorch.

"Oh, no you don't," he cried. "How many times do I have to tell you? If you're at the wheel you can't both go to afternoon tea. You have to take it in turns."

Arthur stared down at the main deck. The Denizens were accepting cups of tea in fine bone china cups that appeared out of the grating, even though there was no one below handing them up. Small biscuits also materialised in the air and were delicately taken and eaten in modest bites. The sight of both made Arthur aware that he was extraordinarily thirsty and hungry, despite the drink of water Sunscorch had given him in the boat. He knew he didn't need food or water, but he felt as if he did.

"How... where are the cups coming from?"

"It's one of the things that didn't change when we remade the counting house," said Ichabod. "Some department in the Lower House is still supplying us with afternoon tea, wherever we are in the House or the Secondary Realms. I would venture to suppose that an order was given long ago and it has never been rescinded. It's quite convenient, of course, and we are the envy of many other ships."

"It's a cursed nuisance," said Sunscorch. He cupped his hands around his mouth and shouted, "All hands come aft! Hold yer cups and saucers!"

The crew was slow to respond and Sunscorch shouted again. The beach was only fifty or sixty yards distant.

"They're best aft. We might lose a mast when we strike," Sunscorch explained to Arthur. "But it'll go for'ard, like as not."

Arthur looked up at the two very tall masts and their mass of spars and rigging. They had to weigh tons, and if one or both of them came down backwards instead of forward, they'd crush everyone.

"Take a hold!" roared Sunscorch.

CHAPTER EIGHT

Arthur hardly felt the *Moth*'s initial impact with the beach. The deck shuddered a little under him, but he was sitting down with his bad leg straight out and he had a very firm grip on an iron cleat next to the rail.

More serious shudders followed, as the ship ground its way up and through the deep sand. Arthur watched the masts carefully, and though they shivered and the rigging rattled and a few ropes and blocks fell down, nothing worse occurred.

After a few more yards' progress, the *Moth* gave a final creaking groan and slid forward no more. It sat upright for a few moments, then slowly heeled over till the deck was at an angle of twenty degrees. Arthur wondered if it was going to go over completely on its side, but the deep sand around the hull held it in place.

Amazingly not one of the crew appeared to have dropped his or her teacup. While Arthur gingerly crawled to the side and looked over at the blue sand, Ichabod went and got a cup of tea to offer to Arthur.

Arthur drank it gratefully, though it was very strong, very sweet and very milky. When the cup was empty, he handed it back to Ichabod, who asked, "More?"

"Yes, please," said Arthur. He was quite surprised when Ichabod simply handed the cup straight back, but the cup was full again. Strangely this time the tea was black and, while still sweet, had been made so by something like treacle. Arthur drank it anyway.

"Just say 'more' if you want more," Ichabod explained. He handed Arthur a biscuit and added, "Similarly, as long as you have a crumb left of biscuit, just say 'more' and you'll get another one. Till afternoon tea is over, which is in about five minutes by my reckoning."

Arthur nodded and concentrated on the business of drinking and eating, with occasional, mouth-full mumblings of "more".

Precisely five minutes later by Arthur's backwards watch, his cup and half-eaten biscuit disappeared. This disappearance was followed by a stream of bellowed orders from Sunscorch, who had clearly bottled them up till afternoon tea was over. As far as Arthur could gather, the orders related to propping the ship up so it didn't fall over, getting out some anchors and carrying lots of different things ashore.

Without imminent danger threatening, and with a full, warm stomach, Arthur found himself yawning. His watch said it was ten past ten, but he knew he must have spent more than seven hours (counting backwards) just sitting in that buoy, let alone the time on the bed in the storm.

Remembering the buoy made Arthur look at his hands. The red colour still hadn't come off. It hadn't got any lighter either. It looked deeply engrained, almost as if it was in the skin, rather than just on it.

"The Red Hand," said Ichabod. "Dr Scamandros might be able to clear it. Feverfew marks all his treasure caches such. The stain is supposed to last forever. Well, until Feverfew tracks the thief down and exacts his terrible punishment. What were you doing on the buoy anyway?"

"I... I was shipwrecked," said Arthur.

"From the *Steelibed*," interrupted Sunscorch as he slid down the deck. "Or so you say. The Captain, Mister Concort and I will want to hear Arth's tale, Ichabod, so hold your questions till dinner. Which will be served ashore, so you can begin by getting the Captain's table on the beach. Arth, you go ashore too and stay out of the way."

"Aye, aye," said Ichabod, without great enthusiasm.

"And look lively, you loblolly boy."

Being called a *loblolly boy* made Ichabod both cross and active. Bent over almost double to keep his balance on the tilted deck, he crawled over to the companionway and hustled below. Arthur was left alone.

He wanted to ask Sunscorch some questions, about almost everything, but particularly about the green-sailed ship that had taken up Leaf. But the Second Mate was too busy, shouting orders and stamping about the quarterdeck.

After a few minutes watching the crew, the boy climbed down from the quarterdeck and made his way through the working crowd of Denizens, equipment and cargo that was being rigged or moved above or through the hatches in the waist of the ship. Eventually he found his way to the forecastle at the front of the vessel. There were several broad rope ladders over each side. Arthur waited for a space in the line of Denizens climbing down with their loads, then carefully lowered himself over the side and climbed down.

It was quite difficult with his leg immobilised by the cast, but he made it. There was still water around the ship, so he splashed into it, and was relieved to find it was very shallow. The blue sand seemed much the same as sand back home. Difficult to walk in, even without a leg in a cast. Arthur found himself imitating one of the Denizens with a wooden leg, not so much walking as stumping his way up the beach.

One of the things the Denizens had brought ashore already was the chest from Feverfew's trove. Arthur walked over to it. It looked ordinary enough, just a big wooden box with bronze reinforcement at each corner and bands of bronze across the lid. He wondered what was inside. What would Feverfew the Pirate value so much?

Arthur sat down and leaned back against the chest. He felt very tired, but he didn't want to go to sleep. He had to work out what to do next. Not that there seemed to be many choices. He felt that he should do something to make sure Leaf was OK, but he couldn't think of anything. And he should try to contact Dame Primus or Suzy. And he should try and get home as soon as possible, but Leaf was right, he ought to sort out Lady Wednesday first and that meant finding the Third Part of the Will, claiming the Third Key...

Arthur's thoughts trailed off into a confused mishmash of different problems and unlikely solutions. His body was too tired and it had finally got its message through to his brain.

The boy slid further into the sand and his head slumped down. As the Denizens toiled to lighten the ship by removing cargo and prop her up with spare yards and topmasts, Arthur slept.

He awoke at sundown. At first, he was totally disoriented. Not only was he lying on a blue beach, but there was an enormous vermilion sun sinking into the sea on the horizon. Its weird light mixed with the violet hues of the sea and the blue of the sand sent alarming messages to his brain.

The reason he'd woken was instantly obvious. Dr Scamandros was sitting next to him, peering at his leg through what looked like a very short telescope. He also had a small bellows with him, a leather-lunged apparatus that looked to Arthur like the original ancestor of an air-bed pump.

"What are you doing?" Arthur asked suspiciously. He sat up and glared at Scamandros. The doctor looked quite different, though it took Arthur a second to work out why. His animated tattoos were gone and he was wearing a woolly cap with a long tassel that hung down next to his neck.

"Your leg has been recently broken," said Dr Scamandros. "And set."

"I know," Arthur replied. His leg was hurting again. He wondered if Scamandros had been prodding it. "That's why it's in a cast. Or was..."

He added the last bit because the ultra-high-tech cast had almost completely fallen apart. There were only thin strips of it remaining, and Arthur could see his pale and puffy skin in the gaps between.

"Usually, I could fix that leg for you," said Dr Scamandros. "But my examination reveals a very high and unusual level of magical contamination that would resist any direct action to repair the bone. I could, however, equip you with a better brace and exert some small magic that would lessen the pain."

"That would be good," said Arthur hesitantly. "But what do you want in return?"

"Merely your goodwill," said Scamandros with a halfhearted chuckle. He tapped the bellows at his side and added, "Though I understand from Ichabod that you might have a cold? If so, I should like to harvest any sneeze, nose-tickle or phlegmatic effusion that you feel coming on."

Arthur wrinkled his nose experimentally.

"No, I haven't got a cold. I just thought I might."

Scamandros was looking through his short telescope again, this time at Arthur's chest.

"There is also a disturbance in the interior arrangement of your lungs," he said. "Most interesting. Again, there is magical contamination of a high order, but I think I could probably lessen the underlying condition. Would you like me to proceed?"

"Uh, I'm not sure," said Arthur. He took a breath. He couldn't completely fill his lungs, but it wasn't too bad. "I think I'll wait. It'll be all right when I get back in the House."

"Just the leg brace, then," said Dr Scamandros. "And amelioration of the pain."

He slid his stubby telescope into one pocket of his greatcoat and, reaching inside, took out a flat tin labelled with the picture of a bright red crab. It had a key stuck to it, which Scamandros now broke off, connected to a tab and used to wind back the metal lid. There was a whole small crab inside, but the Denizen only broke off one of its legs. He put the leg on the sand and passed his open palm across the tin, which disappeared.

Arthur watched with both curiosity and anxiety as Scamandros picked up the tiny crab leg and held it high in his left hand. A thick carpenter's pencil appeared in his right hand and he used this to lightly sketch several lines and asterisks on Arthur's leg. Then he clapped his hands, still holding both pencil and crab leg.

The two objects disappeared and at the same time, the remnants of Arthur's modern cast were instantly replaced by an armoured section of red-and-white-speckled crab exoskeleton, jointed at the knee and ankle.

"As for the pain," Scamandros said, scribbling on a piece of paper with a pen that trailed glowing crimson ink, "take this prescription."

Arthur took the page of heavy, deckle-edged paper. It was very hard to read, but he made it out eventually:

Apply pain-lessening paper to painful area once

Dr J R L Scamandros, DHS (Upper House, Failed)

"What does DHS stand for? And... excuse me... why do you put 'failed' on it?" Arthur asked as he touched the paper to his leg, directly above the break, where it hurt most. The paper crumbled as he spoke, paper-dust forming a miniature tornado that appeared to go straight through his new cast and into his leg. A moment later, the dull pain there started to ebb.

"It stands for Doctor of House Sorcery," said Scamandros. "A very high degree, which I so very nearly possess. Honesty necessitates me to reveal my failure, but it was only in my final year. Seven hundred and ninety-eight years of successful examinations, only to fall at the end. Politics, you understand! But I do not wish to speak of that.

"Let us talk of you instead, Arth. You hold a magical book of great potency in your pocket, too potent for me to even touch without your leave. Your very flesh and bones reek of past magics. You are found on a buoy of the infamous pirate Feverfew, in the Border Sea of the House. Yet you are a mortal, or mostly so. Tell me, on what world in the Secondary Realms do you make your home?"

Arthur almost answered "Earth," but restrained himself just in time. Scamandros had certainly helped him, but there was something about the look in his piercing brown eyes that made Arthur think the fewer secrets he knew the better.

"Passenger Arth! The Captain's compliments and you are to join him for a beachside supper!"

Ichabod's call was very welcome. Arthur struggled to his feet, pleasantly surprised to find that his leg was well supported by the crab armour. Scamandros helped him find his balance.

"We shall speak more, and soon, Arth," the doctor said. Arthur noticed that his tattoos were starting to crawl across his face again, emerging from the skin like a blush. The Denizen leaned in close as Arthur started to step away and added, "Or should I say Arthur, Master of the Lower House and Lord of the Far Reaches?"

CHAPTER NINE

Arthur felt as if Dr Scamandros was watching his back the whole time it took to stomp across the beach to an open-sided tent, where he could see Captain Catapillow, Concort and Sunscorch sitting at a long, white, cloth–covered table. Lanterns hung at the tent's corners, their soft yellow glow in stark contrast to the strange scarlet twilight.

As he walked across the beach, Arthur was thinking furiously. Was Scamandros threatening to reveal his real identity? It hadn't sounded like a threat, but he couldn't be sure. What did the sorcerer want? Who did he serve? He was trained in the Upper House... or so he said. He could easily be a servant of one of the Morrow Days, who would do anything to stop Arthur from liberating any more of the Will.

"Mind the barrels," said Ichabod, leading Arthur between two pyramids of different-sized barrels. There was a huge amount of stuff on the beach, all of it very carefully stacked and ordered. Barrels and boxes and crates and bags. And there in the tent, in front of the table, was Feverfew's chest. Arthur wondered how they'd taken it away without waking him up. Perhaps he'd already slid forward into the sand by that point.

"Bring the passenger forward, Ichabod," ordered Captain Catapillow. He had a writing book open in front of him, and a pen and inkwell, as did Concort. Sunscorch had a huge, thick, leather-bound tome the size of several bricks.

It looked more like a court bench than a dinner table. And "passenger" had sounded awfully like "prisoner".

"Stand in front of the Captain and bow," whispered Ichabod, nudging Arthur forward. The boy complied, inclining his head not just to the Captain, but also to Concort and Sunscorch. Catapillow and Concort gave the slightest nods back and Sunscorch winked, which Arthur found encouraging.

"Now, due to, ah, the irregular nature of the last day, we have not been able to, er, keep up to date the log of our good ship *Moth*," said Catapillow, leaning forward to fix Arthur with his unsteady stare. "Wishing to be, ah, beforehand with such records and intending to inscribe you as a passenger has reminded me that we do not, ah, know who you are, where you are going or what fare you should be charged. There is also the matter of this treasure."

He leaned back when he'd finished talking and folded his hands together.

"You want to know who I am?" asked Arthur. He wasn't sure whether Catapillow's speech actually needed to be answered.

"Indeed," said Concort. "That is of the essence. Who are you? Where are you from? Where are you going? How did you come to be on Feverfew's buoy? Why did you remove the telltale red pitch from the marker so that we didn't know whose treasure it was below? Do you claim the treasure yourself?"

"Well..." said Arthur slowly, stalling as he tried to think of some answers that wouldn't get him into trouble. Clearly, Scamandros already knew or strongly guessed who he was. Would it be any worse if the others knew as well? He needed help – to find Leaf, for a start.

It would be a big gamble. Sunscorch would support him, he thought, because he had the Mariner's disc. Ichabod seemed to like him. Catapillow and Concort were

115

kind of stupid, even if they were technically in charge, so perhaps they didn't matter too much. Dr Scamandros... Arthur really wasn't sure about that Denizen, but after he'd recovered from having his fingers burned by the Atlas he'd been nice enough. The crab armour on Arthur's leg worked really well...

"Speak up!" ordered Concort. His voice suddenly squeaked, which removed all authority from it.

"My real name is Arthur Penhaligon," Arthur said slowly. "I am a mortal from Earth. But I am also Master of the Lower House and of the Far Reaches, though I have given up my Keys in trust to Dame Primus, who was once Parts One and Two of the Will of the Architect."

Catapillow's mouth curled up at one end as Arthur spoke. Then he broke out in uproarious laughter, followed a second later by Concort. Sunscorch neither smiled nor laughed, but looked down at the huge book in front of him.

"Very good, very good," Catapillow chortled. "Master of the Lower House and the Far Reaches! Arthur Penhaligon! Most amusing!"

"But I am Arthur Penhaligon!"

"Yes, yes, you've had your joke," said Catapillow. "Now you must answer our questions."

"Most specifically, do you intend to claim this treasure?" added Concort.

"No, I really *am* Arthur Penhaligon! Why don't you believe me?"

"Don't be silly," replied Catapillow. "Everyone knows Lord Arthur is a mighty fighter! Why, he defeated Mister Monday in personal combat and wrestled Grim Tuesday to the ground and broke both his hands. Besides, I've seen a picture of Lord Arthur. Huge, broad-shouldered chap, carries a bag full of magical apparatus he invented himself."

"Not to mention he always travels with his giant half-bear, half-frog assistant," said Concort. "And an assassin girl who used to be the Piper's bodyguard."

"What?" asked Arthur. "You mean the Will and Suzy Blue?"

"It's all here, you know," said Concort, pulling out a tiny book from his sleeve. It expanded into a large hardcover, bound in red, with the title embossed in enormous gilt letters on both the spine and front cover, *The Epic Adventures of Lord Arthur, Hero of the House.*

"Look, the frontispiece is a portrait of Lord Arthur."

Concort held the book open to show a colour plate that had been stuck in next to the title page. It showed a very tall, handsome man who looked and dressed rather like Monday's Noon. He was posing next to an open carpetbag that was glowing with rainbow-coloured light. A bizarre, hunched-over monster that had the legs of a frog and the upper body and front paws of a bear crouched next to him, and in the background an Amazon woman in silver armour was cutting the head off a misshapen semi-human creature that was clearly supposed to be a Nithling.

"So, who are you?" asked Concort again, snapping the book shut. "And let's be clear this time, what about the treasure?"

"What about the treasure?" asked Arthur as he tried to gather his thoughts. It hadn't even occurred to him that they might doubt his identity. But it was clear that both Concort and Catapillow's main concern was the treasure. "I don't even know what the treasure is. Do I have a claim to it?"

Catapillow and Concort looked at Sunscorch.

"It looks as if that's so," said the Second Mate, tapping the book in front of him. "Dr Scamandros had a reading of the laws for me, and it looks to be that young Arth here is entitled to ninety per cent of the value of this treasure."

"Ninety per cent!" exclaimed Catapillow and Concort. Catapillow added, "Dr Scamandros! How can this be so?"

Arthur hadn't seen the doctor, but the Denizen stepped into the light from beside the table, so he must have followed Arthur and then stood in the shadows.

"According to *The Blue Book of Admiralty*, a fixed buoy treasure marker is itself considered a vessel. This young mortal here was in command of the vessel by virtue of being on it. Mister Sunscorch took him off at his request, but Arth did not relinquish command of the buoy, which marked the treasure, and which was not taken in tow. By taking the chest and not the buoy as well, the vessel is still considered to be afloat and the treasure it marked notionally still of it, though no longer marked by it. The matter is further complicated as the treasure was the property of a pirate outlawed by direct writ of Lady Wednesday. So it is considered immediately forfeit and property of the House authorities, with a reward equal to an amount of ninety per cent of the value of the treasure being paid to the finder. We are not the finder, Arth is, as demonstrated by the unfortunate fact that he is marked with the Red Hand. We are in the position of having salvaged the finder and must come to some arrangement with him. But should Arth wish to be returned to that buoy with the chest, we must do so."

"I'm not sure I followed that," said Arthur. "You're saying the treasure has to be given to Wednesday because it belongs to a pirate? And I'm entitled to a reward equal to ninety per cent of its value because I found it first?"

"Yes," said Scamandros. "However, we do not have to help you. We can simply return you and the chest to the treasure marker. There is also the matter of the original owner of the treasure. So there is room to negotiate, I think."

"Sure." Arthur tried to smile as he spoke. It sounded crazy to him, but no crazier than some of the court reports on the news back home. Murderers who weren't murderers because of weird technicalities. Companies that didn't have to pay debts because of odd loopholes. "What do you suggest?"

"We should first find out what's in the chest," said Dr Scamandros. "Do we have your permission to open it?"

"Yes!" exclaimed Arthur. He was surprised they hadn't opened it already. He would have if they'd been asleep all afternoon.

"I have taken the precaution of examining the chest with various magical instruments," Scamandros continued. "And I have neutralised a number of nasty little traps. So it should be quite safe to open. Just flip back those two catches and turn the key."

"There wasn't a key there before," said Arthur.

"Yes, I had to fashion one to fit," said Scamandros. "Go ahead, open it."

"Why do you want me to open it?" asked Arthur. Scamandros knew who he really was and there was still something slightly shifty about the sorcerer. He wouldn't quite meet Arthur's gaze. "What if there's a trap you missed?"

"I am merely following correct procedure. It is your—"

"Stand back, lad," interrupted Sunscorch, who had left

the table. "Best to let a Denizen bear the brunt of any trickery. You mortals are too fragile."

"Thanks," muttered Arthur. He felt a bit bad now, as if he'd been a coward, but Sunscorch seemed to think it was perfectly sensible of him to refuse. He smiled and nodded at the boy as he walked past and knelt before the chest.

Sunscorch lifted the two clasps at the same time. They snapped back with a loud click, immediately followed by a strange popping noise that made Arthur jump, till he realised that it was actually the sound of the entire crew of the *Moth* drawing in breaths of anticipation. They were all gathered around in a half circle up the beach, beyond the lantern light. The last of the vermilion twilight had faded, so the Denizens were just dark outlines, but Arthur could sense their concentration on Sunscorch and the chest.

The Second Mate turned the key. It played musical notes as it turned several times in the lock.

Ting-ting-ting-ting-ting...

Each note seemed like it would be the last. Finally the key stopped, and instead of a jangled note, there was a soft *snick* as the lock released. Sunscorch leaned forward and lifted the lid.

"Ahhhh!" came from a hundred throats.

"Is that all?" asked Arthur, looking over Sunscorch's shoulder. The contents of the chest looked very disappointing to him. It was full of little off-white blocks carved with letters. They looked like cheap mah-jong pieces.

Sunscorch didn't answer. He seemed quite stunned. Looking around, Arthur saw that nearly everybody else was as well. They were all staring with their mouths open.

Except for Dr Scamandros. He bent down and picked up one of the small blocks and tilted it so the character carved into its surface caught the light.

"A deep, racking cough," pronounced Scamandros. "Fixed in auriphant ivory from Senhein. Good for twenty years or more, as House time flows."

He put it back again and took out another piece.

"A roseola rash around the neck, head and ears," said Scamandros. "Fixed in wood-fired clay. Good for at least a decade in the House."

Arthur knew that human diseases were valued by the Denizens of the House. They would get the symptoms, but not feel the effects. So these little blocks of ivory and clay were how the diseases were actually used by the Denizens, and would presumably be in demand. But what were they worth?

"This is a great treasure," said Dr Scamandros. "A very great treasure. There must be twenty thousand coughs, rashes, swellings and other diseases here, all of the highest virulence and fixed by first-class sorcery. I would guess its value to be in excess of a million simoleons of gold."

His words were met by a vast cheer from the crew, who began to sing and dance around and throw their caps in the air.

"And ninety per cent of it is mine?" asked Arthur. He could barely make himself heard above the uproar.

"Notionally," replied Scamandros. "As I said, if you want both yourself and the treasure to remain salvaged, you must come to an agreement with Captain Catapillow."

"Feverfew will never bear this loss," muttered Sunscorch, who was still staring at the open chest. He pointed at a small bronze plaque set on the underside of the chest's lid. As his finger touched it, the letters engraved there burst into red fire and a booming voice roared across the beach:

"THIEVES! THIEVES! THIEVES! This be the treasure of Captain Elishar Feverfew! The Red Hand marks you! Feverfew's vengeance shall be swift and slow: swift in the taking, slow in the making. Regret and repentance shall prove no—"

Whatever else the voice was going to shout stopped as Dr Scamandros tapped the plaque with an ebony paper knife that materialised in his hand. Silence fell over the beach, the only sound the lapping of the waves on the shore. The Denizens' songs and cheer were gone, replaced by a mood of dread.

"I'm the only one with the Red Hand," said Arthur. "Aren't I?"

"Yes," said Dr Scamandros. "Though Feverfew would kill or enslave anyone sailing with you or giving you aid."

"You're a sorcerer – can't you get rid of it?"

"No. It is beyond my power. Feverfew is an expert in magics I do not wish to know."

Arthur looked down at the treasure, then at his red hands.

"So you're all at risk from Feverfew while I'm around?"

"Indeed. Though, in truth, Feverfew kills or enslaves everyone he encounters anyway. But the Red Hand marks you for a particularly long and unpleasant ending and we would probably share in it."

"Can you send messages to other parts of the House? And can you find out what's happening to someone if they're in the House? I mean, by sorcery."

"Yes, on both counts."

"In that case," said Arthur, turning back to Captain Catapillow, "I am prepared to offer you, and the crew of the *Moth*, all of my share of the reward in return for some help. I want to get a message to Dame Primus..."

Captain Catapillow nodded his agreement.

"I need to find out what's happened to my friend Leaf, who I think is aboard a ship with glowing green sails..."

Once again Catapillow nodded, this time with a smile.

Arthur paused, thinking about what he might need.

"And I might... I might want passage as quickly as possible to wherever I can meet Drowned Wednesday."

"What!" shrieked Catapillow. "Are you totally mad?"

CHAPTER TEN

"Take you to Drowned Wednesday!" repeated Catapillow. "Do you think us fools?"

"Uh, no," said Arthur. "I only said I *might* want to go and see her. I'm not sure where I should go next. But I have been invited to have lunch with Lady Wednesday—"

"You mean to *be* lunch!" scoffed Concort. He paled and added, "Excuse me! I didn't mean to say that!"

"I'm sure we can work something out with regard to the treasure," said Catapillow. "Dr Scamandros will help you find your friend, send messages and so forth. We will even carry you to Port Wednesday. But I'm sure you will be as grateful as we will be to not encounter our most esteemed but sadly submerged ultimate mistress."

"Why?" Arthur asked, wondering why Catapillow and the others seemed unreasonably terrified at the idea. But they were in her service, or at least they operated in her demesne of the House. Presumably she gave them orders or sent them instructions from time to time. But perhaps she was slothful, like Mister Monday, and the administration of the Border Sea was all fouled up like it had been in the Lower House.

"By the way," Arthur continued, "do you have any orders about Lord Arthur? I mean, if you happened to pick him up, what would you do with him?"

"Pick up Lord Arthur? Well, naturally, we should do whatever he wanted us to do," replied Catapillow. "He's lord of two domains within the House!"

"We wouldn't want to cross that half-frog thing," said Concort. "Or the killer girl either."

"So you haven't been instructed by Lady Wednesday or her officers to do anything to Arthur if he does show up?"

Sunscorch snorted. Catapillow and Concort looked at each other. Eventually Concort muttered, "Very busy these days, Drowned Wednesday, what with eating... with various things... unfortunately Noon and Dusk went missing some years ago, the confusion arising out of the flooding..."

"What Mister Concort means," cut in Dr Scamandros, "is that the *Moth* has been largely forgotten these six or seven thousand years. I don't believe we have had any instructions in that time. We simply cruise the Border Sea, take our salvage from it, and sell it and replenish our stores at Port Wednesday or, if we are pressed, at less salubrious anchorages both in the Border Sea and out in the Secondary Realms. Now tell me, have you really been invited to luncheon with Lady Wednesday?"

"Yes," said Arthur. He reached into his pocket and drew out the soggy invitation. Dr Scamandros took it, raised his eyebrows at the almost complete absence of readable type upon it and set it on the table. He took an oval-shaped felt blotter out of his coat and rolled it across the card several times. With each pass, the card dried and the ink returned to its former density and blackness. Catapillow and Concort craned over the table to look, and even Sunscorch tilted his head to get a proper view.

Arthur watched the two officers' faces change as they read the invitation, going from curiosity through puzzlement to shock. Sunscorch, though he moved his lips to read, did not seem unduly affected.

LADY WEDNESDAY

Trustee of the Architect and Duchess of the Border Sea
has great pleasure in inviting
ARTHUR PENHALIGON
to a Particular Luncheon of Seventeen Removes
Transport has been arranged
RSVP not required

"I don't understand," said Catapillow. "Then you must be—"

"But you can't be," said Concort. "You're just a boy!"

"He is," said Scamandros. "Who else might have *A Compleat Atlas of the House* in his top pocket and the mark of the Mariner's favour on a string around his neck? Not to mention this very curious invitation."

"Why is it curious?" asked Arthur. For the first time since the wave picked him up he had time to ask some questions instead of just trying to stay alive or recover from the effort of staying alive. "Why is everyone scared of her? Why do you call her Drowned Wednesday? And what was the Deluge and all that?"

Catapillow and Concort still looked stunned. Sunscorch looked at Scamandros.

"Best if the doctor explains all that to you," said Sunscorch after a moment. "The Captain and Mister

Concort have duties to attend to, as do I."

"I trust you'll join us for supper, Lord Arthur?" murmured Captain Catapillow, without meeting Arthur's eye. "Without any, ah, hard feelings as to our regrettable lack of, er—"

"Sure," said Arthur. "I understand. It's just that the book makes me seem more like a big hero. Who wrote it anyway?"

Concort opened the book again and showed Arthur the title page. Catapillow looked embarrassed and walked off, muttering something to Dr Scamandros as he went past.

"It is, um, written by someone called Japeth, 'Official Biographer, Chronicler, Annalist and Recorder of Lord Arthur'," said the First Mate. "Published by the Dayroom Press of the Lower House."

"I see," said Arthur with a frown. Japeth was his friend, the Thesaurus he'd met in the Pit. He had asked Dame Primus to give him a job, but he hadn't expected it would be writing something that was basically propaganda. He wondered what the point of it was. Why make him out to be such a big hero?

"If you would care to walk with me, I shall attempt to answer your questions about Lady Wednesday and the Deluge," said Dr Scamandros. He lifted his hand and a candle appeared there, lighting up as he blew softly on the wick. "We shall wade in the shallows, so that the sea shall cloak our conversation. There are some matters it is best not to excite the crew with."

Arthur hesitated. While he thought about whether it would be smart to go off with the doctor alone, he looked at Sunscorch and tapped the Mariner's medallion. The Second Mate gave a slight nod.

"All right," said Arthur. "Lead on."

He followed the Denizen out of the bright pool of lantern-light, down the beach and past a line of very neatly organised piles of spare clothing. Each pile was individually labelled.

Scamandros saw him looking at the tidy arrangement and guessed what he was thinking.

"The crew was originally the staff of a counting house," he said. "A warehouse where goods were sorted and valued. They were made for that purpose and, being Denizens of a low order, they change and learn very slowly. Hence they are not very good sailors, but excel at the movement and ordering of cargo. Here we are. I shall just take off my shoes and roll up my breeches."

Dr Scamandros thrust the candle in the sand and sat to remove his shoes. Arthur sat down too and took off his Immaterial Boots.

"We must be careful," Scamandros said as he took up the candle again and waded into the froth. "The beach shelves very steeply. We shall stay near the tidemark."

They started walking along, Dr Scamandros on the lower slope, nearer the sea, so he was almost the same height as Arthur. He was very short for a Denizen, Arthur thought. Shorter even than the miserable Coal-Collaters in the deep cellars of the Lower House.

"Where shall we begin?" asked Scamandros.

"What's the story with Wednesday?" asked Arthur. "Why is everyone afraid of even going near her?"

"I can answer more easily than most, because I am a volunteer on the *Moth* and not in fact in her service," said Scamandros. "I also have made something of a study of both the Border Sea and its ruler. I am sure you are familiar with the Will of the Architect, the breaking of it by the Trustees and so forth?"

"Yes," said Arthur. "You could say that."

"Around that time, Lady Wednesday began to be afflicted by an enormous hunger, something no Denizen usually has to any degree. We merely eat for amusement. She ate and ate and ate, and would normally have grown larger and larger. However, by using the power of the Third Key, she was able to keep this growth in abeyance. This continued for some two thousand years, even though by that time she was eating tons and tons of food every day.

"I am not sure exactly what happened then. Either the power of the Key failed or she misdirected it. In any case, she was transformed into a shape and size appropriate to the amount of food she was eating. She became a Leviathan."

"A what?"

"A Behemoth."

"Um, I don't—"

"A monstrous white whale. A stupendous whale! One hundred and twenty-six miles from tail to head, and thirty-two miles in width, with a mouth when open that is two miles high and ten miles wide."

Arthur stopped walking to think about this. A whale one hundred and twenty-six miles long! Dr Scamandros kept walking and talking so he had to scurry to catch up and missed a few words.

"...transformation and immersion in the Border Sea displaced a vast quantity of water. Fortunately the transformation took place over a week or more, allowing time to prepare the docks and foreshore buildings, most of which were turned into ships like the *Moth*. A new port was partly prepared on the ridge of Wednesday's Lookout, now Port Wednesday.

"But the greatest destruction to actual Denizens was not wrought by the Deluge, but by Lady Wednesday herself. In the shape of a Leviathan she was hungrier than ever, and in her early years, she ate not only the usual plankton, krill and other small creatures by the ton, but also many of her own servants, including her Noon and

Dusk. No one has dared approach her for millennia, save her surviving Dawn, who it is believed she communicates with by moving the pupils of her massive eye in some code, so Dawn need not get too close.

"That is why it is strange that you should be invited to lunch with her. How can you have lunch with a Leviathan? Particularly one that eats everything that comes anywhere near her?"

"Why is she called Drowned Wednesday?" asked Arthur. "I mean, she's obviously not drowned."

"I believe that when she first began to transform she flung herself into the Border Sea and was presumed drowned," said Scamandros. "A nasty fate for a Denizen, since some consciousness would remain until the fishes completely nibbled you away. I also suspect that the term 'Whale Wednesday' is shied away from by her still-loyal Denizens."

Arthur nodded and hopped forward to completely catch up. They were quite a long way along the beach now, the lights of the camp a hundred yards or more behind. Arthur glanced at Dr Scamandros's face. Most of it lay in shadow, only the lower part of his visage illuminated by the candle. His tattoos were moving and shifting, but it was too dark for Arthur to make out what they were showing, save for one of a ship that was cruising across the Denizen's cheek with all sails set.

"Perhaps we should turn around," said Arthur nervously.

Scamandros halted and looked at Arthur.

"We have come far enough to try a little sorcery that may find an answer to your questions," he said, walking up the beach to set his candle down. Arthur followed, the blue sand sticking to his wet feet.

"What was it you wanted first?" asked Dr Scamandros. "A message to Dame Primus or news of your friend?"

"I want to see what's happened to Leaf," said Arthur. Even though she hadn't listened when he'd told her to get out of the hospital room, he still felt responsible... and guilty. He hoped she was all right.

"Your friend was picked up by another ship?"

"Yes," said Arthur. "A bit like the *Moth*, but thinner and longer, with three masts. It had sails that glowed green. I think it was meant to pick me up, like it said in the invitation. 'Transport has been arranged.' Only they got Leaf instead."

"The ship sounds like the *Flying Mantis*. One of the ships of Wednesday's original merchant marine. Which would make sense. Now, do you have anything that belongs to your friend? A lock of hair, perhaps?"

"No!" said Arthur. "I mean, she's just a friend. Like a fairly new friend too."

"Mmm, that makes it more difficult, even though

knowing the ship will narrow things down," mused Scamandros. "Did you shake hands with her? Or have anything she may have touched, like a cup or bottle?"

Arthur shook his head. He tried to think back to the hospital room. Leaf had sat on the bed...

"She did read Wednesday's invitation. Will that do?"

"That will do," said Dr Scamandros with satisfaction. "May I have the invitation, please?"

Arthur handed it over. Scamandros took out a tortoise-shell-inlaid penknife and cut a small, curling sliver off the surface of the card, which he deposited in a tiny tin pillbox. Reaching once more into his greatcoat, he removed a cardboard chessboard – or something divided into coloured squares like a chessboard – which he unfolded. On this board he laid down with some exactitude a small round shaving mirror and a conch shell the size of Arthur's fist. He then placed the tin pillbox down as well, arranging it so mirror, shell and pillbox formed a triangle against the red-and-black-checkered background.

"A trigon on my work-square," he said, taking out a quill pen and a small bronze bottle labelled ACTIVATED INK. BEWARE! "Arthur, please place your hand flat above the trigon, not quite touching."

He indicated the three objects. Arthur complied, holding his hand level just above the mirror, conch and pillbox.

"Now I shall have to write on your hand. It may sting," said Dr Scamandros, in the tone doctors and dentists use when something is going to hurt. He set the bronze bottle down, carefully unscrewed the lid and dipped his feathery pen.

"This is going to help me find out what happened to Leaf?" asked Arthur. He had a strong urge to pull back his hand and run down the beach, back to the camp.

Sunscorch did nod OK, thought Arthur. *So Scamandros must be mostly trustworthy…*

"Yes, yes," said Scamandros. "Hold still."

Arthur held still. Scamandros poised the pen above the back of the boy's hand. A tiny drop of ink fell from the pen and splashed on Arthur's skin like molten metal, sending up a small plume of Nothing-laced smoke.

"Aahhhhh!" screamed Arthur as intense pain shot through him.

CHAPTER ELEVEN

Dr Scamandros didn't pause. With incredible speed, he wrote a word on Arthur's hand even as the boy snatched it away, the ink leaving a trail of fire across his skin.

"It will only hurt for a moment," Scamandros promised, as Arthur rushed to the sea and thrust his hand in. "If I'd warned you, you wouldn't have kept still."

Arthur couldn't speak. The pain occupied his entire mind – but only for a few more seconds. Before Dr Scamandros had finished speaking, the pain ebbed and was gone, as if it had been washed out with the last wave.

Arthur walked the few yards back up the beach. Scamandros had already packed away the board and the pillbox, leaving only the shell and the mirror. He held these out to Arthur, who didn't notice, as he was holding the back of his hand to the candlelight. As far as the boy could tell, there weren't any scars or ink stains. He couldn't see any writing either.

"What did you write?" asked Arthur.

"My signature," said Dr Scamandros. "Most House Sorcery is done with prepared apparatus that will only work for the authorised sorcerer."

"Was there Nothing in that ink?"

"Yes. A very small, refined amount. Not made by me, I hasten to add. I do not work directly with raw Nothing. Though it is true most House Sorcery depends upon apparatus or consumables originally created from or with Nothing."

"Right," said Arthur. He took the mirror and the shell suspiciously. "What do these do, then?"

"I have, I hope, attuned the mirror to show the current situation of your friend Leaf," said Scamandros. "And the conch so you may listen as well. It should work for some days, before the spell degrades and begins to show other persons or places. I should not use it once that occurs, as it may well show you to those who look for such open passages into the mind."

"How do I make it work?"

"Merely hold the shell to your ear and gaze into the

mirror. It will work best somewhere quiet, with a little but not too much light shining into the mirror. Here, with the candle, would be ideal. It is generally best to have someone watching over you, as you will not be aware of what is happening around your corporeal form."

"Thanks," said Arthur. "I think I'll try this a bit later. Closer to the camp."

"As you wish. Now, as to messages, I'm afraid that neither telephone nor telegraph will work for us. Though we are not in the Border Sea, we are of it, and any connection would thus normally go through there and the exchange has been long flooded. However, I can send a message by slower means. Have you paper, pen and ink?"

"No."

"Here you are, then." Scamandros handed Arthur a cracked leather case tied closed with a blue ribbon. "Write a letter while I prepare the messenger."

Arthur opened the case. It was like a pop-up book, with an inkwell, a pile of paper and several pens rising up as he opened it. Arthur selected a pen, dipped it in the ink, which he noticed was turquoise blue, and wrote.

Dame Primus
Monday's Dayroom or Tuesday's Pyramid

Dear Dame Primus,
Lady Wednesday invited me to luncheon
and sent a ship for me, but due to an
accident I am now in another Secondary
Realm with a different, wrecked ship,
called the Moth. A House Sorcerer called
Dr Skamandross is sending this letter for
me. I think I might try to find the Third
Part of the Will, since I'm here. If you can
send help or advice that would be good.
Also my friend Leaf got picked up by
accident and I think is on a ship called the
Flying Mantis. If you can help her get
back home that would also be good.
Yours sincerely,
    Arthur Penhaligon
P.S. Say hi to Suzy for me, and Sneezer
and everyone.

Arthur looked at what he had written. He hadn't even been sure he was going to try to find Part Three of the Will until he'd written it. But the idea must have been growing in his head ever since Leaf had said that he should do something first instead of waiting for the Trustees to do something to him.

The only problem was where to start.

"Finished?" asked Dr Scamandros. "Fold it over and write the addressee on the front. Then press your thumb on the fold and it will seal."

Arthur did as he was instructed. When his thumb pressed down, a spray of rainbow light ran around the edges of the paper, and when he lifted his hand, there was a thick, round seal that showed his own head in profile with a laurel wreath around his temples.

"Now, don't tell Captain Catapillow or Concort," said Dr Scamandros. "Having a shortage of prepared stamps, I have taken something suitable from their collection."

He showed Arthur a large, colourful stamp that pictured a bird with a dark body, a white rump and a forked tail. It was labelled in small type *Leach's Stormy Petrel* and there was a large number 2 and an unfamiliar currency sign.

"From your Earth," said Scamandros. "A nocturnal seabird. I shall just dab a drop of activated ink on its eye and utter a little incantation. You might wish to stand behind me, Arthur. Some of the Architect's words are inimical to mortals."

Arthur quickly moved behind Scamandros and put his fingers in his ears. He remembered the effect of the words the sorcerer had used on the ship.

Scamandros bent over the folded letter, opened his bronze ink bottle and, using a tiny eyedropper, sucked up some ink. He then carefully dropped just a speck of the liquid on the eye of the bird in the stamp, at the same time muttering something that Arthur couldn't hear, though it made his elbows and knees twinge and ache.

The bird twitched and flapped its wings. It poked its head up and out of the stamp and, fluttering its wings furiously, worked its whole body out. As it left the stamp, it grew larger and the letter grew smaller. It continued to grow until it was about two feet long and its wings spanned six feet. The letter was tiny by then, a rectangle only an inch long. The bird, a bright twinkle in its eye, picked the letter up in its beak and swallowed it before waddling down the beach, slowly beating its wings till it was able to take off, immediately becoming graceful and swift.

"Well, I shall just clear up here," said Dr Scamandros. "I have to spread some of this magic-tainted sand around and so forth. If you want to try the mirror and shell, I suggest you ask Mister Sunscorch to watch over you, and sit between the Captain's tent and the sea."

"Thanks," said Arthur. Dr Scamandros was being very helpful.

Maybe I'm too suspicious, thought Arthur. *He must have some reason of his own for helping me... I wonder what it is... I wonder if he can read my thoughts—*

"How long will it take the letter to get to Dame Primus?" Arthur asked quickly, just in case Dr Scamandros *could* read his mind and was offended that Arthur still didn't trust him.

"It's difficult to say. Barring accident or interception, a day or two in our time here. What that would be in the House, I cannot say without considerable calculation. Time does not run true between the House and the Realms."

Arthur nodded. It looked like he was stuck here for a week anyway, till the *Moth* could be repaired. Since there was nothing he could do about that, he might as well use the time to work out what to do. And to do that, he needed to find out what had happened to Leaf.

"I'll go back now," said Arthur. "I will ask Sunscorch to watch over me. Thanks for your help, Doctor."

Scamandros bowed.

Arthur turned away and started to walk back along the beach. It was dark without the candle, but he could see the lights of the camp, which weren't that far. Even so, he started to walk quite fast.

He was halfway there when something made him turn around and look back. He could see the glow of the candle and a partial silhouette that might have been Dr Scamandros. But there was something else there as well. Another shape, a dark cutout against the candlelight. Arthur only saw it for a moment, then it was gone. But in that instant, he thought he recognised what it was.

Another stormy petrel. Dr Scamandros was sending a message to someone else.

I knew it, thought Arthur fiercely. *He's probably trying to sell me out to Wednesday or one of the other Trustees. They might send Superior Saturday's Dusk if that's who it was who attacked me in Grim Tuesday's Pit. If he comes back with his sword I'll be helpless without a Key, though maybe the crew of the* Moth *would defend me because of the Captain's disc. I still don't understand why Saturday would want Nothing to destroy the House. There is definitely something going on with the Morrow Days and Nothing. But what? Why is everything so difficult—*

Arthur's thoughts submerged into his subconscious as he was hailed by a sentry near the camp.

"Halt! Who there goes? I mean, who goes there? Recognise me and advance!"

"Um, I think your name is One-Ear, isn't it?" said Arthur. The Denizen was only partially illuminated by the lanterns on Catapillow's tent, a dozen yards away. "It's

Arthur, I'm just coming back from a walk. Dr Scamandros will be along in a while."

"Advance, friend!" called out One-Ear. He lowered his crossbow and waved Arthur in. As the boy passed, the Denizen muttered, "Actually my real name is Gowkin, but One-Ear sounds so much better. I was a Third-Class Box Shifter before the Deluge. Now I'm a forecastle hand—"

"One-Ear! Watch your front!"

Arthur recognised that shout. Sunscorch came stomping down the beach. Arthur could just make out another sentry behind him, scanning the darkness, his crossbow ready.

"Aye, aye, sir!" called One-Ear. "Just admitting a friend."

Sunscorch gave a slight bow as he met Arthur, which the boy returned.

"The Doc done what's needful?" asked Sunscorch.

"I think so," said Arthur. He held up the mirror and shell. "He's given me something I can use to see what's happened to my friend Leaf. Only I need someone to keep watch while I'm using it. I was hoping you wouldn't mind..."

"Watch over you? Aye, I can do that. I have to finish going round the sentries first, since we don't want Feverfew and his lot arriving unannounced."

"I thought we left them behind!" said Arthur as he

fell into step with the Second Mate.

"Maybe, maybe not," said Sunscorch. "Feverfew's an uncommon clever sorcerer. Dr Scamandros would outdo him in book learning, but that pirate must have dozens of filthy tricks the Doc don't know about. Watch your front!"

The next sentry scrambled to her feet and picked up her crossbow. Sunscorch gave a disgruntled snort and kept on.

"Dr Scamandros told me he was a volunteer," Arthur said. He needed to know more about Scamandros. "What did he mean? Why would he volunteer?"

"Before the big flood there were only Navigator-Sorcerers on the regular ships," explained Sunscorch. "So when all the extra ships were being built, they advertised for volunteers with enough sorcerous training to come aboard. Some of the regular sailors were transferred to the new ships too."

"Like you," guessed Arthur.

"Yes, sir, like me," said Sunscorch heavily. "Fourth Mate of the *Spiral Waterspout* I was, and you never saw a better ship and a finer crew."

"But why would Dr Scamandros volunteer to be a navigator if he was a top-class sorcerer trained in the Upper House?"

Sunscorch shrugged.

"He probably lost something. That's why most folk from other parts of the House come to the Border Sea."

"I don't understand."

"Anything that's ever been lost anywhere turns up in the Border Sea sooner or later," said Sunscorch. "Finding it again can be more than a mite difficult, though. And it has to be lost by accident – not on purpose or stolen."

They were almost down to the sea again. A Denizen stood in the wash, looking out to the water, a crossbow at her side. There were a few very red, very bright stars in one patch of the sky, but it was mostly cloudy and there was no moon of any kind. Possibly no moon circled this world.

"Halt!"

"It's Sunscorch and the passenger," said Sunscorch. "All quiet?"

"Nothing save the waves," said the Denizen. Arthur recognised her voice. It was the one with scales all over her face. Lizard.

"Mind your eye," said Sunscorch. "If they come, like as not it'll be straight from the sea."

"Aye, aye!"

Sunscorch turned back and started walking up the well-trodden patch of sand between two of the larger piles of boxes.

"That's my rounds done. Where do you want to look into that mirror of yours?"

"Somewhere quiet, with a bit of light," said Arthur. He pointed to a patch of sand where there were no resting

Denizens, not too far from the lanterns on the tent. "Over there would do, I guess."

Sunscorch followed Arthur over and stood behind him as Arthur sat down cross-legged on the sand. The boy looked in the shell, holding it up to the light, and shook it a few times to make sure there was nothing inside. Then he gingerly put the shell to his ear, raised the mirror and tilted it so it caught some of the lantern light.

All Arthur could hear at first was the soft roar of the sea inside the shell, and all he could see in the mirror was his own reflection. He tried thinking about Leaf, but for some reason he couldn't remember exactly what she looked like. He could remember her voice, though, and he concentrated on that, recalling what she had said when she'd come into his hospital room.

The roar in the shell cut off, to be replaced by the rattle of iron and the creak of wood. The mirror clouded as if Arthur had breathed on it, then cleared to show not his reflection, but another dark scene, lit by a different light.

Arthur stared at the mirror. He could see Leaf, inside a very cramped, dimly lit room.

She was a prisoner.

CHAPTER TWELVE

Leaf was sitting slumped in a narrow space, with an inch or so of water around her legs. A heavy chain joined the manacles on her wrists to the manacles on her ankles, then ran to a dark iron ring set into the wooden wall. From the way the water gently sloshed from side to side, she was clearly aboard a ship. The only light came from a swinging, smoke-grimed lantern that hung from a hook in the planked ceiling, barely a foot above Leaf's head.

Something moved in the darkness in the corner of the vision. Arthur shifted his head to try to see it, but that didn't work. The mirror was like a TV set or a stage.

Anything that happened to either side or behind it was invisible.

The movement came again. Leaf raised her head and looked around. Seeing nothing, her head slumped forward. It looked like she was totally despondent, till Arthur noticed that she was doing something to the manacle on her left ankle. Trying to pick it, he guessed, catching a glimpse of a nail file or something similar.

Arthur was concentrating so hard on what Leaf was doing to the manacle that it took a moment for him to realise he'd seen movement again. This time, the movement ended within the mirror's frame and Arthur had a clear look at what it was.

A rat. But not just any old rat.

This was a four-foot-tall, brown-haired rat that stood upright on its hind legs. It was also wearing clothes. It had on an old but well-kept swallow-tailed coat of dark blue with gold facings over a cream shirt and silver waistcoat, with white breeches that were rolled up to be out of the sloshing water. Its feet were bare and its pink, hairless tail flicked around behind.

The rat lifted its broad-brimmed but low-crowned hat of oiled leather and said in a voice that squeaked when it took in a breath, "Excuse me, miss. Are you by any chance a mortal from Earth?"

Leaf started and scuttled back, her chains rattling.

"I beg your pardon," said the rat. "I didn't mean to startle you. I would not intrude, save that I have a commission regarding a mortal from Earth."

Leaf shook her head and blinked a few times.

"Sorry," she said. "I just kind of... wasn't expecting... a... a visitor."

"Allow me to introduce myself," said the rat. "I am Commodoure Monckton, officer in charge of the Raised Rats of the Border Sea."

"Raised Rats?" asked Leaf weakly. "Border Sea?"

Commodoure Monckton's whiskers twitched before he answered.

"The Raised Rats, young lady, are those rats that formerly served the Piper and were brought by him to the House. The Border Sea is a demesne of the House, notionally ruled over by Lady Wednesday, self-styled Duchess of the Border Sea and Trustee of the Architect."

"Oh, I see," said Leaf sarcastically.

"I beg your pardon?"

Leaf shook her head again. "Never mind. Yes, I suppose I am a mortal from Earth. A pretty dumb mortal."

"Yet you speak."

"I mean *dumb* like *stupid*," said Leaf. "Anyway, what do you want with a mortal from Earth? Can you help me get out of here?"

Monckton took a paper out of his coat pocket and

held it out to Leaf. It was Post-it note size when he handed it over, but as Leaf picked it up it grew to full letter size.

The paper showed an engraved portrait of a boy. It was quite a good likeness of Arthur. Underneath it were a few lines of type:

REWARD

**INFORMATION AS TO THE WHEREABOUTS OF ONE
ARTHUR PENHALIGON,
A MORTAL BOY FROM EARTH.
SEND PARTICULARS BY TELEGRAM OR MESSAGE TO
MONDAY'S TIERCE, SUZY TURQUOISE BLUE**

"Arthur!" said Leaf. "And Suzy was the girl... the one with the wings."

"Ah," said Monckton. "You know Arthur? Do you know where he is?"

"I might," said Leaf. Arthur could tell she was thinking from the way her eyes had narrowed a bit. "I guess you want the reward?"

"Naturally," said Monckton. "Though in this case we have already been paid a small retainer. We are known to be expert searchers and finders."

"I'll tell you what I know if you help me escape," said

Leaf, holding up her manacled wrists. "And help me get in touch with Suzy Blue."

"Hmmm," mused the Rat. "We can't help you escape, as that would be counter to several agreements we have with various authorities within the House. However, I would be honoured to act as your counsel in the forthcoming court of inquiry into your criminal activities."

"Criminal what? What! The only thing I've done is let them drag me on to this ship! They took one look at me, asked my name and then threw me down here in chains!"

"I believe that you will be charged with being a stow-away," said Monckton, adding emphasis with a flick of his tail. "The penalty is likely to be one or two hundred lashes, which I suspect you would not survive. Or, to be quite frank, being mortal, you would *definitely* not survive."

"Lashes? You mean like whipping?"

"Indeed. With the cat-o'-nine-tails. Perhaps you've heard of it?"

"I don't want to hear about it! Or feel it either! This is crazy. There must be something I can do."

"It depends upon the court," said Monckton. "I suspect there is a logical flaw in the charge, which if correctly argued would result in you being spared punishment."

"What is it?"

Monckton inclined his head a little to the side and looked at Leaf with one bright eye.

"We are mercantile rats, miss," he said. "That is to say, you tell me what you know about Arthur and I shall act as your counsel at the court."

"How do I know that you'll do anything for me once I tell you about Arthur?" asked Leaf.

"I give you my word as a Raised Rat and former mortal inhabitant of Earth," said Monckton, placing one claw over his neatly waistcoated heart. "In the name of the Piper, who brought us here."

Leaf looked at the Rat carefully. He met her gaze and didn't blink.

"OK," said Leaf. "I suppose I don't have much choice. You sound convincing, at least. Better than the guy who sold my dad his last car. I was visiting Arthur in his hospital room, back on our... back on Earth. Arthur had an invitation from Lady Wednesday, to have lunch, and he was telling me about the House and everything. Then a giant wave came through the hospital room and swept us out to sea, on Arthur's bed. We were getting washed up and down these really big waves when a ship with bright green sails picked me up with a rope, but they missed Arthur. I guess he's still floating on his hospital bed somewhere. If it hasn't sunk or been picked up by someone else. That good enough for you?"

"It is an excellent lead, thank you," said Monckton. "It also explains why the Captain and crew of this vessel have been so tediously closemouthed and have chosen to raft up here at the Triangle. Were it not for some of the regular rats, I would not even have known there was a mortal aboard. I suppose the *Mantis* was meant to pick up Arthur for Lady Wednesday, and having failed in their mission, Captain Swell is biding his time trying to work out what to do next. Besides get rid of you, the unfortunate evidence of having picked up the wrong mortal."

"Raft up? The Triangle? Where are we?"

"We are aboard the *Flying Mantis* on the orlop deck," said Monckton. "A ship of Wednesday's regular merchant marine. The *Mantis* is rafted up, which is to say moored to another ship, which is moored to another ship, and so on, all of them ultimately joined to a giant triangular mooring-post that is all that remains above sea level of the old Port Wednesday lighthouse. Hence, the Triangle. Which is, of course, in the Border Sea of the House."

"Which is the centre of the universe," said Leaf. "At least that's what Arthur said. My parents'd freak if they knew it was like this."

"I beg your pardon?"

"They think there's some big tree at the centre of the universe, with little branches going off everywhere. And animals living in harmony and being nice to each other and everything."

"It sounds rather pleasant," said Monckton. "If only it

were so. Now, I must be getting back to my ship. I shall stop off on the way and inform Captain Swell that I shall be your counsel. I imagine the court will sit anytime within the next few days."

"The next few days!" exclaimed Leaf. "They haven't given me anything to eat or drink. I could starve or die of thirst!"

"Not in the House," said Monckton. "You may get hungry and thirsty, but you won't die from it."

"So you're just going to leave me here chained up? That's it? To wait for the court or whatever?"

"Yes," said Monckton. "You have it exactly. A pleasure doing business with you. Goodbye."

"Wait!" shrieked Leaf. But the Rat was gone. Arthur caught a flash of his tail as he left the mirror's field of view.

"Wait! You can't just leave me! What if the ship sinks—"

Leaf's shout was suddenly cut off and the mirror flickered between Leaf's situation and Arthur's face in the lantern light, before settling on the latter. Arthur felt a wave of nausea at the sudden change of perception, but that was banished in an instant as Sunscorch clapped him on the shoulder and whispered, "Arthur! Get ready, lad. There's something coming in from the sea!"

Arthur blinked, stood up and hurriedly put the mirror and shell in the pockets of his dressing gown. That reminded him briefly that he really needed to change into something more sensible, the thought only lasting for a second before it was gone.

"What's coming in from the sea?"

"Dunno," replied Sunscorch. "Lizard saw a light far off. I've seen it too. It's getting closer. Could be the *Shiver*, though why they'd show a light I don't know. Here, take this knife."

Sunscorch had a cutlass at his belt, Arthur saw. He took the long knife the Denizen offered him, still in its sheath, and tried to fasten it to his dressing-gown belt. Sunscorch shook his head.

"That won't serve. Come on, back to the Captain's tent. Ichabod can find you some decent slops."

"Slops? I'm not hungry, particularly for something called—"

"Slops is clothes. Come on. We haven't much time."

The camp was quite different now, Arthur saw as he followed Sunscorch over to Catapillow's tent. The Denizens were all up and getting ready for a fight. They appeared more confident and better organised than they'd been at sea.

"Landlubbers," whispered Sunscorch as they passed a group of Denizens checking over their crossbows. "They'll put up a better fight here than on any deck. Ichabod! Help Lord Arthur into some shipshape clothes!"

"Aye, aye!" called Ichabod. He came over and gave

Arthur a very low bow. "Is there anything in particular milord requires?"

"Don't waste time!" instructed Sunscorch. "Give him whatever fits and be quick about it. I'm off to the guns. Arthur, join me there when you're ready."

Ichabod sniffed.

"Really, he has no idea the difficulties one has maintaining a proper standard of dress."

He looked Arthur up and down, walked around him, and wrote some figures down in a small notebook. Then he indicated the standing screen with the nautical pictures in the corner of the tent. Arthur had last seen it in Catapillow's impossible room aboard the *Moth*.

"If you would care to stand behind this screen, milord, I shall endeavour to present a number of articles of attire that may approach some level of suitability for one of your most eminent position."

Arthur went behind the screen. Almost immediately, Ichabod handed him a huge pile of clothes.

"Undergarments. Choice of three shirts. Collars, choice of four. Neckties, choice of six. Waistcoat, choice of three. Breeches, choice of three. Stockings, choice of five. Shoes or boots?"

"Uh, I don't need any. My slippers are Immaterial Boots."

"Sea-duty belt or ceremonial?"

"Sea-duty, I think..."

Ichabod continued to ask questions, handing Arthur an item of clothing or equipment every few seconds. Finally he fell silent, and Arthur quickly got undressed and put on his new clothes. Surprisingly, everything fit him perfectly. Arthur hadn't deliberately chosen any particular combination, but when he was mostly dressed he found that he had on pretty much the same uniform as Catapillow. A blue coat over a white shirt and blue waistcoat with white breeches.

As Arthur had half-expected, as soon as he changed clothes his Immaterial Boots transformed from hospital slippers into knee-high boots, the left one wider in the leg to accommodate his crab-armour cast. Arthur thought for a moment, then slipped the Atlas and Wednesday's invitation down inside his right boot and the shell and mirror down the left boot. Immaterial Boots were proof against water, as they were to almost everything, and they would keep these articles safe and dry.

"I don't know what to do with this collar," Arthur said a few minutes later. The collar was separate from the shirt and he couldn't figure it out.

"Allow me," said Ichabod. He quickly stepped in and fastened Arthur's collar. Before the boy could protest, Ichabod had wrapped a red cloth around his neck and tied it as a necktie as well. "Arms up, sir, for the belt."

A broad leather belt seemed to be the last thing to put on, but when it was buckled up and Arthur tried to take a step out, Ichabod held up his hand and gave a slight bow. "Your sword, sir. One mustn't venture into a prospective battle without one's sword."

"I suppose, er, one mustn't," repeated Arthur.

I'm even starting to sound like Catapillow, he thought. *I hope I don't turn into someone like him. I'd rather be like Sunscorch. Someone who gets things done.*

Ichabod picked up a scabbarded sword from the floor and fastened it to Arthur's belt on his left hip. At the same time, Arthur tied the knife he'd been given by Sunscorch on to the other hip.

"This is a naval pattern sword, reduced in length and weight by the armourer specifically for your lordship," said Ichabod. He stood up and saw Sunscorch's knife, his mouth twisting a little in distaste. "If I may say, milord, the knife does little for the ensemble. Perhaps if you allow me—"

"I want to keep the knife," Arthur said quickly. "And I have to go and join Mister Sunscorch now. Thanks for your help, Ichabod. I don't know how you got the clothes my size so quickly."

"Oh, I cut them down from the Captain's and Mister Concort's best while you were off with Dr Scamandros," said Ichabod proudly. "Then a few minor tweaks were all that was required, as I have a very good eye, even if I say so myself. 'Always anticipate!' That's the motto of the true gentleman's gentleman!"

"Um, thanks," muttered Arthur. He hoped Catapillow and Concort wouldn't mind their best clothes getting cut down. "Thanks again."

"And should your lordship be wounded in the forthcoming action, be assured that I have applied my motto to my other profession," said Ichabod.

"What?"

"Surgeon's Mate," said Ichabod. "Or as the *extremely vulgar* call it, Loblolly Boy. I assist Dr Scamandros. We have never had to operate upon a mortal, but I have all my equipment ready. Knives, saws, drills – all newly sharpened!"

"Great!" said Arthur, faking a cheerfulness he didn't feel. "Well done! Keep up the good work!"

He hurried away before Ichabod had a chance to show him any newly sharpened surgeon's tools. He was halfway through the camp to where the two cannons were pointing out to sea when he heard the sudden clang and clatter of the ship's bell, and Sunscorch's bellow.

"Stand to your guns! Make ready your crossbows! Cutlasses and boarding pikes to the tidemark!"

Chapter thirteen

Arthur broke into a limping, partly rolling run, joining a dangerous crowd of cutlass- and pike-wielding Denizens heading towards the sea. Two of the *Moth*'s cannons had been taken off the ship and emplaced there, facing the waves.

Near the guns, the crowd split to either side of the emplacement, while Arthur stopped next to Sunscorch and one of the cannons. The weapon didn't look too sturdy or safe to Arthur. The black iron of the long barrel was pitted and rough and its wooden carriage was splintered and cracked, with uneven wooden wheels. Both cannons were stationed on a kind of wickerwork carpet laid over the sand, and that didn't look very solid either.

"Stand away from the gun," warned Sunscorch. "She'll buck when she fires. Break your other leg or your back if you're behind."

Arthur hastily walked over to Sunscorch's right, putting the large Denizen between him and the guns.

"Can you see them yet?" Arthur asked as he peered into the darkness. Apart from the lanterns further up the beach and the glow from the gunner's slow matches – smouldering lengths of what looked like big fat shoelaces – there was no other light. Or was there? Arthur shaded his face with his hands and squinted to get a proper look straight ahead.

"There is a faint glow in the distance, isn't there?"

"Sure enough," said Sunscorch. "But it's too low in the water to be a ship. And it's moving too fast to be a raft or a longboat or suchlike. I can't fathom it, myself. Unless it's those Rats..."

"Rats?" asked Arthur. "Raised Rats?"

"Aye," said Sunscorch. "They have some uncommon vessels. But I dunno—"

He broke off as the glow in the sea suddenly shot up in the air, eclipsing a red star low on the horizon with its sudden brightness. Then it arced down again, re-entering the sea and diminishing.

Sunscorch muttered something and Arthur heard the gunners nearby whispering nervously.

"What is it?"

"It's a Denizen with marine wings and a veritable glimlight of sorcery about him," said Sunscorch quietly. "Most likely Feverfew has come by himself to reclaim his treasure."

"By himself? But surely we're... we've got these cannons... and there's a hundred of us and Dr Scamandros..."

"We've little powder for the cannons," said Sunscorch. "And Feverfew is a master of dark sorceries the Doc wouldn't touch. He'll turn the sea and the sand against us, like as not, same as he made the rigging of the *Oceanus* choke the life out of its crew. But we've a better chance ashore with our lot than in a sea fight, so you never know. If you get a go at him, Arthur, try to take off his head with a single blow and get a handful of sand or grit on the neck-stump. Or lay the flat of your blade there, if there's nought better to hand."

Arthur swallowed and looked back at the rapidly approaching light in the water. Then he drew his sword, resting the blade on his shoulder like the Denizens with their cutlasses.

I will cut off his head, Arthur told himself. *I have defeated Mister Monday and Grim Tuesday. I've been wounded before. I know I can take it. I'm not going to be killed by a pirate... I hope my leg doesn't give way suddenly... This crab armour is good and the joints work well but what if it locks up or it just gets weak as I'm fighting Feverfew and...*

"Stop it!" Arthur whispered to himself. "Whatever happens, I will make the best of it. I will win."

"Wait for it to leave the water!" roared Sunscorch as the light grew even closer. "Point-blank!"

The glow streamed towards them, growing brighter and brighter, like the headlights of an oncoming car. Arthur felt transfixed by the light, unable to move as it got closer and closer. He could make out a dark shape inside the light, inside the wave. An inhuman figure, like a shark, with huge wings propelling it along. It broke the surface and began to surf in on a wave. The gunners grunted and cursed as they shoved and levered at the cannons with handspikes, trying to point them just where the thing was going to come out of the water.

Sunscorch took a breath and opened his mouth, the word "Fire!" already forming there, when suddenly Dr Scamandros came capering about in front of the cannons, shouting.

"Hold! Hold hard! Don't! Don't fire!"

At his last word, one of the cannons went off with a tremendously loud bang, a spray of sparks and an eruption of thick white smoke that completely enveloped Arthur. Coughing and choking, he stumbled away, only to find his feet suddenly wet.

He was in the wash of the surf, and the thing from the sea was standing over him, its light shining through gunsmoke and darkness. It had not been hit.

It wasn't a "thing" any more, though it still had huge wings of metallic yellow-gold feathers. It was a very beautiful, very tall woman, with bright yellow hair tied back in a wire net. She was wearing a green velvet dress with a darker green, fur-trimmed jacket that hung loose on her left shoulder, the arms swinging behind. She held a short, white, scaly whip in her right hand.

She looked down at Arthur and at the unscathed Dr Scamandros, who had come up next to him, and at Captain Catapillow, who Arthur hadn't even seen around, but was now bowing and scraping and mumbling.

"Dr Scamandros?"

Her voice was cold and clear. It made Arthur's ears hurt slightly, as if they were being touched by an icy breeze.

"Yes, ma'am. I am Scamandros."

"I received your message. Introduce me to Lord Arthur. I am in a hurry."

Scamandros bowed to her, indicated Arthur with his right hand and bowed again to both of them.

"Lord Arthur, may I present Lady Wednesday's Dawn?"

Arthur bowed. He had already half-guessed the identity of their surprise guest. She had the hauteur that all the chief servants of the Trustees possessed. A kind of look that said, *I am superior and you had better admit it.*

"Greetings, Lord Arthur," said Wednesday's Dawn. "Please accept Lady Wednesday's apologies for the sad miscarriage of our transport arrangements. Unfortunately I have not yet been apprised of the exact nature of the incident that led you here, but I trust that you are now ready to accompany me to the promised luncheon?"

Arthur looked up at Dawn's beautiful but cold face.

She would cut my throat if ordered to, Arthur thought. *But what choice do I have?*

"I'm not sure," he said aloud. He still had his sword on his shoulder, and Sunscorch's advice about dealing with Feverfew would probably apply equally well to Wednesday's Dawn. He tensed, ready to strike, as he slowly said, "I've heard some scary talk about how Lady Wednesday is kind of... well, you know... a giant whale that eats everything. And I don't want to get eaten."

"It is a temporary indisposition," said Dawn. She looked at Scamandros and Catapillow. "Which those of lesser orders would do well not to gossip about. However, you may be assured that Lady Wednesday intends to resume her traditional human form for this luncheon. That is in indication of the importance given to your visit, Lord Arthur. It is currently a regrettable strain for milady to take human shape. She has not chosen to do so for many centuries."

"What does she want from me?" asked Arthur. There seemed no point beating around the bush. "She's in with the Morrow Days. She's a Trustee who didn't do what she was supposed to. I'm the Will's Rightful Heir."

"These are not matters to discuss in public," sniffed Dawn. "Is it enough to say that my mistress recognises a need for negotiation, not battle?"

"Maybe," said Arthur.

"Excellent. Then I take it, Lord Arthur, that you are ready to come with me?"

"Where exactly?"

"Back to the House," said Dawn. "To the Border Sea. I have many duties, so we must not waste any time. Do you need to breathe?"

"What?"

"Do you need to breathe? You are a mortal of sorts, are you not? If I am to carry you back, we shall spend large amounts of time underwater. If you have not already been ensorcelled to need less air, then I shall have to take care of that before we depart."

"I'm not and I don't think I want to be," said Arthur. "I have asthma and I don't want my lungs messed up any more with magic or anything. And I don't want to turn into a Denizen."

"It is a very straightforward spell," said Dawn. She gave a small flick of her riding crop, as if to illustrate how small a matter it was. "It merely allows you to survive on far fewer breaths. Perhaps, Dr Scamandros, you can allay Lord Arthur's concerns. You are a university-trained sorcerer, I note, though I do not recall your name and station in the Index of Navigator-Sorcerers in the employ of Lady Wednesday."

"Ah, dear lady, I was a volunteer after the Deluge," said Scamandros. He made some nervous shuffling motions and almost tripped over his own feet. "So the paperwork may be a little, that is, not quite in order. But, as to the breathing spell, it is one of suspension, I take it? Perhaps the formulation known as 'A Thousand and One Breaths'?"

"It is a peg, purchased at Port Wednesday," said Dawn, removing a small cloth bag from her sleeve and proffering it to Scamandros. "I am unaware of its provenance. I believe it is worn on the nose."

Scamandros took the bag, opened its drawstring and emptied a small wooden clothespeg on to his palm. He held it up to Dawn's light and looked at the tiny writing on it with his unaided eyes and through his smoked-quartz glasses.

"It is a straightforward spell," he said to Arthur. "One breath will serve for a thousand, till it wears off. There will be a little magical residue, but far less than that already within your flesh and bone."

Arthur took the clothespeg dubiously and opened and

shut it, feeling the strength of the spring.

"How will I know when it wears off?"

"It will fall off your nose," said Dr Scamandros. "You may take it off, of course, and reapply it – though in that case I should be careful not to be too far away from a source of air. It will work less and less well with each reapplication."

"Can't the *Moth* take me to meet Lady Wednesday?" asked Arthur. "I don't think I want to use this spell. Or be carried underwater. No offence, it's just I don't like the idea."

"Time is of the essence," said Dawn. "Lady Wednesday cannot hold her human shape long and the luncheon is scheduled to begin at noon, House time, on the day I left. We must hurry. No ship can carry you there in time, and unless I am mistaken, this '*Moth*' needs considerable work. I also have numerous important tasks that need my attention. The Border Sea must be constantly tended, lest it spread into the Realms or conjoin with Nothing."

"Do you swear that I will be returned somewhere safe after meeting Lady Wednesday?" asked Arthur. "Swear by the Architect, and the Will, and Lady Wednesday."

Wednesday's Dawn scowled and her riding crop whistled back and forth through the air. But finally she said, "Yes. I shall do everything in my power to ensure you are returned to a place of safety after your luncheon with

Lady Wednesday. I swear this by the Architect who made me, by the Will and by my mistress Lady Wednesday."

"OK," said Arthur. "I guess I'd better go."

He looked at Dr Scamandros, who shuffled again and bent his head close to Arthur.

"Captain Catapillow thought it best to inform Miss Dawn," muttered the sorcerer softly so only Arthur could hear. "Not wanting the *Moth* to be entangled in things beyond us, and afraid of what the Red Hand you bear might bring. I have to follow orders, you know. But I made sure your letter went first. Only Miss Dawn was already looking for you."

Arthur shook his head, but when Dr Scamandros offered his hand, the boy sheathed his sword and took it. He still wasn't sure if the Denizen was lying, but Dr Scamandros *had* fixed his leg up. Hopefully Arthur's letter really *was* going to Dame Primus.

"A pleasure to have you aboard the *Moth*," said Captain Catapillow, who was practically hunched over with his constant bowing to both Arthur and Wednesday's Dawn. "Farewell."

Arthur nodded but didn't offer to shake hands. He looked around instead. There was Sunscorch up by the cannons, surrounded by what looked like the whole crew, gathered in close to stare at the luminous Dawn.

"I won't be long," Arthur said. He raced up the beach to

the Second Mate. This time, he did offer his hand, which was taken in a firm grip and shaken so soundly that his shoulder ached.

"Thanks, Sunscorch," said Arthur. "For picking me up from the buoy and everything."

"Fare thee well," said Sunscorch. "Mention Second Mate Sunscorch of the *Moth* to the Mariner, if you ever walk a deck with him again."

"I will," Arthur promised. He saw Ichabod standing primly amid a gaggle of tattooed, unkempt salvagers and waved.

"Thanks for the clothes, Ichabod!"

Ichabod bowed deeply. Arthur waved again and ran back to the sea.

"Take a deep breath and peg your nose," said Dr Scamandros. He leaned close again and Arthur felt him drop something in the pocket of his coat. "And if I may be of service, do not hesitate to send word. I should like to serve the Rightful Heir."

Arthur felt in his pocket as he stepped back. The object was round, heavy and metallic. Before he could investigate further, Dawn spread her wings and gestured for Arthur to approach.

"I shall have to take you under my arm," she said with a fleeting look of distaste. "We shall achieve the best speed if you remain still and don't squirm. Please also ensure your sword stays at your side."

Arthur nodded and stood next to Dawn. Before she picked him up under the arms like a parcel, he took a deep breath, as deep as he was able, and put the peg on his nose. It hurt, but not enough for Arthur to need to take it off.

Dawn spread her wings and, with one mighty flap, launched into the air. As she rose, she began to change. She grew larger and longer, skin and clothing transforming into rough sharkskin with a golden sheen. Her arm changed too, becoming a thick tentacle, its many suckers sticking on to Arthur with nasty pops of displaced air.

Arthur shut his eyes. He didn't want to see the tentacle.

He kept them closed as they dived into the sea, the cold shock of the water smashing into his chest. For a moment he was scared that the peg spell had failed and he would drown. But he felt no need to draw breath, and as long as he kept his eyes closed, he could almost kid himself that he was just in the bath, or mucking around in a swimming pool.

Almost. The water was rushing past too quickly and the tentacle felt too strange. Arthur suddenly thought of something he should have asked.

How long is it going to take to get back to the House? How long will I be underwater? How long will my thousand breaths last?

CHAPTER FOURTEEN

It was a terrible journey, one that seemed to Arthur to last for days, though he knew it was merely hours. At intervals, Dawn would erupt from the water for a long, gliding flight, at the same time calling out to Arthur, "Breathe!"

He would take a breath, then down they would plunge, back into water of varying temperature, though always more cold than warm. The light changed too, often quite radically, from total darkness to daylight of different hues. Arthur realised that Dawn was taking them through several different Secondary Realms. How, he didn't know, since there were no obvious portals and they didn't go through the Front Door. He supposed it was something to do with the nature of the Border Sea and of Wednesday's Dawn. Perhaps she could go wherever there was a sea of some kind.

Arthur survived the experience by going into a state where he was neither awake nor asleep. He kept his eyes closed most of the time, and his mind retreated into semi-consciousness, so he had almost no coherent thoughts or memory of any particular time within the journey. It all felt like one ghastly, overtired waking nightmare.

Finally, Dawn leapt up from the sea. Arthur heard the crack and boom of thunder and saw lightning bolts scrawl jagged paths across the entire horizon. He screwed his eyes shut and tucked his chin in tight, holding like that as the thunder got louder and louder and the white light broke through his eyelids. All of it was just too much to bear and then... it was gone.

They were through the Line of Storms and in the House, spiralling up and up as Dawn climbed higher into the sky, till they were many thousands of feet up. Arthur started to get worried about hitting the ceiling, then realised it was much higher here than the parts of the House he'd been in before.

Fortunately it wasn't cold. In fact, it seemed to be warmer, which was strange, until Arthur figured out that while there was no sun, the ceiling, no matter how distant, must provide heat as well as light. And he couldn't tell whether the air pressure was decreasing, because he wasn't breathing. The peg was still securely on his nose and his last breath had been only twenty minutes before.

"Nearly there," said Dawn, her voice strange and horrible from her shark-toothed maw. "Look to the left."

Arthur looked down. All he could see for miles and miles was the sea, a blue expanse flecked here and there with white. Then as his eyes blurred from the rush of the wind, he saw something long and white, reaching up to the horizon. A mountain chain. No, a mountainous island. It was long and narrow, and the snow-covered central ridge looked like it rose higher than Arthur and Dawn were flying.

"We're going to an island?" he shouted, his words almost smothered by the constant flapping of Dawn's wings.

Dawn laughed, a scornful laugh that made Arthur shudder. There was something intrinsically wrong with a laugh coming from a winged shark.

But there was reason for her scorn, Arthur saw as he looked again. What he'd thought was an island was moving. He could see the vast white wash behind it, which he'd mistaken for surf breaking on a very long reef. And the size and shape of the island changed, as it rose and fell in the water.

It wasn't an island. It was a gigantic white whale. A

Leviathan. One hundred and twenty-six miles long. A Behemoth. Thirty-two miles wide. A mouth ten miles wide and two miles high—

Dawn stopped flapping her wings and began to glide slowly down.

Down towards Drowned Wednesday.

"Hey!" Arthur shouted. "You said Wednesday was going to be in human form!"

"She will be. She eats tons of fish and krill until the last moment, to satisfy her hunger. You see the ship in front of her?"

Arthur peered down. He could see a tiny brown fleck at least a hundred miles ahead of the vast white whale. It was like a speck of dust on the floor, with a commercial cleaner's mop heading straight for it.

"Yes!"

"Milady has already begun to reduce and will be fully in human form by the time she reaches it."

"What happens when she needs to change back?" asked Arthur.

Wednesday's Dawn did not answer, instead diving more sharply, her wingtips lifting and angling to control their descent.

"I said, 'What happens when she needs to change back?'" Arthur repeated, knowing it was important.

"We flee," said Dawn.

"What about the people... the Denizens on the ship?"

"There are none," said Dawn. "The ship was readied at my orders and the crew taken off. It is not an important vessel."

"Right," muttered Arthur. More loudly he said, "Don't forget your promise."

"I will not forget," said Dawn. "In any case, you are probably milady's only hope."

"What?"

This time Dawn did not answer at all. As they glided steadily down, Arthur watched the approach of the Leviathan. Maybe she was getting smaller, but she still looked like a mountainous island, with enormously high cliffs of chalk at the front. Something too big to be mobile.

Then she raised her tail. Even though they were still twenty miles away or more, Arthur flinched in Dawn's tentacular grasp. The tail rose up at least a mile and came crashing down with a rumbling explosion that Arthur could feel through the air as much as hear. He could see the wave it generated too, and was surprised that by the time the wave got to the ship it was just a slightly higher crest in the swell.

"She's changing," said Dawn confidently. "Already only half her normal size."

Arthur found that hard to believe, but he supposed Dawn would know. They were circling above the ship now, still a long way up, but disturbingly no higher than Wednesday's mighty white brow. It loomed closer and closer, and Arthur started to use his hand as a measure, holding five fingers out at arm's length and counting the number of fingers from sea level to the top of the whale's head. It wasn't very scientific but Arthur was somewhat relieved to see that by this crude measure, the whale was reducing in size.

Not that it looked any smaller.

"Shouldn't we fly up a bit?" he asked, repeating the question in a shout when Dawn did not answer.

"No," Dawn roared. "That would show disrespect. I trust milady!"

Arthur took another measure from sea level using his fingers. The whale was definitely getting smaller, but she was still what he could only think of as humongous.

"I don't think it would be disrespectful to not go any lower," shouted Arthur. "I mean, I'm the visitor. Shouldn't we let her get on the ship first?"

Dawn didn't answer. But she also didn't fly any lower.

Arthur kept looking at Drowned Wednesday. Because of her enormous size, he hadn't really taken in how fast she was approaching. The distance between them was rapidly disappearing, and she still loomed higher than they were flying. He felt like an ant watching a freight train approaching, and he was stuck to the railway line.

At least she's got her mouth shut, thought Arthur. She was close enough for him to see one of her huge eyes now, a thing the size of a racetrack. There were oily tears the size of buses rolling across the face of the eye, each one leaving a rainbow trace behind.

The pupil in the eye suddenly moved up and down a few times, then left and right. It looked like a weird code.

Instantly Dawn's wings pumped the air and she veered away from the onrushing whale, circling to gain height. Arthur, taken by surprise, rotated in Dawn's grip and found himself staring at her sharkskin belly. He urgently pushed and pulled himself around, desperate to see what was happening.

It took him a minute or more, a very long minute, with the expectation that when he next looked he would see the giant mouth open and them going straight into it, no matter how hard Dawn tried to fly away.

But he didn't. He saw the top of Drowned Wednesday's head, only a hundred feet or so below. A huge expanse of white whale blubber and, a few seconds later, a blowhole that looked like a billionaire's sauna.

Which was not that big, Arthur thought. The Leviathan had shrunk considerably. She was now no more than a mile long and he could actually see the shrinking taking place. It was like watching a balloon slowly losing its air, while it still kept its basic shape.

"A minor miscalculation," said Dawn as they began to glide around and down again. There was something in her tone that suggested to Arthur that she'd done it on purpose to scare him, perhaps on Wednesday's orders.

Whether it was intentional or not, Dawn made no mistake with the landing on the ship. She circled a few times, watching the approaching white whale get smaller and smaller. Then, when Drowned Wednesday was no more than fifty feet long, Dawn swooped down on to the poop deck, dropped Arthur and transformed herself back into human shape.

"Go down to the main deck," said Dawn. "Milady will meet you there."

Arthur unpegged his nose and slowly climbed down the companionway to the quarterdeck and then to the waist of the ship. Tables had been laid end to end on both the port and starboard sides, from the forecastle back to the mainmast. They were covered in fine white tablecloths and loaded with many different kinds of food on fancy silver platters and trays and china plates and bowls.

This, Arthur guessed, was the luncheon of seventeen removes, though all seventeen courses were already laid out and, as far as he could see, there were no places set, or chairs.

The slap of water on deck made him look to the side ladder. A pulpy-fingered, dripping hand gripped the top rung, followed by another.

Drowned Wednesday was coming aboard.

She did not look good. Her skin was pallid and strangely lumpy, and her arms and legs were of different sizes, the left much puffier than the right. She was wearing a one-piece garment that looked like a huge flour sack with holes cut for her head and arms. Her hair hung limp and wet like a bunch of brown seaweed on her head, obscuring much of her face. Arthur could see that once she must have been beautiful, as were all the superior Denizens, but the fine bones of her face were lost in fat.

She had a rope tied around her waist in place of a belt, and thrust through the rope was a long silver fork – perhaps a short trident. Arthur's eye was drawn to it at once, and he knew without being told that this was the Third Key. Right in front of him! He could run forward and snatch it out—

"Greetings, Lord Arthur," muttered Lady Wednesday as she staggered past him to the table and picked up a huge, meaty bone. She immediately began to gnaw at it, tearing off huge chunks of meat, which she swallowed down with barely a chew. "Wouldn't believe how tired... I am of krill and... microscopic shrimps!"

Arthur tried to keep the look of disgust off his face as she threw the bone away and picked up an enormous cake and forced it into her face.

"Repulsive, aren't I?" mumbled Wednesday. "Not my choice, you understand. Can't stop eating."

"Why?" asked Arthur. "I don't understand. What's wrong with you? What do you want with me?"

"Cursed," came the indistinct reply, as Wednesday moved to a huge silver tureen of soup and started to drink it down. "Or something similar. Never should have gone in with the other Trustees. Started getting hungry back then, almost as soon as I took my part of the Will. But held it in check with the Key. Pass me that turkey."

Arthur looked at the table. It took him a moment to locate a huge roast bird that had to be the turkey, though it was twice the size of any he'd ever seen. He lifted it up with some effort and handed it to Wednesday, who grabbed it one-handed and managed to get her jaws around two-thirds of the huge bird in one go.

Arthur had thought of snatching the Key as he handed over the turkey, but he couldn't bring himself to get close enough. Lady Wednesday's hunger was really frightening and it took all Arthur's courage just to stay and listen to her – from a distance.

"As I was saying... this good... started getting hungry but held it in check for a couple of thousand years without too much trouble... sauce for this duck, ah... ate a huge amount but didn't matter... then I realised wasn't just my appetite getting out of hand... cucumber sandwiches excellent, only four dozen, pity... the Border Sea was spreading without my direction... extending into the Secondary Realms, which was bad enough, but also into Nothing..."

She paused to eat a huge, towering jelly-cake, shoving handfuls of it into her maw in quick time. Then, between mouthfuls of bread torn from a loaf the size of Arthur himself, she continued.

"I could stop the Sea spreading when I noticed it, using the Key... ugh, fish, you can have that... but I didn't like what was going on. Eventually I concluded that the problem went back to our actions with the Will. So I decided—"

She stopped suddenly and flung herself on a platter of small chocolate desserts, smearing chocolate all over her pasty face. Then, through bubbles of chocolate, she continued what she was saying.

"I decided that I would free Part Three of the Will and relinquish the Key. That I was not equipped to deal with whatever was wrong with the Border Sea and with myself."

Wednesday stopped eating for a few seconds. Her face screwed up with a look of pain.

"Unfortunately I also decided to share my plan first with my friend, the so-called Superior Saturday, who I thought might do the same. Two of us would have a better chance against the others. Or so I thought."

She took a deep breath and staggered down the table to a barbecue plate that was sizzling away without any visible source of heat. It was crowded with thick, succulent sausages, which Drowned Wednesday picked up by the half dozen and crammed into a mouth that Arthur noticed was already bigger and wider than it had been moments before. Drowned Wednesday herself had also grown a foot or two in every direction while she was speaking.

"Saturday betrayed me! The other Trustees, save that somnolent fool Monday, called me to a meeting. I was ambushed, five Keys against my one. They stripped me of my power and I was cast down into the Border Sea, my shape lost, my appetite unsuppressed!"

She punctuated her last remark by eating an entire watermelon, rind and all, washing it down with a huge flagon of ale that spilled down her front.

"Ahh! Since then, I have not been fully able to wield the Key. All the power I have is directed at growing no larger, else I eat up everything in the Border Sea and beyond!"

"What about the Will?" asked Arthur. "Why didn't you just release it like you were going to?"

"Stolen!" roared Wednesday as she slavered over a side of suckling pig. "They reached into my mind and stole out the secret of its location, then Saturday or one of the others sent that pirate Feverfew to take it. But you will get it back, Lord Arthur! You will get the Will and I shall give you the

Key, and all will yet be well. Oh, how I long not to... eat! Eat! Eat!"

She threw herself on the table, sliding along with her mouth gaping open like some sort of awful giant vacuum cleaner, scooping up food, plates and all. As she ate her way along the table, her torso grew larger and larger, and her arms and legs shrank back into her body.

"Where did Feverfew take the Will?" Arthur shouted. He started to back even further away from the feeding frenzy, darting glances at Dawn, who did not look at all ready to fly away.

"Aaaarrch homp homp ugh," Wednesday gurgled and spat, bits of mangled silver falling from her jaws. "Don't know! The pirates have a secret harbour. I know it is in my very own Border Sea, I feel it in my gut! But I cannot find it. You must! Now run! Run!"

She focused on the last few yards of piled-high food on the table and swallowed the lot down in one sweep of her now enormous mouth. Then she turned towards Arthur and slid on to the deck, a huge blubbery cylinder that was not yet whale but no longer human, her now vestigial arms and legs writhing and her vast mouth chomping, the ridges of bone that had once been teeth making a hideous clattering sound.

Arthur wasn't on the deck any more. He was halfway up the main mast, almost jumping from ratline to ratline. He climbed so quickly that he made it to the cross-trees and was working himself on to the small platform there when Dawn caught up with him and plucked him away and into the air.

Below them, Wednesday continued to grow and grow, threshing and rolling in her hunger, biting at the timbers of the ship until her own rapidly increasing weight broke the vessel's back and sent it to the bottom.

Dawn did not waste any time letting Arthur have a look at Wednesday's transformation. She started flying directly away, her wings beating rapidly and full, gaining height as well as speed. It took Arthur a moment to understand that even now they might not get away, that Dawn was pushing herself to the limit in order to escape Wednesday's remarkable growth and even more remarkable hunger.

Neither of them spoke for some time, till it was clear that their flight had taken them out of Drowned Wednesday's ravening path.

"Where do you wish to go?" asked Dawn finally. "I will do as promised and take you to a place of safety, if you so desire."

CHAPTER FIFTEEN

Arthur didn't reply immediately. He felt himself at an important crossroads, and his choice here would decide not only his own fate but the fate of many others as well.

"If safety is your prime concern," Dawn continued, "then I must take you to Port Wednesday. It is the only place in the Border Sea where there are elevators to take you elsewhere within the House, and thence wherever you wish to go."

Arthur was silent, thinking this through. It would be so easy to go to Port Wednesday, take an elevator to the Lower House, and then go home through the Front Door or Seven Dials. That would be the safe course to follow. But deep inside he felt that there were no safe courses for him any more. Not in the long run.

"How far are we from the Triangle?" he asked.

"A half-day's journey, by way of an ocean in the Secondary Realms," replied Wednesday. "Or a week or more if we stay within the House. Port Wednesday is even closer, only a few hours away, again by way of a suitable sea on another world in the Secondary Realms. There's nothing for you at the Triangle."

"My friend Leaf is there, and some Raised Rats. Have you asked them to try and find the pirates' secret harbour?" asked Arthur.

"No," said Dawn. "We do not deal with Rats. Milady Wednesday wished to ban them from the Border Sea, but they possess a patent of authority from the Architect herself, allowing them to roam where they will within the House. What can you possibly want with the Raised Rats?"

"They're expert finders and searchers," said Arthur, thinking back to the vision he'd seen of Leaf and the Commodoure. "Or they say they are."

"They are braggarts and not to be trusted," Dawn scoffed. "They sell their services and the secrets of others. They have never answered to any authority within the House, save the Architect's, and since her disappearance I doubt they have grown more obedient to anyone, not even Lord Sunday."

"He's ultimately in charge of everything, right?"

"After a fashion," replied Dawn. "Superior Saturday has the day-to-day management of affairs, as it were. Lord Sunday's mind dwells upon higher things, not for any lesser beings to know."

"They're both traitors to the Architect," Arthur stated boldly. "Saturday and Sunday, and all the other Morrow Days."

"Where do you wish to go?" asked Dawn, her tone even frostier than usual.

"The Triangle," Arthur answered firmly.

"The Triangle," Dawn confirmed. "I cannot approve of this desire to deal with the Rats, but does this mean you will go in search of the Will? To aid milady?"

"Yep," said Arthur. Somehow *yep* seemed the most positive thing he could say. Stronger than *yeah* and more heroic than *yes*. He hoped he could live up to it.

He pushed on. "I'm going to rescue Leaf and get the Raised Rats to help find the pirates' secret harbour. Then I guess I'll work out some way to release the Will and set everything straight. Including Lady Wednesday."

Dawn was silent for a while, save for the sound of her constant wingbeat. In a small voice that sounded strange and half-strangled, she finally said, "Thank you."

Then she folded her wings and dived towards the sea, with Arthur just managing to take a breath and put his nosepeg back on before they plunged through a slow rolling wave.

The journey to the Triangle was much quicker than Arthur had thought it would be. Even the Line of Storms didn't bother him this time. He just shut his eyes and put his fingers in his ears. He figured that if the lightning hadn't fried him the first few times it wasn't going to now.

Shortly after crossing the Line, the sea suddenly changed colour and temperature, and they were swimming through lukewarm, orange-tinted seas full of tiny floating flowers. Sometime later the orange sea transformed to a body of freezing black water, full of small, regularly shaped chunks of faintly luminous ice. It was as if millions of radioactive ice cubes had been dumped into the sea. Fortunately Arthur did not feel the full effect of the cold, for the golden radiance of Wednesday's Dawn surrounded him and kept him warm. In any case, they were not in this chill sea for long, leaving it abruptly for the blue waters of the Border Sea and, very soon after, another crossing of the Line of Storms.

Somewhere just past the Line, the clothespeg suddenly fell off Arthur's nose. Without meaning to, he breathed in a large amount of water and panicked. He had no idea how deep they were swimming, or how long it would take to get to the surface. He just wanted air immediately and instinctively threshed around in the grip of Dawn's tentacle, fighting against her as he tried to push up to where he imagined the surface was.

Dawn didn't release her hold, but she quickly slanted upward. Her huge wings gave one enormous beat that sent her bursting out of the sea and into the air. Arthur tried to take a breath but had too much water already in his lungs, so he broke into a coughing fit that ended in him throwing up what seemed like gallons of water. Even more came out of his nose and ears.

Finally he managed a few racking breaths, interspersed with bouts of coughing, till he hung exhausted in Dawn's grasp, unable to stop thinking about what might have happened if the peg spell had failed when he was underwater in that black, freezing sea.

"We are nearly there," said Dawn. "Though it will take longer now that I cannot go by water."

Arthur nodded, unable to speak. Her flying speed seemed quite fast enough.

Eventually the water stopped coming out of Arthur's nose and he could breathe normally again.

"The Triangle lies dead ahead," Dawn informed him. "Though it is unusually empty. There were reportedly thirty or forty ships there a few days ago. Now, I only count eight…"

Arthur looked down. At first all he saw was the sea, with the white tops of the waves relentlessly moving in the same direction. Then he shifted his gaze and saw eight ships of different sizes floating next to one another, in the lee of what at first sight appeared to be a sheer rock that thrust out of the sea. On closer inspection, Arthur realised the protrusion was actually the top of a pyramid, its stones heavily weathered by wind and ocean. It rose several hundred feet above the sea and was perhaps half a mile long on each side. If it had once ended in a point, that was gone, leaving a flat platform about the size of a tennis court, which was almost completely occupied by a huge iron ring. There was a single six-foot-thick rope tied to the ring, swinging down the lee side of the pyramid into the sea. The ships were either tied up to this rope, or rafted up to a vessel that was.

"Can you see the *Flying Mantis*?" asked Arthur. "Or the Rats? What kind of ship do they have?"

"The *Mantis* is not there," said Dawn. "As for the Rats, one of their putrid, smoky steamers is tied up on the eastern side of the raft, next to the four-masted ship *Undine*."

"A steamship? The Rats have steamships? Why doesn't everyone else?"

"They are forbidden by Drowned Wednesday," said Dawn. "With good reason, for they are foul and unclean. But the Rats have their exemptions. Besides, only the steam vessels made by Grim Tuesday work in the Border

Sea and they are fuelled with Accelerated Coal, made from Nothing. As with everything from Grim Tuesday, the price of this coal is exorbitant."

"That'd be right," said Arthur. "Where is the Rats' ship again? I can't see it."

"Next to the big four-master on the eastern side, as I said."

Arthur looked again. This time, he saw the Rats' vessel. It was only a third the size of the four-masted barque next to it, and his eye had been momentarily confused because the Rats' ship could sail as well as steam, having two masts and square-rigged sails as well as a large central funnel that was not currently smoking.

"We will land on the *Undine*," said Dawn, "and see what is happening. It is unusual for so few ships to be here. Everything looks strangely quiet."

She began to spiral down. Arthur closed his eyes as their rapid descent made him feel dizzy. He didn't open them again until he suddenly felt a solid deck under his feet and Dawn let him go.

She had already transformed back into human form. This time, she was wearing a kind of naval uniform, with a very dark blue coat that was almost black, hung with medals and supporting two very large silver epaulettes. Arthur wondered how she managed to instantly change clothes.

There was no one on board to greet them. Dawn looked around, a frown wrinkling her forehead. There was no one to be seen on any of the other ships either. The only sounds were the groan of the wooden hulls, the high-pitched squeaking of the mooring ropes and the wash of the sea.

Dawn opened her hand and gripped the air, and a flaming harpoon appeared in her fist. Arthur flinched, but though it was obviously magical, it was not like the Mariner's harpoon. It didn't make him feel odd when he looked at it, so he hoped it wouldn't have the horrible side effects the Captain's harpoon did when it was used.

"The guard boat is missing," said Dawn. "This is what comes of having all one's faithful Nisser..."

She restrained herself, but Arthur knew she had been going to say *eaten*.

"I suppose the crews are hiding inside the Triangle," Dawn continued. "Fearful of a pirate attack, no doubt. Which reminds me – put these on."

She pulled a pair of white leather gloves out of her sleeve and handed them to Arthur.

"No need to cause panic at the sight of the Red Hand," she said.

Arthur put on the gloves as Dawn stalked across the poop deck and looked over the port side, across to the pyramid. As she walked away, Arthur heard a shout to starboard.

"Ahoy the *Undine*!"

Arthur went to the rail and looked down. The shout had sounded high-pitched, so he wasn't that surprised to see a four-foot-tall Rat wearing a blue cap, blue breeches and a loose white shirt hailing him from the forecastle of the steamship. A ship, Arthur noticed, that despite Dawn's disdain looked very spick-and-span. It also had a name, painted in white on the bow. *Rattus Navis IV*.

"Ahoy to you too," Arthur called out. "Where is everyone?"

"A score or more ships sailed within the last few hours, and of those that are left, most of the crews are quivering inside the Triangle," replied the Rat. "It started with the sea level dropping four fathoms for half an hour yesterday. Then the *Shiver* was sighted to the south this morning. What with the rumour of someone afflicted with the Red Hand and all, a dreadful fright got among the Denizens. The braver ones decided to chance it on the high seas, preferring not to be sitting here. Those less brave thought to barricade themselves inside the pyramid and leave the pickings to Feverfew."

"But he has not come," interrupted Dawn, looming up at Arthur's side. "Or he has become uncommonly gentle with his prey. Has *Shiver* been seen again today, Rat?"

The Rat doffed his cap before replying.

"No, ma'am."

"Is your captain aboard?"

"Captain and crew, ma'am, awaiting custom."

"Who are you?"

"Gunner's Mate First Watkingle, ma'am."

"And your captain?"

"That would be Longtayle, ma'am. Do you wish to come aboard?"

"No. I have other pressing matters to attend to, but my companion here has business with your captain. This is Lord Arthur, Master of the Lower House and the Far Reaches. For some reason he believes you Rats might be useful. He is an honoured guest of Lady Wednesday and is to be treated with all courtesy."

Watkingle bowed low, but didn't answer.

"Farewell, Lord Arthur," said Dawn, offering her hand. "I hope you succeed."

Arthur wasn't sure what to do, but he took it and gave a kind of half bow and a little shake.

"I'll do my best."

Dawn nodded, withdrew her hand and took a standing jump over the rail and on to the deck of the next ship, without even flapping her wings.

"Just come down the *Undine's* ladder amidships, sir," called up Watkingle. "Then jump down, if you don't object."

As Arthur walked along to the waist of the ship, Watkingle called out something and more Rats came on the steamship's deck, arranging themselves in a line opposite the *Undine*'s ladder. When Arthur climbed down and jumped across to the deck of the *Rattus Navis IV*, one of them played several piercing notes on a silver whistle. All the Rats immediately stood to attention.

Watkingle saluted Arthur, then said, "Welcome aboard, sir. Please follow me. Mind your head."

Though the deck was wooden, as soon as Arthur followed Watkingle through a door between the two quarterdeck companionways, his feet rang on iron. Arthur stopped to look around and felt the rivets in the iron wall. He had to bend his head a lot lower than he had in the *Moth*, as the ship was built to Raised-Rat scale.

"She's an iron ship, sir," said Watkingle. "Timbered up to ease the sensibilities of Wednesday and her officials. Built by Grim Tuesday himself, four thousand years ago, and still as sound a vessel as anyone would wish."

He knocked on a door at the end of the passage.

"Lord Arthur, Master of the Lower House and the Far Reaches, sir!"

The door was opened immediately by another seaman Rat, dressed like Watkingle but rather more neatly. Beyond him, there was a large stern cabin with dinner-plate-sized portholes on three sides, a map table loaded with charts and augury puzzle boxes with pictures of animals on them, several upholstered chairs and a couple of riveted iron chests. Two Rats stood over the table, both in blue coats with gold epaulettes. Arthur recognised one of them as Commodoure Monckton. The other was a black Rat, not brown, taller and younger-looking, his whiskers shorter and not as white.

The black rat said, "Thank you, Watkingle, that will be all. Lord Arthur, welcome aboard the *Rattus Navis IV*! I am Captain Longtayle, and may I introduce Commodoure Monckton."

Both Rats inclined their heads and snapped their tails like whips, the crack echoing through the cabin. Arthur jumped in surprise, then bowed.

Longtayle pulled out a chair from the table and offered it to Arthur. When he sat, so did the two officers. The Rat who had opened the door immediately put a glass in front of Arthur and poured what looked like red wine from a silver jug.

Arthur looked at it and wished it wasn't wine.

"Cranberry juice," said Longtayle, correctly judging Arthur's expression. "An antiscorbutic for our rare ventures into the Secondary Realms. While we are Raised, we are not Denizens. Like the Piper's children, some diseases may still get hold of us out in the Realms. Scurvy is one of them."

Arthur nodded over the rim of the glass. The juice tasted very good indeed.

"Before we go on to discuss your particular business, Lord Arthur," said Commodoure Monckton, "I believe I should tell you that we have been employed by Monday's Tierce, Miss Suzy Blue, to find you and accordingly I have just a few minutes ago sent a message to the effect that you have been found. We have also claimed a reward."

"That's OK," said Arthur. "I knew you were working for Suzy. What I want to know right now is what's happened to my friend Leaf."

The two Rats exchanged a surprised look.

"We are expert searchers and finders of information as all else," said Monckton. "But clearly your sources are as good. It was only five days ago that I entered into an agreement with Miss Leaf."

"Five days," Arthur repeated, mystified. Yet again the weird time shifts between the House and the Secondary Realms were confusing him.

"Yes, five days," Monckton confirmed.

"That was for her court thing, right?" said Arthur impatiently. "What happened?"

"The court was held this morning, before Captain Swell chose to sail away. Miss Leaf was charged with being a stowaway—"

"I know! What happened to her?"

"With the potential punishment being a death sentence for a mortal, I was acutely aware of the stakes. However—"

"*What happened?* Is she... ?"

CHAPTER SIXTEEN

"No, no, she's not dead," replied Monckton. "But she has been pressed."

"Pressed!" Arthur exclaimed. "What do you mean? Like crushed?"

He couldn't believe it. Whipping was bad enough, but to be pressed flat—

"No, no! Pressed, as in forcibly enlisted," said Monckton. "I was able to prove that she did not go aboard the *Flying Mantis* of her own free will, so she was not a stowaway. But she was not a passenger either, nor a distressed sailor. Ultimately the only thing she could be was one of the crew. So she was pressed into service as a ship's boy."

"Ship's girl," said Arthur.

"Ship's *boy*," said Monckton. "They're always called ship's boys, even when they're girls. There are plenty of both aboard the ships of the Border Sea. Though apart from your friend Leaf, they're all the Piper's children, of course, and therefore our brethren. We help one another, where we may."

"But what will happen to her?"

"It's a hard life, but the *Mantis* is a well-found ship and a fair one," said Longtayle. "Your friend might work her way up, become an officer, even captain her own ship in time. Mortals learn much faster than Denizens, so there's no knowing where she'll end up."

"But she won't want to be a ship's boy! She has to get home! She has a family and friends!"

"She signed the ship's articles," Longtayle reported. "There's no breaking them."

"Except by executive order from Drowned Wednesday," corrected Monckton.

"So I could release her once I get the Will to make me Master of the Border Sea," said Arthur. "Or Duke, or whatever it is."

Both Rats nodded in agreement. They didn't seem surprised that Arthur was planning to assume control over the Border Sea.

"I suppose Leaf will be safe enough on board the

Mantis," Arthur said in a hopeful tone. She was probably better off than he was, being out of the trouble he was heading into, but still he wished he'd reached the Triangle earlier and could have helped Leaf get off the ship and go home.

I'll have to check, he thought. *With the mirror and the shell...*

"She'll be safer than most at sea, for the *Mantis* is a good ship, but there's always storm and wrack," said Monckton.

"And pirates," added Longtayle. "The *Shiver* has been sighted too often in recent times for my liking, not to mention some of Feverfew's lesser brethren, such as Captain Blooddreg of the *Nightdream*."

"That's why I'm here," said Arthur. "Kind of. I need to find Feverfew's secret harbour, and I need to go in there and get something. I must ask for your help."

"We are mercantile Rats," said Monckton. "That is to say, we do not do anything without payment of some kind."

"Do you actually know where Feverfew's harbour is?" Arthur asked. "Or can you find out fairly quickly? I mean, there's no point talking about payment if you can't do anything."

"We think we know where it is," said Longtayle. "That is to say we have deduced its location from some evidence, but we have not actually been there ourselves. As for getting you there... if we're right then that's an even more difficult proposition."

"OK," said Arthur, ready to bargain. "What payment do you want for the location, to start with?"

"We deal in information," said Monckton. "So if we answer your questions, we'd like you to answer an equivalent number of ours."

Arthur had been expecting to pay a ransom in gold or treasure. This seemed too easy...

"Is that all?" he asked.

"That may be more than it seems," Longtayle advised.

Arthur shrugged. "I don't have anything to hide. At least I don't think I do."

"Then you shall ask three questions of us," said Monckton. "And we shall ask three of you."

"There's no trick to this, is there?" Arthur asked suspiciously. "I mean, what I just asked doesn't count as a question, does it? Because I'm not agreeing to that."

"Only significant questions count," said Monckton. "So, you want to know what we know about Feverfew's secret harbour?"

"Yes," said Arthur. "That's my first question. Where is it?"

In response, Longtayle unrolled a very large map that took up most of the table. It was labelled THE BORDER SEA and was nearly all blue water, with occasional small flecks of land, each neatly marked in tiny cursive script.

Arthur looked over the map eagerly, taking in place names like Port Wednesday, the Triangle, Mount Last and Swirleen Deep. At first glance, he couldn't see anything labelled Feverfew's Secret Harbour, so he went back to the top left corner to start a systematic search up and down, only to be interrupted as Longtayle carefully placed a small ivory carving of a white whale on the map and tapped it twice.

"It's there," he said. "We believe Feverfew's secret harbour must actually be inside Drowned Wednesday."

"Inside her!"

"More exactly, we believe the secret harbour is a miniature worldlet that is anchored inside Drowned Wednesday's stomach. It can be accessed in only two ways. One is via a unique augury puzzle that Feverfew possesses, made for him by Grim Tuesday, like the worldlet itself. The other is directly from Wednesday's stomach."

"But it can't be inside her," said Arthur. "She returned to her normal human form. How could a whole secret harbour still be in her stomach?"

"I am not a metamathic sorcerer," said Longtayle, "but I believe the explanation is something like this: the secret harbour is contained within a bubble of the Secondary Realm that has been brought into the House. The size of that bubble may change from minuscule to gigantic without affecting the world it contains. When Lady Wednesday used the Third Key to return to her former shape, the bubble shrank with her. When she grew again, it grew. But the world inside the bubble did not change."

"And you can get into it from Wednesday's stomach?"

"We believe so," said Longtayle. "Or out of it. We think Feverfew had the worldlet sorcerously placed inside Wednesday for two reasons. It would be the ideal hiding place, but also would provide unparalleled opportunities for recovering salvage. You are aware that anything lost always turns up eventually in the Border Sea?"

Arthur nodded. He'd been told that by Sunscorch.

"A great part of what is lost lies in the very deeps and is unrecoverable, unless it floats up before it sinks to one of the places where the Sea now impinges upon Nothing and is dissolved. But there is still considerable salvage in shallower water, and it, along with everything else in Wednesday's path, ends up in her stomach, at least for a time. Feverfew uses his slaves to harvest the salvage Wednesday has swallowed, adding greatly to the plunder he takes from the ships of the Border Sea."

"How do you know about this?" asked Arthur.

"One of the advantages granted us by the Piper is the ability to return to our former shape and size for a time," explained Monckton. "It is unpleasant and potentially dangerous, should we forget that we are Raised, but we are able to masquerade as normal rats. One of our number managed to infiltrate the *Shiver* in this fashion and observe the transition to the secret harbour. While there, she also saw slaves being sent out somewhere, the survivors returning with salvage. Later, we deduced the location of that harbour and the nature of the slaves' activities. Captain Longtayle, show Lord Arthur the map and the sketches."

Longtayle took a leather case from under the table, opened it and took out several rolled-up pages. He laid these out on the table.

The first one was a map, drawn in pencil and entitled in large uneven letters FEVERFEW'S ISLAND. It showed a body of land shaped like a skull. Under the title there was a note that read: *The isle is roughly 4,500 double paces long and 3,200 double paces wide.*

The left eye socket of the skull had LAKE LEFT written on it. The right eye socket was broken and open to the sea. This was labelled HARBOUR and there were some smaller notations indicating a jetty, a shipyard, eight warehouses, a dozen large buildings marked as slave quarters and a star-shaped construction called Feverfew's Fort.

The nose cavity was labelled as HOT MUD CRATER, with a scrawled note underneath that said *Nothing?*

Down by the skull's jawbone, there were lots of

squiggly lines described as TEETH MOUNTAINS and *Followers of the Carp. Escaped Slaves.*

There was sea around the island, but it only extended for about 850 double paces according to the indicated scale, till it met a line marked *Extent of Bubble* that circled the map. Not far from the harbour mouth, near this line, there was a narrow peninsula that thrust out into the sea, with a dot on the end of it and the inscription: *Exit to salvage grounds.*

The second page Longtayle unrolled showed several rough charcoal sketches. One drawing showed the harbour with half a dozen ships present, one of them easily recognisable as the *Shiver*. The other ships looked derelict and were all piled up against one another in one corner of the harbour, while the pirate schooner was tied up to the jetty.

The second drawing showed a line of slaves wearing bizarre-looking diving helmets, each of them hobbled with a long chain and equipped with a sack and net.

The third drawing was incomplete, a partial scene captured over the shoulder of a pirate who was kneeling on the deck of a ship. He had the lid of a box next to him, the lid illustrated with something that looked like a cross between a squid and a man.

The fourth and final drawing showed a line of small mountains or large hills, which were covered in thick jungle. The caption under the drawing read *Followers of the Carp must be escaped slaves. Potential here.*

"How did your spy get back out with these?" asked Arthur.

Longtayle shook his head.

"She didn't. The map and the drawings came by simultaneous bottle."

"By what?"

"Simultaneous bottles are a form of communication we developed ourselves, with some assistance from certain parties. Essentially they are pairs of magical bottles. Anything put in one simultaneously appears in the other bottle as well. But they do not work outside the Border Sea and are very expensive to construct, so only our most important agents are equipped with them. Our various vessels also use simultaneous bottles to keep in touch. We have over a hundred simultaneous bottles aboard."

"So these two papers were the last thing to come through from your agent with Feverfew?"

"Not quite," said Monckton grimly. "The last thing to come through before the bottle shattered was a severed tail. So you see, one gallant Rat has already given up her life for this information."

"This drawing, is it of Feverfew himself?" Arthur asked, indicating the sketch of the pirate kneeling on the deck. "And what's on the lid of that puzzle box?"

"We believe it's Feverfew," said Longtayle. "He was once a mortal man, though greatly changed by sorcery and his long existence in the House, and this drawing shows a man of mortal dimensions. The augury puzzle he is using is not one that is listed anywhere we can find. The creature it portrays is a Gore-Draken, a rare form of Nithling that is very occasionally created when certain lost items within the Border Sea come in contact with Nothing. This suggests the augury puzzle was created from the intestines of a Gore-Draken specifically for Feverfew, which could only have been done by a very superior Sorcerer or one of the Morrow Days. Since Feverfew's private bubble was made by Grim Tuesday, it's likely the Grim made the augury puzzle to go with it. Who paid for it to be made is another question, which we do not know the answer to."

"Probably Superior Saturday," said Arthur. "That's who Drowned Wednesday went to in the first place, to get his help to return the Keys to the Will."

"*Her* help," said Monckton. "Superior Saturday is female. Or she was, last we heard. Now, I think you will agree, we have answered your first question. So we shall ask one in return. Why do you want to go to Feverfew's secret harbour?"

Arthur thought for a moment. There seemed to be nothing to be gained from trying to not answer the question or fudging the answer. He liked the Rats. They seemed very straightforward and he knew he would need more of their help.

"I believe the Third Part of the Will is there. Drowned Wednesday doesn't have it any more and she says Feverfew took it, with help from the Morrow Days. I want to get to the Will and release it. Then I can get the Third Key from Drowned Wednesday, fix her up, get Leaf back and..."

The two Rats leaned forward as Arthur hesitated.

"Then... I'm not sure. I guess I'll need to go back home for a little while, to make sure everything's OK. But if I manage to get the Third Key, I suppose I'll have to work out what to do about Sir Thursday and just... get on with it."

"That is a generous answer, Arthur. Please, your next question."

"It's not exactly a question," said Arthur. "I need to get to that secret harbour. If there are only two ways in, and one of them is Feverfew's augury puzzle, it looks like I'll have to get in through Wednesday's stomach. Which means I have to survive getting swallowed up. The only way I can think of doing that would be to be in a submarine or something like it. I've heard you have lots of strange ships, so my question is this: "Do you have a submarine or know where one is, and can I borrow it?""

CHAPTER SEVENTEEN

"A valuable question, Lord Arthur," said Monckton. He hesitated, his whiskers shivering, then went on. "We do indeed have a submersible boat, a craft we keep secret. But I am afraid it is laid up underneath our dock at Port Wednesday, for lack of an essential component, which we have been waiting on for some time."

"What kind of component?" asked Arthur. "And who's making you wait? Uh, only answer if that doesn't count as another question."

"That can be accounted as part of your second question, Lord Arthur," replied Monckton. "The submersible boat was made for us in the Far Reaches, by Grim Tuesday's minions. The component it lacks is, in fact, a canister of Accelerated Coal, which must be replaced every century or so. However, since the fall of Grim Tuesday, very few of our orders are coming through from the Far Reaches."

"Yeah, well, I'm sure Dame Primus is doing her best to sort everything out," said Arthur defensively. "Grim Tuesday was using way too much Nothing—"

"That was not a criticism, merely an observation," said Monckton. "We are aware that changes were necessary in the Far Reaches, and we have been advised that we will get a new fuel canister within the next thirty or forty years."

"Thirty or forty years! That's hopeless," said Arthur. He thought for a moment, then said, "How about I get you a new fuel canister? Will you then let me use the submersible to get into Drowned Wednesday's stomach?"

"Will you allow me to confer with Lieutenant Longtayle for a moment?" Monckton asked. "The submersible is very valuable, and it would not be easy for even it to survive a passage into the Leviathan's interior – and out again."

"Sure, go ahead."

Monckton and Longtayle retreated to the other side of the cabin to whisper, while Arthur studied the drawings and the map again. His head was full of rapid thoughts darting around and linking together to lead him into new ideas.

OK, if I can get into Wednesday's stomach and then into Feverfew's private worldlet, I still need to find the Will and release it and get back out again. Presuming the place will be full of pirates, it would be dumb to go in there by myself... This is kind of like working out how to rob a bank or something... I need to get a team together to help me...

There're the Rats, of course, to run the submarine... I wonder if the Rats can fight... I probably need some Denizens who can fight the pirates, though we should try and sneak in, but just in case... I wonder if Dawn would come along... Then there is the sorcery angle, so if I could get Dr Scamandros to help out... and Sunscorch, he'd be a good fighter, though the rest of the Moth's *crew wouldn't be up to much—*

Monckton and Longtayle came back to the table and sat down. Arthur looked at them expectantly.

"We have agreed," said Monckton. "You may have the use of the submersible *Rattus Balaena* and its crew if you can secure a new power canister for it. We will do our best to deliver you into the belly of the whale."

"Great!" exclaimed Arthur. "And they'll take me out again too, right? With the Will."

"Yes, if at all possible, the *Balaena* will stand by to take you off the worldlet again and return out to the Border Sea. But the crew will not be able to help you against Feverfew in the worldlet itself. That is too great a risk."

"What about taking on extra passengers, as well as me? I'll need to get some help."

"There is limited space aboard the *Balaena*. It was built

for us Rats, but there is room for you and perhaps another six normal-sized Denizens, if no one minds being a little cramped. There might be some bumped heads too."

"Great! I'd better write a message to Dame Primus to get that power canister delivered. Do you have someone in Port Wednesday with one of your bottles, so I can send it to them to pass on?"

"Certainly," said Longtayle. He opened a drawer and offered Arthur a thick sheet of paper, a quill, a bottle of ink and a small pot of sand. "We shall consider our next question while you write."

Arthur dipped the quill in the bottle and wrote quickly. The smooth black ink ran a little too freely, causing blots and blotches along the way.

Dear Dame Primus,
I don't know if you got my other letter. Anyway, I'm in the Border Sea and I talked with Lady Wednesday and she explained how she got turned into a whale by the other Trustees and how she wants to release the Will and give the Key to me. But the Will got stolen by a pirate called Feverfew who works for the Morrow Days. I've done a deal with the Raised Rats and

they've told me that Feverfew's secret harbour is inside her and they'll let me use their submarine to go there so I can try to get the Will and fix everything up. Only the Rats need a power canister from the Far Reaches for the submarine, so can you please hurry that up so they get it straight away. I mean, really straight away, not next year or whatever. Immediately. Right now.

Also can you send Suzy to help me out? And if you can get in touch with the Mariner, can you ask him to come and help me out too?

Regards,

Arthur

P.S. Send a reply via the Rats at Port Wednesday and their simultaneous bottles, so I get it quicker.

P.P.S. Can you check what's happening back on my world? I want to know what the Border Sea did to the hospital. Thanks.

Arthur finished by spreading some sand over the paper to dry up the ink, as he'd seen done in the offices of the Lower House. He lifted the page to pour the sand back into the pot, then folded the paper, wrote Dame Primus's name on it and sealed it with his thumb. As before, his thumbprint shone and rippled like a rainbow and became a proper seal, showing Arthur's laurel-wreathed profile.

"If the power canister is delivered quickly, how long will it take before we can get going in the submarine?" asked Arthur.

"Well, the *Balaena* is at Port Wednesday, so we will have to get there first," said Longtayle. "Under full steam, that will be five days. The *Balaena* can be readied in that time, so we would be able to depart in her immediately."

"Five days!" exclaimed Arthur. "I guess there's no choice... I hope I still get back home just after I left, like I've done before. I suppose I might need the time to get in touch with the helpers I need..."

"Our simultaneous bottles are at your service," said Longtayle. "I presume we can send the bill for their use to Dame Primus?"

"Yes," said Arthur. "But no jacking up the price or anything – we'll only pay the regular fee."

"That is understood. Are you ready for our second question?"

Arthur nodded.

"What has the Will told you about the disappearance of the Architect?".

Arthur was surprised by the question, but tried not to show it. He wondered if he was supposed to be repeating what the Will told him. But a deal was a deal – and in this case, he didn't think giving out the information would hurt. "I think it just said She went away," he told the Rats, "leaving the Will behind."

"Are you sure of the exact words?"

"Pretty sure. Yeah, it was back when the Will was a frog in Suzy's throat. It said something like 'The Great Architect went away' or 'The Architect then went away.'"

"It never said that She was killed or slain by her own servants, the Morrow Days?"

Arthur dropped the cup he'd just picked up, the cranberry juice spreading like spilt blood towards the papers, till the liquid was hastily blotted up with a cloth by the Steward.

"What?! No! The Will said something about choosing to go away or it was Her own choice. It never said anything about Her getting killed... Do you think the Morrow Days killed Her? The Architect of everything? How would they do that?"

"Some authorities claim She is dead or returned to Nothing, which is the same thing," said Monckton. "We wanted to know what the Will had said to you, because the

Will probably knows and it would not lie to the Rightful Heir."

"I don't know about that," said Arthur. "I reckon it would lie if it suited it. And the First Part of the Will used to say it didn't know enough because it was only one-seventh of the whole Will. Though I have to say since it became Dame Primus it acts like it knows everything."

"You really think the Will might lie to you?"

Arthur thought for a moment. He couldn't think of any time when the Will had told him an outright lie, but he still had the feeling that it would if it thought it might help its cause. It would certainly lie by omission, choosing not to tell him things if he didn't ask for them.

"Yes, I think it would, but only if it thought it needed to. You know, to make me do something the Rightful Heir should do."

"That is interesting. We had hoped to learn definitively what has happened to the Architect, but clearly that is not yet possible. Thank you, Arthur. Do you have your third question?"

"I might save it for the time being, if that's all right." Arthur didn't want to waste his last question and he needed to think things through.

"You may do so," said Monckton. "Of course that means we will also still have a question for you."

"That's fine," Arthur agreed. He sat quietly for a

moment, going over a rough plan in his head. "I want to send some other messages as well," he finally said. "Do you have a bottle on board the *Moth*? The salvage ship I was on."

"I don't think so," replied Longtayle. He pulled out a small book from his pocket and started to flick through it. "I'll check the list."

"Is there any other way to get a message to them?"

"There are numerous ways," said Monckton. "But most rely on sorcery and we do not practise House sorcery, save for navigation. If Wednesday's Dawn is still here, she might send a message for you. She has many powers within the Border Sea."

"I'd like to talk to her," said Arthur. "But she told me she had urgent business to attend to."

"We don't have a bottle or anyone on the *Moth*, but I'll send someone to check if Wednesday's Dawn is still over at the Triangle," said Longtayle. He opened the door and spoke quickly to the Rat who stood at attention there.

"Sorcery..." said Arthur. He suddenly remembered Scamandros had put something in his pocket. Arthur had meant to transfer it to his boot so it would be safe, but he'd forgotten. Was it still there? He reached into the deep pocket and for a moment thought it was gone. Then his fingers closed on something cool and metallic in the corner.

He realised then that Longtayle and Monckton were looking at him curiously, so he hastily pulled his hand out. The Rats were probably trustworthy, but they didn't need to know everything, particularly if they were going to be trading information with him. Arthur needed to keep some secrets in reserve.

"Would you care to be shown to your cabin?" asked Longtayle. "It will take an hour or so to build up steam, then we will be on our way. Earlier, if the wind shifts and we can sail. The breeze is against us for Port Wednesday at the moment, but it may change."

"Thanks," said Arthur. He thought he could take a look at whatever Scamandros gave him in the cabin, and maybe use the shell and mirror to check out how Leaf was doing.

"You shall have my cabin, which is opposite," said Longtayle as he opened the door and indicated another one across the passage. There was already a replacement sailor Rat on sentry outside, who stood aside and saluted. The Rats ran a much more disciplined ship than the *Moth*, Arthur noted.

Arthur bowed to the sentry, crossed the passage and went into his cabin. It was smaller than the room he'd been in, no more than fifteen feet long and twelve feet wide, with a folded-up bunk on one bulkhead and a folded-down desk and chair on the wall.

Arthur sat down and pulled his boots off as part of the

process of retrieving the Atlas, Wednesday's invitation, the shell and the mirror. He put all these things into his inside coat pockets, then took out the metal object Scamandros had given him.

It was egg-shaped and made of gold, and there was a small curved catch on the side. Arthur flicked this up and the egg opened. One side was a watch, with an ivory face and ornate numbers picked out in tiny emeralds. The two hands were made from some kind of faintly glowing blue metal. The other side had a miniature portrait of Dr Scamandros. It was very lifelike. As Arthur looked at the painting, the tattoos on his face began to move, and the pale blue sky behind him changed to show a background of dark smoke and dimly lit figures that were either fighting or dancing. At the same time, the doctor's head turned away, as if he was looking behind him.

Arthur gasped and Dr Scamandros looked back. His wild eyes met Arthur's.

"Arthur!" shrieked the tiny figure, barely audible over the sudden din of screams, shouts, explosions and clashing metal that came through as well. "Help! Give me your hand!"

Without even thinking about it, Arthur touched the miniature with his finger. It was instantly seized and drawn in somewhere, along with Arthur's other fingers and then his whole hand. He felt someone – or something

– grip it fiercely. Panicked, Arthur pulled back as hard as he could.

It was like trying to pick up a very heavy weight – Arthur felt his elbow and shoulder joints stretch and almost crack. He leaned back and put his feet against the wall, pulling with all his strength. Then suddenly he was lying on his back and Dr Scamandros was sprawled next to him on the floor.

"Shut the watch!" squealed Scamandros. "Shut the watch!"

Arthur leapt up. Just as he reached for the watch, he heard a strange zinging sound and a long, oily flame shot out of the open watch and struck the iron ceiling, the flames burning off the paint and sending billows of choking smoke everywhere.

Arthur, thankful he was still wearing gloves, swiped at the watch, shutting it with one blow. The oily flame disappeared as the watch shut, but there was still lots of smoke. Arthur, coughing and rubbing his eyes, opened the door and the porthole to let it out, then turned to Scamandros, who was still lying on the floor.

"Are you all right? Where did you come from – and how?"

"Just recovering my strength," gasped Dr Scamandros. "You called at an opportune time, Lord Arthur. Thank the Architect I had the foresight to give you my transfer watch!"

"Is that what it is?"

"Yes, one of my graduation projects." Scamandros tried to get up, but got tangled in the tails of his yellow greatcoat, till Arthur gave him a hand. "I had thought I might need to merely talk with you again, but the transfer was most fortunate."

"Why? What's happened to the *Moth* and everyone?"

"The *Moth* has been taken," said Scamandros, his eyes downcast. "By the pirate Feverfew."

"What—"

Arthur was interrupted by shouts of "Fire!" from outside, followed a few seconds later by several seamen Rats bursting in with buckets and a hose, fortunately not yet fully up to pressure so it only dribbled water.

"Where's the fire?" shouted the first Rat into the room.

"It's out," said Arthur. "Don't worry about it."

"Who's this?" asked the Rat suspiciously, looking at the bedraggled, yellow-overcoated, surprisingly short Denizen who had so mysteriously appeared. Dr Scamandros bowed, but this didn't help. The Rat looked around, made sure there really was no fire, then nodded to Arthur and backed out.

"Stay here, please, sir, while I fetch the officer of the watch," the Rat said as she shut the door.

Arthur wasn't sure what would happen next.

CHAPTER EIGHTEEN

No more than a minute later, there was a knock at the door. Arthur opened it and found Lieutenant Longtayle standing there, now wearing a sword. Behind him were half a dozen Rats wearing steel cuirasses and helmets, and carrying short crossbows or cut-down boarding pikes.

"You have a visitor, Lord Arthur?" asked Longtayle politely, but his eyes were cold and did not stray from Dr Scamandros, who was sitting in the chair mopping his forehead with a yellow silk handkerchief.

"It's Dr Scamandros, from the *Moth*," Arthur explained. "He came through a transfer watch."

"Are you sure it *is* Dr Scamandros?" asked Longtayle. "It

could be a Nithling masquerading as him. Transfers can be intercepted or redirected."

Arthur looked at Scamandros more carefully than he had before. The doctor certainly looked the same...

"I *am* Dr Scamandros!" the Denizen protested weakly.

"Prove it," said Longtayle.

"You Rats! Never prepared to take anyone's word for anything," Scamandros complained. "Well, if you must insist upon proof, here are some documents for you."

He reached inside his greatcoat and pulled out a thin leather document case tied together with pink legal ribbon. He undid this and pulled out a parchment, which he handed over to Lieutenant Longtayle, who carefully looked it over. Arthur couldn't see what was on it clearly, but he caught a glimpse of a kind of three-dimensional portrait of Dr Scamandros that moved and turned, with flowing type scrolling underneath the picture.

"This is merely a student accreditation from the Sorcery Scholar Assistant Registrar of the Upper House," said Longtayle. "If it's a true document, what are you doing here in the Border Sea?"

"Up until very recently I have been the Navigator-Sorcerer of the ship *Moth*," said Dr Scamandros. "A post I have held for several thousand years, giving complete satisfaction, I may add. I have a letter here to that effect from Captain Catapillow."

He handed over a folded sheet of paper. Longtayle read this one too.

"What brought you to the Border Sea in the first place?"

Angry storms rolled across Scamandros's cheeks and his fingers twitched.

"That's none of your affair, young Rat!"

"You've come aboard without permission," said Longtayle grimly. "If you don't answer my questions we shall have to—"

"He's my guest!" interrupted Arthur. "I kind of... I guess I brought him aboard."

Scamandros waved his hand weakly. The storms on his cheeks dispersed and the ships tattooed there rode gently at anchor. A sun shone on his forehead, turning green as it slowly sank towards his right ear.

"Never mind, Lord Arthur. It's well known that these Rats never rest without prying out everyone's secrets. I came to the Border Sea to find my final exam papers, which were supposedly lost before they could be marked. I thought that if I could find them and have them properly assessed, I could gain my degree and once more be admitted into the halls of learning in the Upper House. A foolish hope, I now acknowledge. I suspect my papers were never truly lost and so will not reappear in the Sea."

"That confirms your identity," said Longtayle. He bowed and added, "We like to be sure who we have aboard, Doctor. As it happens, your 'secret' was already known to us. If Lord Arthur wishes to confirm you as his guest, we are happy to welcome you aboard the *Rattus Navis IV*."

"I do confirm him as a guest," said Arthur. "I was hoping to enlist Dr Scamandros for my... my expedition anyway."

"Expedition?" Scamandros asked. "Well, if I could have a cup of tea and a biscuit first, I daresay I could manage a small expedition..."

"We have to get to Port Wednesday before we really get started," said Arthur. "So you'll have a few days to recover—"

"Excellent!" Dr Scamandros beamed. He cast his eyes about the cabin. "Perhaps I might lie down on that bunk over there? I feel a little weak."

"Uh, I guess you can," said Arthur. "But I want to know what happened with the *Moth*! Was... was anybody killed? Is Sunscorch all right?"

"They'll all be slaves now," said Dr Scamandros gloomily as he climbed into the bunk. He looked down at his stomach, then pulled his greatcoat closed. "Those that survived. Sunscorch? I don't know. Everything was confused. There was smoke everywhere and Feverfew cast a spell that made the planks bite at our ankles. The Captain and Mister Concort retreated to the main cabin, while Sunscorch led the defence.

The *Shiver* fired a broadside of grapeshot as she closed, raking the deck, then suddenly there were pirates everywhere, all around. I ran to the forepeak, thinking to jump, when I heard the chime of my transfer watch..."

"But how did Feverfew know where you were? Was the *Moth* still on the beach?"

"On the beach? No, no, we were only there for two weeks, though of course that was a week too long for Sunscorch. After the ship was fixed up we started back for the Border Sea. That was when Feverfew got us. The *Shiver* was waiting, right where we came through the Line of Storms. I don't know how Feverfew knew where we'd cross. Though one naturally loathes and detests him as a pirate, one must admire his sorcery."

"You were on the beach for two weeks? But it's only been hours for me since I left."

"Time runs true in the House and—"

"—meanders elsewhere, yeah, I know," interrupted Arthur. He was thinking about getting back home before he was missed. "But that's a big time difference."

"I've known bigger," said Scamandros. "Why, one time we left the House for a year and came back only fifteen minutes after we left. The tea was still warm in the pot I left on the corner table of Aunt Sally's Café in Port Wednesday. Quite disturbing, I have to say. Now tell me, what is this expedition you plan, Lord Arthur?"

"It's a very difficult one," said Arthur carefully. "And getting more difficult. You see, I'm going to sneak into Feverfew's secret harbour and steal something from him. Only now I guess I'd better try to rescue the survivors from the *Moth* as well."

"That would not be wise, Lord Arthur," said Longtayle. "We consider you would have some small chance of infiltration for the purpose of finding and retrieving the object you seek. That chance would be greatly reduced if you try to free slaves as well."

"I guess I'll have to see for myself," said Arthur stubbornly. "What do you think, Dr Scamandros – will you help me?"

"Naturally I am at your service, Lord Arthur," said Scamandros. "May I ask where the fabled secret harbour of Captain Feverfew actually is?"

"Inside Drowned Wednesday."

Scamandros's head fell back as Arthur spoke, hitting the pillow with a loud thud.

"Dr Scamandros?"

Longtayle went to the bed and looked down on the doctor, peeling back one eyelid.

"Fainted," he pronounced. Then his whiskers twitched and he peered more closely at the Denizen's midsection. Reaching inside the doctor's coat, his paw came out covered in blue blood.

"Fetch Mister Yongtin!" he barked to one of the sailor Rats.

"Is he all right?" asked Arthur.

"Peppered with grapeshot," answered Longtayle. "Strange that his coat isn't... I wouldn't have thought he'd have fainted, though, just from these wounds. He's a Denizen..."

He bent down still closer and sniffed, his whiskers all aquiver. Then he recoiled and wiped his snout with a clean white handkerchief.

"He's poisoned with Nothing," Longtayle pronounced. "Feverfew must have doctored the grapeshot. I don't know how he'd make it stick together—"

He stopped talking as a tall, piebald Rat wearing a long apron over his frock coat rushed in. This new arrival went immediately to Dr Scamandros, pushing Longtayle out of the way. He sniffed at the Denizen, opened up his Gladstone bag, and began to pull out a number of instruments, including a large pair of pincers, which he laid on the table.

"Got to get the Nothing-laced lead out of him," said the Rat. "Clear the room so I can work, Longtayle."

"Mister Yongtin," whispered Longtayle as he ushered Arthur out and across the passageway into the great cabin where he'd met with Commodoure Monckton, though the commodoure wasn't there now. "An excellent surgeon, but no conversationalist."

"Is... do you think Dr Scamandros will die?" Arthur asked.

"Probably not," said Longtayle. "It's very hard to kill a Denizen. It depends on whether Yongtin can get the Nothing out before it dissolves too much of him. But he'll be weak for quite a while, so I doubt you can count on him for the expedition."

"I hope he'll be OK," said Arthur. He felt a bit bad because he knew he wanted Dr Scamandros to recover as much for the expedition as for his own sake.

"I'll show you to another cabin," said Longtayle. "It might be an idea to rest, if you can. We found long ago that though sleep is not absolutely essential within the House, we mortals and semi-mortals are happier if we do rest our tired minds and bodies."

"I could do with a rest," admitted Arthur. "Only there's one thing I have to do first, but I need someone to watch over me. Maybe, if it's OK, you could do that."

As they went into the new cabin, Arthur quickly explained to Longtayle the watching spell Scamandros had made for him so he could check that Leaf was all right. He showed the Rat the mirror and the shell.

"I can't watch myself," said Longtayle. "I am the Captain of this ship, after all. But I shall assign someone trustworthy. They will be with you in a few minutes."

He sounded a bit offended.

"Oops," muttered Arthur to himself as the Rat left. Obviously you didn't ask the Captain of a ship to do something so basic as stand around watching a passenger stare into a little mirror.

As promised, a few minutes later there was a knock on the door. Arthur opened it and let in a familiar-looking rat.

"Gunner's Mate First Watkingle," Arthur said as the Rat saluted and opened his mouth to talk.

"Bless me! You remembered, sir."

"Thank you for coming so quickly," said Arthur. "Did the Captain explain what I want you to do?"

"Stand sentry-like while you whip up some magic," replied Watkingle, tapping the cutlass at his side. "And if your eyes turn yellow and you start acting strange or yabbering peculiar, then I'm to give you a tap on the head with the pommel of this 'ere cutlass."

"Uh, that's not exactly..." Arthur started to say. Then he shrugged and nodded.

I guess if my eyes do turn yellow and I start yabbering peculiar it probably would be best to hit me on the head, he thought.

Sunlight – or the light from the ceiling of the Border Sea – streamed in through the porthole. Arthur sat down, got out the mirror, angled it to the light and raised the shell to his ear.

Once again, Arthur tried to think of Leaf. A few images rose up in his mind. When he'd first seen her, refusing to run, with her brother, Ed. Then in her house, with the Scoucher cutting its way through the front door.

These images briefly crossed the surface of the mirror, then it went dark. Arthur heard the hiss inside the shell change. He caught the sound of footsteps, followed by a match striking. Light flared in the mirror and the darkness ebbed.

Arthur saw a pale hand transfer the match to a lantern. Then, as the wick caught and flared, another view of a small space aboard a ship. Not the same prison area Leaf had been in before, though the ceiling was only four feet high. This was a long, narrow room.

Leaf was there. She looked quite different. She had a blue bandanna tied around her hair and was wearing a blue-striped shirt and black breeches, with the tops of her high sea-boots folded down over her knees. Even in the flickering light, Arthur could see her skin was much darker than it had been, burned brown by some otherworldly sun.

There was a boy with her, dressed in the same style. He was the one who had lit the lantern, which now hung by a hook in the ceiling.

"I don't see why we have to fight, Albert," said Leaf. "It seems kind of dumb to me. I mean, it's not as if we don't get along OK."

"Tradition," replied Albert glumly. "I don't want to fight either, but the Captain told me we have to. 'Ship's boys always fight,' he said, 'and Miss Leaf has been aboard a month without a drubbing. See to it or you can both have twenty of the best over the twelve-pounder.'"

"What?"

"Twenty strokes of Pannikin's cane over one of the cannons," explained Albert. He was rolling up his sleeves. "Which would hurt a lot more than anything you could do."

"You're just trying to make me angry," said Leaf. She didn't bother to roll up her sleeves, instead leaning back against a curved internal strut. "Which won't work. I've studied psychology. I know what you're trying to do."

"You don't know much else," said Albert, though there wasn't much heat in his words. "I get tired trying to teach you everyday stuff you should already know."

"What, like the difference between the mizzen gaff and the mizzen topsail yard?" snorted Leaf. "As if I'd ever need to know that back home."

"I keep telling you, you won't be going home," said Albert. "That just doesn't happen. You might as well face up to the fact that you're one of the Piper's children now, or good as."

"Arthur will find me," said Leaf. "He's the Master of the Lower House and everything. I'll be going home, sooner or later."

"Sure, and Pannikin will give us extra plum pudding for good work," Albert scoffed, then suddenly darted forward and punched Leaf fair in the face.

"Ow! What the—"

Albert darted in again, but this time when he threw a punch, Leaf ducked aside and trapped his arm with an obviously well-practised move using her left hand and right arm. She followed this up with a swinging movement of her body that propelled Albert into the side of the ship.

He hit hard and Leaf let go. But instead of falling down or giving up, Albert turned around and punched her again, this time in the stomach. Leaf fell back, gasping, the wind knocked out of her.

"That'll probably do it," said Albert, wiping his bloodied nose with the back of his hand. "S' long as the Captain sees blood he'll be satisfied, and if you can walk around all hunched up like that for a hour or two—"

"I might have to, you idiot," complained Leaf. "If you just needed a bloody nose why didn't you say so?"

"I thought it'd be better if *you* had the bloody nose," said Albert. "Didn't know you could fight, did I? What was that wrestling trick?"

"Judo." Leaf straightened up and took a breath. "And that's not all I know either, so you watch it."

"We can be friends again now," said Albert, holding out his hand. "For about another three months or so, I reckon, before the Captain decides we should be fighting. Or if we get any more ship's boys aboard. Or we get washed between the ears and have to start all over again."

"Washed between the ears? That doesn't sound good," replied Leaf as they shook hands.

"It isn't. It's strange, now I think about it. I mean, the Border Sea is all messed up, what with Wednesday turning into a great big fish and all, but the washing between the ears is still regular. Someone always turns up to do it, every couple of decades. Never thought about that before. Can't see why anyone would bother. We're just the Piper's brats, after all."

"I'll have to ask Arthur," said Leaf. "I want to know why the Piper brought you all here in the first place too. And the Raised Rats."

Albert shrugged.

"Never thought about it all myself. Too much to do. Speaking of which, we'd better get back topside before my nose stops."

He lifted down the lantern and blew it out. Arthur listened as it was replaced, and to the soft footfalls as the two children walked away. He was about to stop watching, when a narrow beam of light entered the frame and he saw the silhouettes of Leaf and Albert against it. They were opening a hatch and climbing out, but as they did so, there was a lot of shouting from up above. It took Arthur a few seconds to separate out some specific words from the general tumult.

"Beat to quarters!"

"It's the *Shiver*!"

As Arthur heard the words, a strange red wash crossed the mirror, like a crimson oil spreading on water. The dark image of the inside of the *Flying Mantis* was replaced with something lit by a very bright, green-hued sun, so glaring that Arthur had to squint.

"You may wear gloves," said a voice from somewhere within the bright light. "But I can still see the mark of MY RED HAND!"

CHAPTER NINETEEN

Arthur tried to look away, but an unseen force gripped his head, keeping him staring at the mirror.

"You will come to me," ordered the voice in the light. It was little more than a whisper, but it echoed in Arthur's mind. "Reach through the mirror with your red-splashed hand."

Arthur's fingers twitched. He felt them slide across the surface of the mirror without his control, his whole hand preparing to plunge through the silvered glass. At the same time, through squinting eyes, he saw a face emerge from the light. A shrivelled face that looked like an ancient bog corpse that had been burnt.

"You have stolen from Feverfew – now you must make reparations," whispered the face, which Arthur knew with dread was Feverfew's own, sorcery-ravaged and twisted by Nothing. "Reach through the mirror!"

"NO!" Arthur screamed. He couldn't shut his eyes, but he managed to turn his head, dislodging the shell. Still, Feverfew's voice remained, whispering inside his skull.

"Reparations... reach through the mirror... reach through the mirror—"

There was a sharp pain in Arthur's head and the voice vanished. Arthur blinked several times and just managed to raise his hands in time to stop Watkingle from hitting him for the second time with the pommel of his cutlass.

"No! Don't! I'm all right!"

Watkingle lowered his cutlass.

"Wasn't sure I hit hard enough," he said. "Thought I'd start with a little tap, like on a table for ordering a drink."

"Thanks," muttered Arthur, feeling the sore spot on the top of his head. He felt a small wash of nausea pass over him and gulped. Seasickness, he figured.

"You were screaming softly," said Watkingle. "Fair gave me the shudders."

"Me too," replied Arthur. He sat up and looked around, ignoring a momentary attack of dizziness. The mirror was lying on the floor, a huge crack running across it. The shell was crushed under his foot.

A fixed gaslight burned in the corner of the cabin and there was no longer any sunshine coming through the porthole. The ship was vibrating with a low, regular hum and he could hear a distant sound like someone hitting a punching bag, not in time with the slight roll and pitch of the ship.

"How long was I looking in the mirror?"

"From four bells in the afternoon watch to six bells of the first," reported Watkingle. "Nine hours, more or less."

"It seemed like minutes. I guess they were a long way out in the Secondary Realms. I wonder where..."

Arthur's head throbbed and his throat was sore, probably from the soft screaming Watkingle had described. He shivered again as he thought of Feverfew's horribly burned face and his whispering voice.

Don't think about Feverfew, he told himself. *Think about what must be done.*

"The *Flying Mantis* was about to be attacked by the *Shiver*," Arthur said aloud, still thinking to himself.

"The *Mantis*?" said Watkingle. "That'd be a rare fight. She's a regular ship. Pirates don't normally go for the regulars. They might win, but they'd get mighty cut up."

"Feverfew's already taken the *Moth*," said Arthur. "And now he's gone for the *Mantis*. I wonder if..."

He knows I have something to do with those two ships, Arthur thought, the shivers coming back. *With his sorcery, he's seen the connections. I'm marked by his Red Hand and he's looking for me. I'll never get away, I'll never...*

"Stop!" said Arthur, stamping his good foot. His own mind was getting out of control.

"Stop what, sir?" asked Watkingle.

"Never mind." Arthur forced the little voice of fear in his head to shut up. He was going to strike first, and once he had the Will released and the Third Key, he could sort out Feverfew without any problems. Probably. Almost for sure...

"Is Lieutenant Longtayle awake?" he asked.

"*Captain* Longtayle," corrected Watkingle. "Not his watch, but I could wake him if it's urgent."

"No, I guess there's no point waking him," said Arthur. He massaged his temple with his fingers as he often saw his mother doing. Perhaps that would make his headache go away. "What's wrong with calling him lieutenant, anyway? The Commodoure called him that."

"He's a lieutenant in the service," explained Watkingle. "But he's the captain of this 'ere ship, so he's always called Captain on board, except by higher-ranking Rats discussing matters not to do with the ship. Understand?"

Arthur shook his head. He couldn't concentrate on weird details like this.

"I'll just call him Captain all the time to be on the safe side. I suppose I should try to get some sleep."

"I would if I were you, sir," agreed Watkingle. "Always sleep when you can, that's my rule. Now, as the Captain has ordered me to keep a sentry on you for your own protection, I might just lie down on this 'ere floor if you've no objection?"

"Be my guest," said Arthur. He lay down on the bunk. There was no chance of going to sleep, he thought. He had too many ideas floating around in his head and too many nervous fears knotting up his stomach. All kinds of worries: about Leaf, Scamandros, Sunscorch and the crew of the *Moth*, about insanely driving a submarine into the mouth of a monstrous whale...

Arthur woke with a start. There was sunshine streaming through the porthole again. Watkingle was propped against the door with his tail across his lap, apparently asleep. But as Arthur sat up, the Rat opened one eye and his tail flicked over.

"What time is it?" Arthur asked.

"Just past four bells of the forenoon watch," Watkingle replied. He got up, straightened out his shirt, and brushed some cheese fragments and crumbs off his breeches.

"Which is what in normal hours?"

"Ten o'clock in the morning."

Arthur rubbed his eyes. He still felt incredibly sleepy.

"So I slept for about eleven hours, right?"

"No," said Watkingle. "You've been asleep for the last four days."

"Four days! I – I can't have," stammered Arthur. "That's impossible."

"The Captain had Mister Yongtin in to look at you when you didn't wake up the first morning," said Watkingle. The Rat shuffled a bit and his tail flicked nervously. "He said that a combination of a sorcerous insult and a... um... blow to the head had laid you low and you ought to come good in a few days. After a few days, he said he wanted to open up your head and take a look—"

Arthur hastily felt his head. There were no bandages and he couldn't feel any scars or stitches.

"He was going to do it this evening if you didn't come around," said Watkingle. "So as you'd be right for when we arrive in Port Wednesday."

Arthur stopped feeling his head.

"Are we nearly there?"

"Approaching the harbour bar as we speak," said Watkingle. He scratched his nose and added, "If you're fit, the Captain and the Commodoure would like to have a word."

Five minutes later, Arthur was in the great cabin sipping on cranberry juice. He felt surprisingly good. His broken leg didn't hurt at all and moved more freely, the crab cast adapting to his increased mobility. He also felt fresh and quite optimistic, no longer so weighted with fear for Leaf and the others.

I will do what I can do, he thought. *There's no point worrying about anything till I've tried my best.*

"We regret the blow to your head, Lord Arthur," said Longtayle. "Watkingle was following orders, but perhaps his idea of a little tap—"

"It's fine," said Arthur. "If he hadn't hit me, Feverfew would have totally taken me over."

"Feverfew? You saw him?"

"I saw Leaf first. The *Mantis* must have gone out into the Secondary Realms, because she'd been aboard more than a month. I guess she's fit in pretty well, from the look of things. But right at the end they were getting attacked by the *Shiver*. That's when I saw Feverfew. He was... pretty ugly."

"The *Mantis* was definitely being attacked by the *Shiver*?" asked Monckton. He looked at Longtayle, his tail rising up in an agitated question mark. "Feverfew grows very bold. We have no separate confirmation of this."

"Watkingle said the *Mantis* might be able to hold off the *Shiver*," said Arthur.

"It's impossible to say," said Monckton. He was obviously troubled. "If Feverfew was determined, he would probably win out. From talking to Dr Scamandros, you were very fortunate to get away from him the first time."

"Is he all right?" asked Arthur. "Dr Scamandros? I forgot to ask..."

"He recovers well," replied Longtayle. "He will be joining us shortly. So you say that the *Mantis* was being attacked by the *Shiver* four days ago, by House time? Do you know where?"

"I think it was in the Secondary Realms, but I'm not sure."

"If Feverfew is out cruising for victims, then he and his pirates will not be in his harbour," said Monckton. "Greatly increasing your chances, Arthur. But four days ago by House time... he could be anywhere."

"It doesn't matter where Feverfew is," said Arthur, hoping he sounded braver than he felt. "I have to get into that secret harbour. Even more now, if Feverfew has taken Leaf and the crews of the *Moth* and the *Flying Mantis* to be slaves."

I hope that's what happened, Arthur thought. *Better than being killed. Though maybe the* Mantis *defeated Feverfew...*

"There is some good news," said Longtayle. "The Accelerated Coal has arrived and the *Balaena* is fully operational. I have just had a message via bottle from her, confirming that the submersible will rendezvous with us offshore in about ten minutes."

"We're not going into Port Wednesday?" asked Arthur.

"No," confirmed Longtayle. "Commodoure Monckton

and I decided that it would be best to keep your presence secret and your transfer to the submersible even more so. Feverfew certainly has informers in the port and they are bound to have sorcerous means of communicating with him."

"That makes sense. Did any messages for me come through while I was sleeping? Dame Primus must have got my letter if you've got your fuel canister already."

Longtayle shook his head. "No messages have come through by bottle. However, there is a representative from Dame Primus aboard the *Balaena*. She has probably brought messages for you."

"She?" asked Arthur eagerly. "Is her name Suzy Turquoise Blue?"

Longtayle took a paper scroll from the pocket of his coat, unrolled it and scanned the text.

"No name," he said. "Just 'a representative from Dame Primus'."

"I hope it is Suzy," said Arthur. "No one else has come aboard the sub as well, have they? Like a tall, grizzle-bearded old guy with a harpoon?"

"I presume you refer to the Mariner," said Longtayle stiffly. "If he chose to grace any of our vessels with his presence it would be reported instantly. We hold him in only slightly less esteem than his brother, our noble creator, the Piper."

"So he's not aboard, then," said Arthur. Instinctively he touched the Mariner's medallion on his throat, to make sure it was still there. Not that it had done anything anyway. At least as far as he could tell. He'd always known it was unlikely the Mariner would show up to help him, but he had hoped. Now that small hope had all but disappeared.

"Where is Dr Scamandros?" he asked. It was looking more and more likely that he'd have to sneak into Feverfew's secret worldlet by himself, without the team he'd been imagining would be there to help him.

"He should be here by now," said Longtayle. He strode over and opened the door to look in the passageway, startling the sentry. "Ah – here he comes."

Dr Scamandros entered a few seconds later. He looked the same as he always had, but was walking with the aid of an ebony walking stick that had a carved parrot head for a handle.

"Lord Arthur!" he exclaimed, using his stick to balance in order to offer a low bow. "I am most pleased to see you recovered. I cannot thank you enough for my timely rescue, as it is clear that without the friendly and most expert attentions of Mister Yongtin – worth every silver real, I may add – I would have expired quite rapidly from Nothing poison."

"I'm glad you're OK," said Arthur. "I mean, that you're

all right. You are basically all right now, aren't you?"

"Indeed 'basically all right' describes my condition quite well."

Arthur looked dubiously at the little Denizen. Scamandros hadn't fully straightened up after his bow, and the tattoos on his face showed derelict hulks barely afloat amid the wreckage of battle, with sunken masts poking up through matted rafts of debris populated by desolate castaways.

"I was hoping you might be able to help me get into Feverfew's secret harbour," said Arthur. "But you don't look well enough—"

"Poppycock!" snorted the doctor, wincing as he put his shoulders back and stood to attention. A tattooed wind blew across his face and the hulks sprouted jury-rigged masts and sails. "Why, an hour or two of rest aboard these kind Rats' submersible and I'll be right as a trivet."

"You'll be at least a day aboard the *Balaena* unless Drowned Wednesday changes her course dramatically," said Longtayle. At the same time, Arthur asked, "What's a trivet?"

"There you are, at least a day's more rest and I shall once more be fighting fit. As to trivets, they are three-legged stands that are notionally most sound but in practice tend to fall over, so perhaps I erred in my metaphor. Right as rain is what I meant."

"What – oh, never mind. I'll be happy with whatever help you can give me. Particularly if you can disguise me. With sorcery, I mean. To fool the pirates."

"Sorcerous disguises? A snap!" declared the doctor. "Though to be entirely accurate, while I could weave a most excellent disguise over you, it would not stand up to Feverfew's burning gaze. Ordinary pirates, yes. Feverfew himself, no."

"I don't plan to let Feverfew get a look at me," muttered Arthur. He glanced over at Monckton and Longtayle, who were taking delivery of another scroll from a messenger, clearly the latest arrival from a simultaneous bottle.

"One of our ships is shadowing Drowned Wednesday," said Monckton, indicating the ivory whale on the chart. "She is maintaining her usual course for this time of year, following fish patterns, and the *Balaena* should be able to intercept her without trouble. But we need to get you on board immediately. Drowned Wednesday moves far more swiftly than any ship, so the submersible will have to get in position directly in front of her and then steam full ahead in order to navigate the great intake of water through the straining bones of the great creature's mouth."

"Straining bones?" asked Arthur. No one had mentioned anything about straining bones. "What... what are they?"

"Drowned Wednesday in her Leviathan form is not just

an overgrown Earth whale," said Monckton. "But she has some similarities with the larger types. As far as we have been able to ascertain, she does not have teeth as such, nor the typical baleen structure of some whales. But her upper and lower jaws hold vast vertical sheets of perforated bone, which form a lattice that strains the water that rushes into her mouth. The holes aren't big enough to admit any ship larger than a brig, but the submersible should fit easily. Provided it can aim at one of the holes, of course. It is possible that the rush of water may be too fast for the submersible to have any steerageway, and it will smash into the bone. Or end up between the upper and lower plate and be ground to pieces."

"But you think your submersible has a good chance of getting through?" Arthur hadn't thought getting swallowed by Drowned Wednesday was going to be easy, but he hadn't considered the possibility of smashing into some weird whale-teeth or getting crunched up. "What comes after the straining plates? Do we just keep on going with the flow into her stomach? And is that completely full of water or does it ebb and flow like a tide?"

"We don't know," said Monckton. "One of the reasons we have agreed to supply the *Balaena* to your expedition, Lord Arthur, is that it will provide us with new information. The *Balaena* will send us reports via simultaneous bottle for as long as it – that is to say, we will be very interested to see what else is inside Drowned Wednesday in addition to Feverfew's private worldlet."

"We'd best be getting aboard," said Longtayle. One of his ears twitched and Arthur realised the Rat was listening to the sound of the ship's engines, which had just grown softer. "We've heaved to. The submersible must be about to rendezvous."

"Submersible *Rattus Balaena* alongside!" reported a Rat a second later.

"Are you coming with us, Captain?" Arthur asked Lieutenant Longtayle.

"I am assuming command of the submersible," said Longtayle. "Due to the nature of the expedition, all the crew are volunteers. Are you ready to go, Lord Arthur? And you, Dr Scamandros?"

"I'm ready," said Arthur.

"Yes, I believe I am," replied Scamandros.

"Good luck!" said Commodoure Monckton. He stood and saluted as they left, as did the Steward and sentry Rats.

"And to you too," muttered Dr Scamandros as he followed Arthur out of the door.

CHAPTER TWENTY

The submersible's conning tower was the only part of the *Balaena* visible above the surface. The sub had tied up on the starboard side of the ship, and Port Wednesday lay to port, so Arthur only had a brief glimpse of that harbour, made even less visible by the fading light from the distant ceiling as the Border Sea's strange night came on.

He saw a dark granite mountain that had been terraced into a dozen or more levels, with hundreds of houses and buildings sprawled along each terrace. Beams of light shot up and down from the higher terraces, marking the paths of elevators to other parts of the House.

Arthur couldn't see the harbour mouth, but he could

see a telltale forest of masts in the middle of the lower terraces, so the harbour clearly cut deeply into the mountain and the terraces wound around it.

"Mind your step, sir!" called a Rat.

Arthur gratefully accepted a helpful paw to jump from the ship to the conning tower. The Rat's paw felt just like a human hand, at least through Arthur's glove.

Arthur's boots rang like a bell on the ladder as he quickly climbed down into the hull. The access tube was quite narrow and would have been difficult for a fully grown man, but it posed no problem for Arthur.

The inside of the submarine was not what he expected. Though it was a grey, dark metal above, inside it was panelled with a cherry-coloured timber and there was a richly patterned carpet on the floor. Arthur peered at the design in the relatively dim light from what appeared to be electric lamps set into the bulkhead. It took him a moment to work out that the flowing lines contained text and that the whole carpet was some sort of epic poem. Or a mission statement. He'd heard of some weird companies doing that in their headquarters. But he didn't have time to puzzle it out.

There was a door forward and a door aft, the forward one open. It was wood-panelled too, but Arthur could see the metal beneath, as it was easily six inches thick.

A crew Rat beckoned Arthur ahead. He was a brindled

Rat, a kind of brown-and-black mixture, wearing a blue woollen turtleneck sweater with *Rattus Balaena* embroidered around the neck in gold. He also had on a leather helmet, like the ones pilots wore in really old, open biplanes, but without the goggles.

"Welcome aboard, sir. If you would just come forr'd to the bridge. There's not much room elsewhere."

Arthur ducked as he stepped through the bulkhead door. The Rat led him along a very narrow corridor that had doors and hatches of varying shapes and sizes along both sides, till they came to another bulkhead door.

This opened to a chamber about twenty feet long and fifteen feet wide. It was also carpeted, but you could see where the carpet had been cut so the furniture could be bolted to the metal deck beneath.

The front of this chamber was dominated by a bank of glass-covered dials and instruments, numerous wheels and levers, and a crystal globe about two feet in diameter atop a central plinth. Two tall-backed leather chairs were positioned on either side of the globe, facing the controls.

The rear two-thirds of the bridge, as this room clearly was, could have been transplanted from an expensive hotel or café, though one with limited space. There were six elegant, narrow chairs, bolted to the deck in groups of three, each with a little table between them.

Longtayle and another submariner Rat were down at

the controls, intent on going through a checklist. The only other person – or sentient being – there was an exquisitely dressed girl sitting demurely in one of the forward chairs, with her back to Arthur. She was wearing a pearly-white dress with puffed-up sleeves and numerous ruffles and flounces, topped with a very broad-brimmed white hat that had a spray of peacock feathers that almost touched the ceiling. She was drinking very slowly and precisely from a gold-rimmed teacup.

Arthur's heart sank. She was too small to be a Denizen, but Dame Primus had obviously sent someone else, one of the Piper's children more to her liking. Not the ragamuffin Suzy Blue.

Still, she would have messages, which could be important. With a sigh that he didn't even try to suppress, Arthur slid between the chairs to approach the girl.

She turned her head very elegantly as Arthur sighed. Though the huge hat shadowed her face, Arthur recognised the sharp, dark-eyed face underneath. He tripped over his own feet and hit the shin of his good leg on the chair next to her.

"Lord Arthur, I presume?"

Arthur recovered his balance and frowned. She looked like Suzy Blue, but her voice didn't sound quite right. She certainly didn't dress like Suzy Blue.

"Suzy?"

"My name is Suzanna," said the girl.

"Suzy Turquoise Blue," said Arthur, with more conviction. It was Suzy, just all cleaned up and nicely dressed, and putting on a different voice.

"Suzanna Monday's Tierce," corrected the girl. "That is my name and station."

"What's happened to you?" burst out Arthur. "I can't believe you're acting like... like..."

"A properly brought-up young mortal," said Suzy. "That is the standard Dame Primus has set for me and that I try to attain. Please, do sit down, Lord Arthur. Would you like a cup of this rather strong, but quite refreshing, tea?"

Arthur sat down with a thump. He'd really been looking forward to seeing Suzy again and having her help. This beautifully dressed, ramrod-straight girl might look like Suzy, but she might as well be an imposter. He couldn't see her being much help. She probably wouldn't want to leave the submarine.

"Do you have any messages from Dame Primus?" he asked abruptly.

"Tea?" responded Suzanna.

"Just the messages, if you have any."

"La! You are in a fearful rush!" protested Suzy. She put her teacup down with agonising slowness and took a small silk handbag out of her lap. It was a delicate shade of pink. Arthur almost couldn't bear to look at it. Suzy Turquoise

Blue was a brave adventurer, not someone who carried around a tiny pink handbag and said "La!"

Suzy reached into the bag and withdrew a tiny square of paper that grew as it came out, to become a larger envelope of stiff, heavy paper, sealed with a huge red wax seal that showed the stern profile of Dame Primus. Without a laurel wreath, Arthur noticed.

"With the compliments of Dame Primus," said Suzy, passing it over with a very fake-looking smile.

Arthur snatched the letter. As he bent it to break the seal, he saw Dr Scamandros out of the corner of his eye. The little sorcerer was being assisted to one of the chairs by the same Rat who'd shown Arthur in.

Up the front, Longtayle and the helmsrat sat down in the control chairs. Longtayle raised a pipe to his mouth and spoke into it. His amplified words crackled out of a speaker hidden somewhere above Arthur's head, and could be heard echoing up from the corridor behind as well.

"All hands to diving stations! Sections report when secure!"

Arthur opened the envelope. Like most letters in the House, there was no separate sheet of paper. The writing was all on the inside of the envelope. Arthur unfolded it completely and paused to listen as other Rats' voices crackled and echoed through the loudspeaker system.

"Engine room ready."

"Auxiliaries ready."

"Air circulation ready!"

"Tower secure!"

"Foresnout ready."

Longtayle spoke to the helmsrat. Arthur started to read his letter.

To Arthur, Rightful Heir to the Keys to the Kingdom and Master of the Lower House, the Middle House, the Upper House, the Far Reaches, the Great Maze, the Incomparable Gardens, the Border Sea and those Infinite Territories beyond the House commonly called the Secondary Realms

Greetings from your faithful servant, Dame Primus, Amalgam of Parts One and Two (comprising Paragraphs Three to Thirteen) of the Will of Our Supreme Creator, Ultimate Architect of All and Steward of the Lower House and the Far Reaches in trust for the Rightful Heir

This missive is conveyed to you by the hand of our good and faithful Miss Suzanna Monday's Tierce. We trust it finds you well.

Get on with it, thought Arthur.

We are delighted to hear that you have once again

chosen to prosecute the campaign against the vile and treacherous Morrow Days. We are not pleased that you have chosen to make alliance with Drowned Wednesday, as we fear that she clouds her true purpose. Do not trust her!

We are currently besieged by papers, as the Morrow Days seek to render us immobile and ineffective under a deluge of administrative tasks – a clever tactic made easier for them by Monday's many millennia of sloth.

However, we are pleased to report that progress is being made to return the Lower House to efficient operation. Rehabilitation of the Far Reaches has begun, with the Pit already 0.00002% filled in.

We have not been able to locate the Mariner as you requested, but as is no doubt evident, Accelerated Coal has been provided to the Raised Rats.

On the matter of these Rats, you must be wary in your dealings with them. It is possible they are still following some obscure and eccentric plan of the Piper's, which may be in opposition to our own aims. Do not answer their questions! Their curiosity knows no bounds and they always seek knowledge forbidden to them. Unlike the Piper's children, no effective means has been found to wash between their ears, so they have gathered far too many secrets.

Arthur stopped reading and looked surreptitiously at Suzy.

That's what happened to her, he thought. He felt both sorrow and anger rising up inside him. *She got washed between the ears and Dame Primus let it happen! Or made it happen. Dame Primus never liked Suzy!*

Suzanna noticed his look. She gave him that fake smile and said, "Dame Primus requested that you read her letter most carefully."

It's not her fault, thought Arthur as he bit back a sharp retort. The sadness overcame the anger he felt. He couldn't look at Suzy, so he went back to reading the letter.

One thing may be said for the Raised Rats. They do keep their agreements. One must merely be careful what one agrees with them.

We await further news from you, Lord Arthur, and trust that we shall soon be united, by your hand, with the Third Part of our supreme Mistress's Will.

Until then, we remain your obedient and respectful servant.

May the Will be done.

"That's a fat lot of help," Arthur said to himself. He started to fold the letter, but it folded itself instead, ending up no larger than a postage stamp. Suzy held out her hand for it, so Arthur gave it to her and she replaced it in her pink handbag.

Up in front, Longtayle was issuing more commands.

"Extend top-eye!"

The helmsrat flicked switches and, in answer, the crystal globe began to shimmer. After a moment or two, it showed a picture of the sea outside the submarine. The bottom half was just blue water, but the top half showed a view of the *Rattus Navis IV* steaming away.

"Rotate top-eye."

Arthur caught another glimpse of Port Wednesday as the scene shifted through 360 degrees, ending up back where it started, with the *Rattus Navis* still heading directly away.

"Extend snout-eye."

The snout-eye view was all blue water.

"Tail-eye."

The view in the globe changed again. It was still mostly water, but one corner of the great dark mountain of Port Wednesday was visible.

Longtayle swivelled in his chair to face the rear.

"We're ready to go, Lord Arthur. At your convenience."

Arthur looked around. There was Suzanna, calmly sipping her tea. No longer the devil-may-care, ready-for-anything friend. There was Dr Scamandros, looking unwell, his tattoos barely visible, hardly moving. The Mariner hadn't come.

And then there's me, thought Arthur. *With a bruise on my head, one leg in a crabshell and no real idea what I'm going to do even if we do get into Drowned Wednesday's stomach and I can sneak into Feverfew's secret little world.*

Longtayle twitched one ear.

Arthur took a deep breath and said, "Let's go!"

CHAPTER TWENTY-ONE

The helmsrat moved his levers and the distant hum became a louder vibration, rattling Suzanna's teapot till she laid a firm hand on it.

"Full ahead both engines," commanded Longtayle. "Helm steady as she goes. Dive to twenty fathoms."

The view in the crystal globe became full of bubbles and blue water that slowly changed colour from a light azure to a deep blue-black. The submersible angled down and Suzanna's tray slid along the table, till it was arrested by the raised lip, a feature Arthur hadn't noticed before. The incline was gentle and didn't last long before the submarine levelled off.

"Twenty fathoms," reported the helmsrat. "Cruising speed achieved. Eighteen knots."

"Very good," confirmed Longtayle.

"Phew!" said Suzanna loudly, startling everyone. She ripped off her large white hat and threw it on the floor. "Fair thought I'd never see a ceiling again with that on!"

"Suzy!" exclaimed Arthur. He started to get up and was surprised to find a restraining belt had automatically slid around his waist when the submarine dived. It had a buckle, but it took him a few seconds to work out how to release the old-fashioned bronze hook and clasp.

Suzy, in that short time, had torn the puffy sleeves off her dress and was reaching into her pink handbag to pull out a much larger, much scruffier leather suitcase with a broken strap. She undid her belt, put the case on the floor and rummaged around in it.

"What were you doing?" asked Arthur. He felt quite cross that she'd been pretending, though he was also relieved. "What was with all that Suzanna stuff?"

Suzy pulled out her favourite squashed top hat and stuck it on her head with a pat to the crown that made it even more dented.

"Promised, didn't I? Old Primey wouldn't let me go excepting I swear to be all ladylike and proper on the Border Sea. So I swore, but we ain't on the Border Sea any more, are we? We're under it."

"I'm glad to see you," said Arthur. "The real you, I mean."

"Good to see you too, Arthur," declared Suzy. She spat in her hand and held it out for him to shake. "Be even better once I get out of these ridiculous duds. I reckon you couldn't even run in this, let alone climb a wall."

Arthur took her hand with some hesitation.

"I didn't really spit," whispered Suzy as they shook. "Just did it to stir up the Rats. They're awful particular for folk who started out as vermin. Not that I hold that against them. They're good mates to all the Piper's children, long as it don't cost them any hard cash or real secrets."

"Dame Primus didn't say much in her letter," said Arthur as they sat back down. He tried not to flinch as his seat belt crept back around and refastened itself. "How is everything? How long has it been since I left you in the Far Reaches?"

"Over a twelve-month," said Suzy. She carelessly poured some more tea, letting it slop over the top of the cup. "And a busy time it's been. I reckon the Morrow Days have fair got the wind up about you, Arthur. And Dame Primus. You should see the stuff they're sending down to try and keep her busy. One of the forms was eighty-two feet high when all the pages were stacked up! Mind you, that old Primus doesn't really read like normal folk. She just sits there absorbing it. Like dropping a biscuit in tea. Oops!"

"So they're just sending lots of paperwork? That doesn't sound so bad."

"Well, there's also been assassins, sabotage and tons more Nithlings boiling up out of the floor, and no help to deal with them," said Suzy, fishing for her biscuit with a spoon. "It's been much more exciting than it used to be. Not that Dame Primus lets me anywhere near anything if she can help it. Lessons, lessons and more lessons, that's her idea of what's good for me. Surprised she let me come along here, though I s'pose since you asked directly she couldn't say no. Thanks."

"You do know what I want to do?"

Suzy nodded airily.

"Course I do. We sit here in comfort scoffing tea and biscuits till we get swallowed up by old Wednesday whale. Then we have to get into some crazed pirate's private world, which is stuck in her ladyship's guts, grab the next bit of the Will and then the usual, only you reckon Wednesday's just going to hand over the Key."

"I guess that covers the main points..."

"And you've got your own sorcerer along this time," said Suzy approvingly. She waved at Dr Scamandros. "How-do. I'm Suzy Blue. Used to be an Ink-Filler."

"Pleased to meet you, young lady," said Dr Scamandros. He leaned forward in his chair and came up against his seat belt. He looked puzzled, then subsided back again, obviously considering the three-foot distance too far to travel. "I am indeed a sorcerer, though sadly not in full bloom. Dr Scamandros is my name. I shall be assisting Lord Arthur and yourself, I believe, by constructing sorcerous disguises to ease your entry into Feverfew's hideaway."

"Disguises! What kind?" asked Suzy. "I wouldn't mind a pirate rig myself, with some tattoos like yours."

"Actually," Arthur said, "I was wondering about disguising ourselves as rats. Ordinary rats, if that's possible. I mean as an illusion, not as some kind of shape-change. I don't want to get turned into a rat. Not that it wouldn't be great to be a rat, if I had to be one—"

Arthur stopped before he got himself into any further embarrassment, since he was sure Longtayle and the helmsrat were listening to every word.

"You want anyone looking at you to see a rat," said Dr Scamandros.

"Yes."

"It can be done," said Scamandros. "But I don't have anything prepared, so I shall have to start from scratch. It will take time. The first things we will need are noses and tails."

"Noses and tails?"

"Yes. Rat noses and tails."

Arthur winced as Longtayle's right ear rotated and quivered in attention.

"Uh, I don't think—"

"No, no. Not *real* noses and tails. We'll have to make some, and I shall imbue them with sorcerous intent as we go. Now let me see. We shall need a quantity of nice thin paper, a simple glue, some cardboard. Activated Ink."

As he spoke, the doctor pulled all these things out of his coat pockets, along with a pair of scissors, several quills, a quill-sharpening knife and an enamelled snuff box.

"Are you familiar with the craft of layering paper and glue that when dry is quite solid and three-dimensional?"

"You mean papier-mâché," said Arthur. He'd made masks for the end-of-year play at his old school. "I've done some."

"We shall make rat noses for you and Suzy out of glue and paper. I shall write on each layer of paper with Activated Ink, impressing it with a spell of illusion and misdirection. This spell will build in strength with each layer, which when complete will create a fully fledged illusion that will cloak your body and present the appearance of a rat to anyone who looks at you. I estimate that to produce two such rat noses will take at least five hours."

"I think it's going to be at least twelve hours before we even get to Drowned Wednesday," said Arthur. "So we've got plenty of time."

"We shall need it," said Scamandros. "For the rat noses

will merely fool the eyes of the pirates – excepting Feverfew, as I previously mentioned. To present them with the sounds and smells of a rat, we shall need to work on another spell, which will be housed in tails. Tails that must be woven expressly for the purpose on looms created for that spell and that spell alone."

"Looms? Ain't they great big wooden things with lots of threads in a frame?" said Suzy. "Could be tricky to get one in here, even if you've got it tucked away in those pockets."

"Looms are not always large," said Scamandros. He reached into his coat and came out with two cotton reels, no more than three inches high and two inches in diameter. They each had four nails hammered into the top of them.

"Allow me to introduce you to the wonders of the Arkruchill circle loom," said Dr Scamandros.

"That's what you use for French knitting," said Arthur. "I know how to do that. Or I did know, once."

"French knitting?" asked Scamandros. "I learned it as Arkruchillor circle-weaving. But doubtless, as with most good ideas, it came from your Earth and was transplanted to Arkruchillor by travellers from the House. You will need small hooks and the yarn."

He handed over two small, silver, hook-ended needles and two balls of brown, fuzzy wool, then quickly explained how to run the wool through the cotton reel, arrange it around the nails and start weaving or knitting, with the occasional use of the hook. After a few false starts, Arthur and Suzy quickly began to produce lengths of knitted wool.

Once they had the knack, Scamandros took the reels back.

"I have to write the spell on them first, so you'll need to start again," he explained. "In any case, we should do the noses first. They will take the most time and will also need to dry."

The next eight hours were taken up entirely in craft activity, interspersed with occasional breaks for tea or to look at something interesting in the crystal globe. Once they passed through a large sargasso of salvage, and all kinds of things bumped past the submarine. Long-lost possessions, treasured by their owners. Many of them were children's toys, dimly seen stuffed animals and wooden figures, floating in the darkness of the sea.

Finally the work was done. The rat noses looked like papier-mâché cones with paper whiskers. The rat tails looked like three-foot-long braids of brown wool. But if you looked closely, you could see the words of Scamandros's spell moving about in the paper or on the wool. Tiny letters marching around, joining up into words. Arthur couldn't read them, but when he looked at them his mind was filled with images of rats. Normal rats, the kind he used to see occasionally slipping out of the gutter near the central railway station in his old home city.

"Try them on," urged Scamandros. "But please remember, you must have both nose and tail on for the complete illusion, and if you only wear one of the two, there might be some imbalance in the spell."

"Like what?" asked Suzy.

"Suffice to say that if you put a nose on, put the tail on quickly thereafter," said Scamandros. "And vice versa."

Arthur picked up a rat nose and stuck it over his own, tying the cord at the back of his head. It felt ridiculous, a feeling made even worse when he fastened the rat tail to the back of his trousers.

"Marvellous!" said the doctor. "Say something."

"I feel stupid," grumbled Arthur. As far as he could tell he looked just the same and his voice sounded normal. But Scamandros clapped his hands and Suzy laughed.

"I'll try mine!" she said.

Arthur slipped off his rat nose and undid the tail as Suzy put hers on. As she tied the cord at the back, she disappeared. Arthur blinked and it took him a moment to think of looking down. There was a rat near his feet, looking up at him and waving a pink paw.

"It works!" exclaimed Arthur.

Suzy reappeared, the rat nose hanging around her neck like a strange necklace.

"I could have done with one of these years ago," she

said. "How long will it last?"

"A few days," said Scamandros. "The Nothing in the Activated Ink will eventually eat through the paper and the wool. But it is a reliable, well-made charm, even if I say so myself. It might even last a little longer."

Arthur looked at Suzy. Her eyes were dreamy, indicating some thought about an additional use for the rat disguise, beyond sneaking into Feverfew's worldlet.

"Pilchards," said the helmsrat. "Or sardines."

Everyone looked at the crystal globe. It was suddenly full of flickering silver shapes, so many that Arthur had to stare and focus to work out that the *Balaena* had struck a huge shoal of fish.

"We must be approaching Drowned Wednesday," said Longtayle ten minutes later, when there was no sign of any lessening of fish. "She concentrates the fish in her path, using her powers."

He picked up the speaking tube.

"All hands! Secure for ramming stations! Close all watertight doors! Stand by all pumps! Everyone strapped in back there?" Longtayle called out.

"Yes," said Arthur.

"Indeed," said Scamandros.

"Reckon so," said Suzy.

Longtayle did not leave his chair, but he leaned around to talk to the others.

"Drowned Wednesday usually cruises near the surface, and according to our observations her mouth extends from four hundred fathoms above sea level to an estimated six hundred and fifty fathoms underneath. We have calculated that if we go in at about thirty fathoms below sea level, we should have a very good chance of finding a hole in the upper straining plates and should have no risk of being caught between her jaws. The plates are mostly holes, in fact, but we will have very little time to see one and steer for it, if we are not in the grip of too strong a current."

"We're getting a current now," reported the helmsrat. "Speed in the water has increased to twenty-six knots."

Longtayle turned back to concentrate on the controls.

"What do we do if we don't go through a hole?" asked Suzy.

"I think we get smashed to bits," said Arthur. "But like Longtayle said, it's mostly holes. And the current must aim for the holes, or get directed through them. We'll be all right."

"What happens if we don't get smashed completely to bits, but just a bit smashed to bits?" asked Suzy after a while. "I mean, so we're still alive but drowning?"

"Suzy, please don't ask me these questions right now," said Arthur with as much restraint as he could manage.

The silver fish in the globe were rushing past at a faster and faster rate, and he could feel the *Balaena* rocking up and down and from side to side, as it was swept up by the inrush of water into Drowned Wednesday.

Suddenly, all the silver fish disappeared and the globe went dark.

"We're in her shadow!"

"Emergency power!" snapped Longtayle. "Snout-eye lights to maximum!"

Light glimmered in the crystal globe and grew brighter. The silver fish were no longer streaming past. They were going backwards, along with masses of seaweed and other objects that had to be salvage. Like the submersible, they were all being sucked into Drowned Wednesday's maw.

Something hit the *Balaena*, the sound echoing through the hull, a deep, long *bong*! It was followed by a whole series of impacts that together made a noise like hail on a tin roof. The submersible rocked and rolled, the helmsrat and Longtayle both working the levers furiously to keep it stable.

Arthur saw the glint of something white up ahead.

"The straining plate!"

Longtayle saw it too. He and the helmsrat redoubled their efforts, the submersible rolling over to thirty degrees and into a steep incline, then levelling off just as quickly. Arthur saw the solid white ahead of them replaced by a dark hole. The submersible headed straight for it, surrounded by silver fish and hundreds of pieces of flotsam and jetsam of many varying sizes.

"We're in!" called Longtayle as he flicked between the views in the crystal ball. All of them showed distant white walls. "We're going through the straining plate!"

He spoke too soon. With a resounding crash, the *Balaena* hit an obstruction big enough to really slow her down. Everyone was thrown forward, tight against their seat belts, then hurled back again as the submersible screamed to a full stop.

The water and all the smaller debris kept rushing past, not quite so quickly, but the submersible didn't move at all, even though the engine vibrations began to shake the hull.

"We're stuck," whispered Arthur.

Stuck deep underwater, in a tunnel of bone.

CHAPTER TWENTY-TWO

"Stop both!" shouted Longtayle.

The engine vibrations ceased, but the sound of debris hitting the hull continued and Arthur could see a constant stream of small objects flowing past in the crystal globe.

"There's an obstruction in the tunnel," said Longtayle over his shoulder. He raised the voice-pipe again and snapped, "Damage report!"

Rat voices answered, crackling and echoing overhead. All confirmed that there was no significant damage.

"What are we up against, Foresnout?" asked Longtayle.

"The ramming spike has gone through a timber wall," reported the petty officer in charge of the submersible's front section. "Looks like the side of a big merchant vessel, wedged across the tunnel. Very solid."

"Retract the ramspike."

There was no answer for about twenty seconds. Arthur watched the view in the crystal globe. It was hard to make out what lay ahead because of the great cloud of debris flowing past, but there was a shadowy view of algae-covered timber.

"We can't retract it, Captain. Even low gear won't budge it, with everyone on the windlass."

"We'll back out, then," said Longtayle. "Helm, what's the speed of the current?"

"Nineteen knots."

"Nineteen?"

"It's varying between eighteen and twenty knots."

Longtayle's tail whipped out from behind his chair and slapped the floor in agitation.

"What's the problem?" Arthur asked nervously. He decided that he didn't really like being in a submarine. It was all so enclosed, and if anything went wrong, there was just nowhere to go...

"There's a wreck wedged in this particular hole through the plate and we've run straight into it," explained Longtayle. "Our ramming spike is stuck in it. Normally we could reverse and pull it out that way. But our maximum backing speed is eighteen knots and the current is stronger than that."

"So we really are stuck?"

"Temporarily," said Longtayle. "Fortunately we have time to deal with the situation. A number of options present themselves—"

"We're deeping, sir," interrupted the helmsrat.

"What?" asked Longtayle. "Within the tunnel?"

"No, sir. It must be the Leviathan herself. She's diving."

"But she hardly ever dives! How deep?"

"Forty-five fathoms. Forty-eight. Fifty-three..."

"Emergency diving stations!" snapped Longtayle into the voice-pipe. "Brace all watertight doors!"

A chorus of "aye, ayes" came over the speakers. Longtayle leaned over to watch the depth meter with the helmsrat, who kept calling out the depth anyway.

"She's levelling off," reported the helmsrat. "Level at sixty-seven fathoms."

"How deep can we go?" asked Arthur.

"Deeper than this," said Longtayle. "The danger is that a very small movement for Drowned Wednesday might take us down too far. We counted on her just cruising along the surface like she normally does."

"I bet she saw something to eat," said Arthur. "But we're OK for now, aren't we?"

"We have to get out of this hole in the plate," said Longtayle. "Once we have freedom to move within her, we'll be fine. But we're too deep to send divers out now, to chop away the obstruction. Perhaps, Dr Scamandros, you might have some sorcerous solution?"

Scamandros cleared his throat.

"Hmmph, can't say anything springs to mind, sadly. Most of my practical knowledge is for wind and wave, on top of the sea, not underneath it."

"We'll try to shake ourselves out then—"

"She's diving again, Captain."

"Depth?"

"Seventy-two fathoms and getting deeper. Eighty-two fathoms. Eighty-seven fathoms. Ninety fathoms. Ninety-five fathoms."

The helmrat's impassive voice was suddenly drowned by a horrible, metallic booming that sounded like someone hitting an enormous bell. It was so loud it completely drowned out all other noise. Then it slowly eased into a host of different booms and squeals, none of them as loud, but all of them very frightening.

"We can go deeper," said Longtayle. He sounded confident, but Arthur saw that the Rat's tail had gone completely white.

"One hundred fathoms. One hundred and two fathoms."

"Send a bottle message," ordered Longtayle suddenly into the voice-pipe. "Test depth reached. DW still diving."

"Aye, aye," came the disembodied response.

"Dr Scamandros!" Arthur turned to the sorcerer. "What about communicating with Drowned Wednesday? Is there anything you can do to... to, I don't know... cast a light in the sky so she'll look up at it?"

Scamandros was mopping his forehead with his yellow silk handkerchief. He put this away and started hunting through the numerous inside pockets of his coat. In fact, he seemed to have more pockets than it was possible to have inside a coat.

"No, no, that won't do... won't work from down here... never quite mastered that one... perhaps, no, used that up... have to be able to see the target..."

"How about you bung an illusion of a big hunk of roast beef on top," suggested Suzy. "I reckon she'd go for that."

"I can *make* the illusion," said Scamandros peevishly. "But I can't get it outside!"

"One hundred and six fathoms," reported the helmsrat. He turned to look at the Captain and said, without a tremor in his voice, "Estimated crush depth is one hundred and ten fathoms."

Arthur didn't need to ask what the *crush depth* was. It was obvious from the horrible booming and screeching sounds coming from all around them. He jumped as a new sound started, and turned to see water spraying up from the floor.

"One hundred and eight fathoms."

"Can Drowned Wednesday hear underwater?" asked Suzy.

"Crush depth exceeded," reported the helmsrat. "One hundred and eleven fathoms... and getting deeper."

As if in answer to his voice, all the lights suddenly went out. Arthur stared into the darkness, expecting any moment to hear the hull completely buckle... followed immediately by the cold shock of tons of water and almost instantaneous death. At least it would be quick...

Everyone else seemed to be expecting the same thing. They were totally silent for about ten seconds, then Longtayle spoke.

"Switch to circuit B!"

The helmsrat moved. Through the constant booming and whistling, Arthur heard a switch click and the Rat swear under his breath. Then there was a glimmering of light in the filaments as the bulbs heated up, gradually brightening to cast a strange red glow over the submariners.

"Depth!"

Once again the passengers held their breath. Surely they couldn't still be going down or they would already be crushed.

"One hundred... one hundred and thirteen fathoms! And steady!"

"What did you say, Suzy?" asked Arthur.

"I said, 'Can Drowned Wednesday hear underwater?'"

"I bet she can," said Arthur quickly. "Whales have sonar! They sing to one another! If we can make a really high-pitched loud noise, then she'll... she'll know there's someone stuck in her jaw... That's probably not going to help, is it?"

"Why not?" asked Suzy.

"Well, she might just dive even deeper to get rid of whatever's making the annoying noise."

"One hundred and fourteen fathoms!" reported the helmsrat. "She's diving again!"

"It's not going to make things worse, is it?"

"Do whatever you can," ordered Longtayle. "The crush depth is an estimate, but—"

His voice was cut off as several jets of water burst out of the walls at the same time, accompanied by a terrible, deep groan from the hull.

"Doctor!" yelled Arthur. "Can you make a really long, really high-pitched squeal?"

Scamandros was already unscrewing the parrot head of his walking stick. He nodded as he reached inside the head and made some adjustments.

"Block your ears!"

Arthur just had time to put his fingers in his ears as the parrot head suddenly shone with a bright light and its beak opened, emitting an incredibly piercing shriek that went on for several seconds, completely cutting through the groans and bellows of the distressed submarine. Scamandros worked the parrot head like it was a puppet, pulling on little levers, and its shriek began to go up and down to a regular rhythm.

The helmsrat was trying to shout something but Arthur couldn't hear him. The parrot shriek was so loud and so high-pitched that it actually hurt. He could feel it making his cheekbones ache.

Water touched Arthur's feet. He yelped and pulled his legs up. There was at least a foot of water in the compartment and it looked like it was rising. So it hadn't worked, and they were all going to be crushed and drowned—

The screech stopped. Hesitantly, Arthur pulled one finger out of his ear, just enough to hear a confused babble of voices that included the helmsrat shrieking, all calm gone.

"One hundred fathoms and rising! She's going up! She's going up!"

Whether it was in response to the parrot shriek or not, Drowned Wednesday rose up far faster than she'd sunk. Not that either motion had been very significant for her, Arthur thought. A bit like him bobbing his head down an inch.

"Ten fathoms and shallowing! Six fathoms! Sea level!

We're out of the water. We're right out of the water."

Everyone stared at the crystal globe. All the water was running out of the hole they were in, to reveal the obstruction as a barnacle-encrusted wall of copper-sheathed timber.

"She must be lifting her head up," said Longtayle. "That'll make things easier."

He lifted the voice-pipe.

"Cox'n, prepare a diving party for outside work. Four rats with axes. Damage control, get all pumps going."

"Aye, aye!"

Arthur was watching the crystal globe carefully, so he was the first to notice the water streaming back from inside the whale. At the same time the submersible shook and tilted down at the stern, the water still in the bridge sloshing around everyone's ankles.

"We're in the sea again. Nine fathoms!" called the helmsrat. "But the current has reversed. It's coming out of her now, at six knots."

"Belay that diving party!" called Longtayle. "Full back both engines!"

The vibration of the engines had just begun when there was suddenly a much bigger and more dramatic vibration, a shock wave that shook the whole submersible with a sound like a china cabinet falling over. Arthur held his hands against his ears as he felt his stomach flip-flop and the blood rush to his head.

"What was that?"

"Jaw clash," said Longtayle. "Guess she really didn't like that parrot noise. It might help us get free."

"Or shake us to bits," said Suzy cheerfully.

The shock wave came three more times, each more violently than the last. Arthur was very glad to be sitting down and belted in, as even so he was thrown about in his chair. The teapot and cups were long since smashed to pieces and they combined with various other bits and pieces to fly dangerously around the bridge. Arthur was cut slightly across the cheek before he covered his face with his arms.

"We're backing free!"

Arthur stared at the crystal globe. The wooden wall was receding as the submersible backed out. All the bits of flotsam were still flowing back out of Drowned Wednesday, rather more slowly than they'd streamed in, so it seemed she had stopped moving and lowered her mouth.

"Tail-eye!"

The view changed to show the open sea behind them.

"If she'll just stay still long enough for us to back right out and go through another hole..." muttered Longtayle. "All we need is a minute. One minute..."

No one spoke as they all watched the tail-eye view. It slowly changed, the debris floating more freely and the white walls of bone being left behind.

"Snout-eye."

The globe flashed and there was the immense wall of white bone ahead of them, riddled with holes.

"Do you want to pick a hole, Lord Arthur?" asked Longtayle as they continued to back through the sea.

"No! Just aim for one!"

"Port thirty and take her up," ordered Longtayle.

The submarine rattled and groaned as the engines returned to forward thrust. Ever so slowly the *Balaena* began to move towards a new hole. Then there was a strange rush of speed, and both white walls and dark hole rushed towards the submersible.

"She's moving forward again!"

"Steady helm, straight at that hole!"

"Let's hope this one's not bunged up," said Suzy.

"The currents would clean them out," said Arthur distractedly. He was trying to watch the crystal globe. They were lined up OK for the new tunnel, but it would only take a slight shift for them to miss it. "It must have been a big ship to get stuck. We were just unlucky to hit that one."

"But very fortunate to come back out again," said Dr Scamandros nervously.

"Here we go!" cried Suzy. "Straight as an arrow!"

CHAPTER TWENTY-THREE

There was no obstruction in the new tunnel. The *Balaena* passed through it at a steady pace, helped along by the steadily increasing current. Drowned Wednesday was on the move again and sea water, food and debris were once more rushing into her gullet.

The tunnel through the plate was only a hundred yards long. As they emerged from the far end, Arthur found that he had been holding his breath. He let it out, but didn't gain any real feeling of relief. There were bound to be so many troubles and obstacles ahead. And even if they did manage to get the Will, they'd still have to come back out.

Which is going to be difficult, Arthur thought. *I reckon we can go faster forward, but if the current is too strong, the* Balaena *won't be able to get out unless Drowned Wednesday stops for long enough...*

Once through the straining plate, the *Balaena* followed the current into the broad lake that was the inside of Drowned Wednesday's mouth. They crossed that in twenty minutes, the engines straining to maintain steerage way as the current grew swifter, the food-laden waters gathering to pass into Drowned Wednesday's throat.

But this was almost routine work for the submersible, like navigating a tidal estuary. The throat was very wide, and though there was a lot of material being carried along, there was nothing that posed a threat to the *Balaena*. Much of it was fish and sea creatures of all kinds, mixed in with salvage.

Arthur had even started to relax a little as the pumps cleared the bridge of water and both Longtayle and the helmsrat resumed their usual calm dialogue of orders and information.

Then, about two miles down the throat, without any warning, the *Balaena* was suddenly picked up and flipped over in a complete somersault. Arthur nearly slid out of his straps and once again was struck by flying debris, including the lid of the teapot, which gave the ring of pure silver as it hit him on the head.

At the same time, a strange electric tingle passed

through Arthur's body and the ends of his fingers burst into smoky green flames that disappeared a moment later, just as he cried out and started shaking his hands.

The whole thing happened so quickly that no one had time to react. It was like being on an unfamiliar fairground ride that had suddenly whipped around and no one was sure whether it was going to do it again.

"We've passed through a sorcerous membrane of some kind," wheezed Dr Scamandros. His greatcoat had ridden up around his throat and got tangled, and he was having difficulty pulling it back into place.

"Pressure gauges have all reset," reported the helmsrat. "According to this, we're only five fathoms down and there's air above us. No current to speak of either. Still water or near enough."

Longtayle scratched his ear.

"Guess we went through some kind of valve. Take us up to top-eye depth."

"Aye, aye, sir."

A few minutes later, the top-eye view in the globe revealed the surface of a sea within Drowned Wednesday, or a large lake. It was illuminated by a pinkish glow from the stomach roof high above, a glow Dr Scamandros suggested was from the reaction of specks of Nothing with particles of the House, both of them eaten by Wednesday and caked on to her stomach lining.

"Very dangerous," the sorcerer added, staring into the globe with fascination and dread. "Too much Nothing. If enough of it managed to unfix from the House particles and it became concentrated..."

"Can we look for anything like a... well, anything big enough to be Feverfew's worldlet?" asked Arthur.

"Rotate top-eye."

The view in the crystal globe slowly moved around. At first it revealed only more monotonous, greenlit sea. Then there was a sudden flare of colour, bright enough to make Arthur blink.

There, a few miles away, was a shining dome rising out of the sea. A dome easily a thousand yards high and five or six miles in diameter, its rainbow sides shimmering with all the colours of the spectrum, like a giant soap bubble in the sun.

"Immaterial Walls," commented Dr Scamandros. "Very fine work, particularly on such a scale."

"That's it," said Arthur. "It has to be. Now we need to find the entrance."

"Keep us at top-eye depth," instructed Longtayle. "We'll do a circumnavigation, see if anything is visible. Snout-eye view."

"Probably be guards somewhere," said Suzy. "Or traps or the like. I mean, it is a pirate's secret worldlet, ain't it? If it were mine, I'd have guards and traps all over the place."

"Let's hope not," said Arthur. "I mean, it *is* inside a giant whale, to start with, and Feverfew comes and goes by sorcery. It's not as if they'd be expecting anyone to come in except the salvage slaves they sent out."

"Speaking of salvage slaves, I think that might be one there," said Longtayle. He pointed at a dim shape in the globe. "Not moving, though..."

Arthur leaned forward to get a better look. There was a human-shaped figure standing still on the stomach floor. As the submersible edged closer and its lights shone through the murky water, the figure became clearer. It was humanoid, rather than human. About seven feet tall, it had a human face with a beard and long hair, but its muscular bare arms glittered with green scales and there was webbing between its fingers.

"A Nisser," said Longtayle. "But petrified or frozen."

"What's a Nisser?" asked Arthur. The creature had been stilled in the act of reaching out for something, his webbed fingers ready to grab. He looked angry, his mouth open, showing many small, sharp teeth.

"Drowned Wednesday's guards," said Longtayle. "Like the Commissionaires in the Lower House or the Winged Servants of the Night in the Middle House. She ate them up."

"This one made it through," said Suzy. "Do you reckon we can wake him up, Doc?"

Scamandros put his quartz-lensed glasses on his forehead and peered at the globe. Then he shook his head.

"He is tightly wound with a very sophisticated binding. I could unpick it, but not easily and not underwater."

"Feverfew, I guess," said Arthur. "Hey! There's another one, closer in."

"Port ten and slow ahead," instructed Longtayle.

The submersible gently turned and progressed closer to the rainbow-hued dome. Its light spread through the water now, dimming the white beams from the submersible's front. In this ripple of colours, there was a dark silhouette. Another Nisser, this time frozen in the instant she had raised a trident for a killing thrust.

"And another two," said Suzy. "Over there, right near the dome."

She pointed at two tiny dark specks on the very edge of the snout-eye view. But when the *Balaena* drew closer, the two figures were not Nisser. They were Denizens, or rather the skeletons of long-drowned Denizens, dressed in rags and manacled at the ankles, a long, algae-covered chain stretching between them. Both clutched long rakes, the metal heads blooming with rusty flakes and curls.

Arthur was both horrified and fascinated to see that the Denizen's bones were, as far as he could tell in the rainbow light, a dull golden colour.

"Interesting," said Scamandros. "Denizens don't usually decompose. I suppose this water must have stomach acids in it, like a mortal creature. Or it may be the result of Nothing contamination. I presume this pair must be enslaved flotsam rakers."

Longtayle's tail twitched. Arthur saw him look around the bridge, as if he might see signs of the corrosive sea already affecting the submersible.

"That brings up an important matter," said Longtayle. "We must presume that the waters of this stomach are dangerous to the *Balaena*, so we cannot linger. I'm afraid we can only give you twelve hours, Lord Arthur. After that, we must attempt to leave the Leviathan."

"Is that twelve hours from when we find the way in?" asked Suzy.

"Twelve hours from now," said Longtayle.

Arthur nodded. He was still staring into the globe. There was something about the rainbow-hued wall just beyond the two skeletons. If he looked from the corner of his eye, he could see something that might be an arched doorway. But when he looked straight on, all he could see were swirls of colour, shifting and changing like oil in a puddle on the road.

"Can anyone else see a door?" he asked. "An archway, about eight feet high, just behind the left-hand skeleton?"

"Nope," said Suzy.

"No," said Longtayle.

Dr Scamandros put his glasses on his forehead and looked closely where Arthur was pointing.

"Mmmm, an archway... yes... yes, there is a two-way membrane through the Immaterial Wall. Very cleverly concealed. How did you spot it, Arthur?"

"I was just looking," replied the boy. "But I can only see it out of the corner of my eye."

"A useful talent," said Dr Scamandros. "Particularly for you, Lord Arthur. I should make a habit of looking out of the corner of your eye. You never know what might be there, unseen."

"If there is a doorway there," said Longtayle, "we'd best drop you off, Lord Arthur, and find somewhere to hide the *Balaena*."

"How will you know when to come and get us?" asked Arthur.

Longtayle reached into his pocket and pulled out a small wooden box. Opening it, he showed Arthur a tiny green bottle packed in cotton wool.

"This is a one-shot bottle," he said. "Paired to one here. It can send only a single word, which is already in it. All you have to do is pull out the cork and the message will go. As soon as we get it, we'll come in for the rendezvous. Also, if anything happens to us and we can't pick you up, the bottle will crumble to dust."

"Thanks," said Arthur. He turned his head to look sideways at the globe. The arched door was still there, about fifteen feet away. "Dr Scamandros, this membrane thing in the Immaterial Wall – does that mean there'll be air on the other side of the door?"

"Probably. But not certainly."

"Have you got one of those clothespeg charms? You know, the 'thousand and one breaths' thing?"

"I fear not, Arthur. Has the one Wednesday's Dawn provided already failed?"

Arthur nodded and looked at the globe again.

"It's not far," said Suzy, correctly guessing that Arthur was worried about the distance underwater from the submersible to the door. "Bound to be air on the other side, even if we have to go up for it."

"Providing the water doesn't dissolve us or burn us," said Arthur. He knew he was procrastinating, but he couldn't help it. "And what if there's a trap, like you were talking about before?"

"Nah, you're right," said Suzy. "Why bother, if you're inside a whale?"

"I hope you're right," said Arthur. "Or I'm right. OK, I guess we'd better get going."

He picked up his rat nose and rat tail and started to put them on.

"Are these things waterproof, by the way?"

"Hmm?" asked Dr Scamandros, who was looking at the dome wall again.

"Are they waterproof?"

"Of course! I am a marine sorcerer, remember. Every charm and spell I have made since I signed on to the *Moth* has been highly resolute in the face of dissolution by the universal solvent!"

"So they're not exactly waterproof," said Suzy, while Arthur was still trying to work out what Scamandros had said. "How long will they stand up to a good soaking?"

A ship tattoo that was sailing across Scamandros's face suddenly hit a rock and sank, though it did manage to launch its boats, which rowed away towards his chin.

"It is very unusual to demand complete waterproofing," sniffed Scamandros. "I would expect these charms to withstand an immersion of four or five hours in normal sea water. Less in this noxious brew. It is the paper, of course, that is most at risk, though woollen yarn, once sodden, is also—"

"Thank you, Doctor," interrupted Arthur. "If we're going, let's go."

Better to get this part over with, he thought. *At least I'll be out of this metal coffin...*

"There is an escape chamber towards the stern," said Longtayle. "You'll have to go out one at a time."

"I'll go first!" said Suzy.

"No, you won't," said Arthur. "I'll go first this time. It's my responsibility."

Suzy shrugged and tipped her hat, allowing Arthur to go ahead of her to the rear bulkhead door.

The submersible was longer than Arthur had thought. Having only seen from the conning tower to the bridge, he was surprised by how much corridor they had to go along, and how many doors they went through. But they encountered only one other Rat, waiting for them at a door marked DORSAL ESCAPE AFT. Arthur was surprised to see it was Gunner's Mate First Watkingle.

"Did you volunteer?"

Watkingle grinned, which looked rather fearsome on a four-foot-tall rat.

"Always volunteer, that's my motto, sir," he said. "None of this 'don't get into trouble' namby-pamby stuff. Why, when I think of the things I might 'ave missed—"

"Thank you, Watkingle," said Longtayle quellingly. "Show Lord Arthur and Miss Suzy to the escape chamber."

"Aye, aye," said Watkingle. He turned his head slightly so Longtayle couldn't see and winked at Arthur before undogging the door and opening it. The chamber beyond was like a very small shower stall with a hatch in the ceiling instead of a showerhead. On the side of the hatch were two handles. One was painted yellow and one painted red. A brass plaque on the hatch said in inch-high letters PULL YELLOW. WAIT FOR IMMERSION TO THE RED LINE. PULL RED.

"The procedure for emergency evacuation from the craft is simple and straightforward," lectured Watkingle in a singsong voice. "First, you will enter the chamber and close the door behind you. It will automatically latch and cannot be reopened from inside. Second, grasp the yellow handle with one paw and pull. This will open a valve and water will enter the chamber. Third, when the water level reaches the red line painted around the wall of the chamber, take a normal breath. Do not take many breaths or take a deep breath. Then, grasp the red handle with one paw and pull. This will open the exit hatch. Fourth, kick off from the floor and swim out. Understood?"

Arthur looked into the chamber. The red line was about four inches from the top. He would have to crouch a bit and keep his head back to have his face out of the water for that last breath. The hatch was big enough for him to fit through without a problem.

"OK," he said. "Get in. Pull yellow handle. Wait till the water reaches the red line. Take a breath. Pull red handle. Swim out."

"That's it, sir," said Watkingle.

"I'll swim to the door and go through," Arthur told Suzy. "I'll meet you on the other side."

"This looks like fun," said Suzy. She rubbed her hands

together and added, "Sure I can't go first?"

"No," said Arthur. "As in 'no, you can't go first'. I think we'd better put on our disguises now."

He tied on the rat nose and fixed the tail. When he looked around, Suzy was near his feet, already a rat. Arthur presumed he appeared to be a rat as well.

"I'm ready," he said.

Suzy squeaked something back at him.

"What?" asked Arthur. Then the realisation hit him: They looked and sounded like rats to each other as well as to everyone else.

Arthur lifted off his rat mask and unhitched his tail.

"We won't be able to talk to each other when we're wearing these," he said. "So once we're inside, follow me."

Suzy squeaked, then was herself again, holding her rat nose.

"Whatever you say," she said.

Before Arthur could make sure she really meant it, she'd turned back into a rat.

"I mean it," said Arthur. "Follow... as in, stay behind me."

He slipped the rat nose back on and refastened his tail, then stepped into the escape chamber. The door shut behind him and he heard a heavy bolt or latch sliding across.

Arthur rubbed his suddenly sweaty hands against his

breeches, checked that the Atlas and Wednesday's invitation were secure in his Immaterial Boot, and reached up to pull the yellow handle.

Water flowed in with shocking speed. It didn't sting or dissolve his clothes, but it did smell very strongly of ozone. Arthur barely had time to register this and take a breath before the water hit the red line. It was up around his eyes before he even pulled the red handle. Instantly the hatch above flicked open.

Arthur clumsily kicked the floor, favouring his bad leg, so that he didn't get clear of the escape chamber in one go. He had to push against the wall till he rose up in a froth of bubbles from the small pocket of air that had been left, mixed with the atmosphere trapped under his clothes.

Orientating himself from the line of the submersible's hull, Arthur struck out for where the door was supposed to be. The rainbow light from the dome was much brighter when seen directly, so for a moment Arthur couldn't see the archway even from the corner of his eye. Panic started to rise in him, until he calmed himself with the simple thought that even if he didn't find the door, all he had to do was rise to the surface. Though if he did that, it might be hard to dive back down again.

Then he saw the archway, a little bit to the left of where he thought it was. Arthur already felt as if he needed a breath, but he was used to that feeling. He kicked harder, feeling the strangeness of his crab-armoured leg, and scooped harder with his arm stroke.

The archway drew nearer. Looking down, Arthur saw that the layer of fine debris and muck below him contained many bones, broken skulls and pieces of rusted chain. Evidence of the scores, possibly even hundreds, of slave salvagers who had either failed to return to Feverfew's worldlet...

...Or who had been thrown out, to die in the belly of the Leviathan.

CHAPTER TWENTY-FOUR

Arthur reached the doorway. As he touched it, the rainbow colours drifted away, to be replaced by a featureless grey. Even more disturbingly, his hand went through it as if there was nothing there.

The boy didn't stop. He kicked again, and went through the grey archway, to land sprawling on a wet stone floor.

"What was that?" asked a voice.

Arthur rolled over and sat up, ready to move. He saw that he was in a large, timber-walled room – more of a shed or barn really, since the far end was completely open and there was bright sunshine streaming in.

There were four Denizens sitting on a wild variety of

chairs of different styles and eras, around a highly polished table that even to Arthur looked like a priceless antique. The Denizens were all dressed in flamboyant and ill-matching finery, mixing up everything from twentieth-century Earth military tunics to glittering, lumpy, alien-looking helmets. Every inch of their visible skin was tattooed, and they all had at least three knives in their belts, as well as short, pistol-grip crossbows on the floor next to their chairs.

"What was what?" another Denizen asked.

Arthur moved very slowly towards the wall. There was no cover at all, nothing in the room save the table and chairs, but there was a narrow band of shadow along the edge where the floor met the wall.

One of the Denizens stood up.

"I thought I heard something near the water gate."

Arthur crouched in the shadow.

It'll take a while to pump out the escape chamber ready for Suzy to come through, he thought. *But maybe she'll swim faster than I did. If she comes through now, the Denizen will see her for sure, even as a rat...*

"Sit down! It's your turn!"

The Denizen slowly sat down and turned his attention to whatever was on the table. Some sort of game, Arthur saw, being played on a board with glittering pieces made from gold and gems. Not chess, because he didn't recognise the pieces, and all four Denizens were playing. They each had piles of paper in front of them too, which changed hands frequently. Not bank notes, but badly torn-up scraps and pieces with scrawled writing on them.

Arthur crawled along the wall, thinking furiously. If Suzy came out now and they heard her, he'd try to distract them.

"What was that?"

The same Denizen stood up again. Arthur looked around and saw a rat scuttle across the floor, out of the archway.

"A rat!"

All of the Denizens erupted out of their chairs, sending them flying. As they bent down to grab their crossbows, Arthur ran straight at them. Not daring to hesitate, he jumped on the table, kicked the board over and jumped again to the far side, almost stumbling as a sharp pain shot through his bad leg, despite the crab armour's support.

"Another rat!"

"It's mine!"

"Ware crossbow!"

A crossbow bolt zinged to the left of Arthur, sending chips of stone flying. He zigzagged and another bolt whisked past his ear. Then he was outside, in the bright sunshine, standing on sandy ground strewn with rocks. There was a stand of palm trees nearby, the first of a whole line that stretched along the narrow peninsula back to the island proper.

Arthur hurled himself towards the closest palm, continuing to zig and zag, but there were no more crossbow bolts. Once he got behind the trunk, he risked a glance back.

The four Denizens were standing by the entrance to the shed, reloading their crossbows. They didn't look like they were going to pursue Arthur.

There was no sign of Suzy. Arthur scanned the ground, his breath coming in ragged gasps as he grew more afraid that she had been hit by a crossbow bolt. After a few breaths that didn't get properly into his lungs, Arthur tried to calm down.

This is a bubble from the Secondary Worlds, he told himself. *The bubble is inside the House but the bubble contains a fragment of a Secondary Realm. Maybe even of Earth. It looks like it. So I'll get asthma here. Have to be careful. Don't push too hard...*

A sudden squeak near his foot made Arthur jump. He looked down. A rat was looking up at him, making gestures with her paws.

"Suzy!" Arthur exclaimed, before he remembered she would only hear a squeak.

Suzy squeaked some more, insistently. Arthur correctly translated this as "Get a move on!"

He turned and, jogging rather than running, moved to the next palm, and then the next. As he jogged, he looked ahead, trying to match up the geography with the map he'd seen.

There was the harbour off to the right. Arthur could see the hulks of at least a dozen vessels all piled up on the far side. Total wrecks, or near enough. But closer, floating at anchor, were the *Shiver* and the *Moth*. And worst of all there was the *Flying Mantis*, its sails furled, their green radiance dimmed.

"So Feverfew has captured Leaf," Arthur muttered to himself.

If she isn't already dead.

He stopped, sheltered by a clump of palms, to get his breath back and look around more easily.

There were half a dozen low stone buildings clustered around the quay, clearly warehouses. Up the slight hill from there was Feverfew's fort, a building of earth and stone ramparts shaped like a star within a star, with cannons visible on many levels. Across from that, and under its guns, were three ramshackle wooden buildings, little more than long sheds, with holes for windows.

Slave quarters, Arthur thought.

There were few signs of life. The occasional glint from the helmet of a sentry in the fort and a bit of movement aboard the *Shiver*. But the slave quarters were still. The breeze was blowing towards Arthur, but he couldn't hear anything, save the plaintive cry of some kind of seabird. He looked for that, remembering the black cormorants that had flown from the buoy to warn Feverfew, but no birds were visible.

Arthur looked away, up to the hills, where the Raised Rat spy had noted *Followers of the Carp. Escaped Slaves* on her map.

The hills were a lot higher than he'd expected, perhaps more than a thousand feet, and were also covered in what looked like dense jungle or rain forest. It would not be easy to climb them or to find anyone there, particularly if they were trying to stay hidden.

Suzy squeaked something at him and jumped up and down on the spot, an action Arthur took to mean "get on with it".

He got on with it, walking quickly to the next clump of palms. His breathing was all right, but he knew he couldn't take any risks. He had no medicine here. No inhaler, and no paramedics with asthma medications and oxygen or hospitals nearby.

Suzy squeaked again and did a somersault, showing her impatience.

"I can't go any faster," said Arthur, even though he knew she'd hear only the squeak. He shrugged his shoulders up and down as well.

It did seem to pacify Suzy for the moment. She stopped being agitated and walked along with Arthur peaceably enough. They still went from clump to clump of palms, to be on the safe side, and every fifty yards or so Arthur stopped to listen and look around. The peninsula they were on was about a mile from the harbour, so he figured they should be reasonably safe.

After a while, they left the peninsula and started out across the mainland, where the palms and sandy ground gave way to thick dark earth with lots of rocky outcrops, and stunted, windblown trees with grey-green leaves. These spread low to the ground and made the going more difficult, particularly as Arthur occasionally found himself thinking he was much smaller than he was and hit his head on a branch. This was disturbing, as it suggested Dr Scamandros's rat disguises were having some effect on their wearers as well as observers. But Arthur couldn't worry about it. He concentrated on heading towards the hills, watching out for pirates or cormorants or other things that might serve Feverfew, and keeping his breathing steady.

The stunted, spreading, grey-green trees didn't last long. As the ground continued to rise, the bare earth and stones were replaced by leaf litter, small ferns, larger ferns and big pale-trunked trees that rose straight up for forty or fifty feet before spreading out to make a thick canopy that greatly reduced the light and heat from the sun.

The air felt much more moist too, and there were little rivulets of water to jump across every ten yards or so, usually into soft ground that was not quite mud – or if it was, it had a sufficient layer of leaves, bracken and forest debris to make it more solid.

There were occasional small noises in this verdant undergrowth, but nothing too alarming, and Arthur hadn't seen any footprints or other signs that the pirates ever left their harbourside dwelling. He was also starting to think of himself more and more as a rat, so when they had clambered up to a clearing that he thought marked the first stage of their hill ascent, he stopped and took off his rat mask and tail.

Suzy didn't take hers off. She sniffed around his feet and then sat in a begging posture, squeaking. Finally Arthur leaned down, gripped the rat by the nose and tail, both of which felt totally authentic, and pulled.

Finding himself suddenly pinching Suzy's real nose and tugging on a loose piece of cloth from her ripped-up dress, Arthur let go.

"Cor, what I wouldn't give for a piece of cheese," Suzy said as she massaged her nose. "I reckon the doctor made those charms too strong. I was only following you that last bit cause you were another rat and I thought you might know where some food was."

"At least they worked properly to begin with," said Arthur. He peered up at the sky and then back down the slope. He could just see the topmast of the *Mantis* and a patch of blue that was the outer harbour. The harbour buildings were out of sight, obscured by a ridge lower down. But in the valley below, he could see a huge circular patch of dark brown edged in bright yellow. He realised this must be the nose cavity of the skull he'd seen drawn on the map. A lake of mud that the mapmaker had also annotated with the word *Nothing* and a question mark.

After watching the lake for a few seconds, Arthur saw that the mud must be hot, for huge bubbles appeared and the surface was in constant, low movement as the mud roiled and turned over.

"Bet that fair stinks," said Suzy, looking down at the lake. "Lucky the wind's the other way. Where to now?"

"I think we're about halfway up the first hill," said Arthur. "But I really don't know for sure. I wonder where these Followers of the Carp hang out? I mean, where would you go if you'd escaped from the pirates? Besides away from the harbour, which we've done."

"Up," said Suzy. "They're Denizens, right? They always want to go up. Up is good, inside the House. The higher the better. That's why the superior ones, like the Noons and such, make themselves tall. Got a thing about it. Bit silly really, just makes it harder to get clothes to fit."

"Up," said Arthur. "That makes sense. Unfortunately. I hope I'll be OK to keep climbing."

"What's wrong?" asked Suzy. She hadn't spent any time with Arthur in the Secondary Realms when he didn't have a Key.

"I have a... I guess you'd call it a breathing sickness," said Arthur. "Sometimes it comes on if I do too much exercise. Because this worldlet is part of the Secondary Realms, I might get affected by it."

"Like black lung, is it?" asked Suzy, clearly interested. "Or the greenspit cough?"

"Maybe," said Arthur. "Don't worry about it, though. I feel fine for now. Slow and steady, that's how we'll go."

"Without the rat disguises?"

Arthur nodded. "We should be OK up here. But we'd better hang on to them just in case we need to use them to get back out."

After a brief rest, they continued on. The rain forest drew in again as they left the clearing and there were no obvious paths. Arthur simply went where the undergrowth had a gap in it or was less sparse, but he always aimed uphill.

After another half hour or so of thrashing their way upslope, Arthur paused for another rest. He wanted to wait till they hit a clearing, but there had been no sign of one and he had to take a break.

"Not much to see, is there?" said Suzy. "Smells a bit too."

Arthur sniffed at the rich odour of the forest.

"It's only all the leaves and stuff turning into mulch," he said. "I wonder whether the Followers of the Carp have built houses up here, or found caves or something. You wouldn't last long just camping out."

"Could be worse," said Suzy. "Down in the Pit or in the Lower House Coal Cellar."

"Or collecting salvage for Feverfew," said Arthur. He was thinking of all the golden bones strewn outside the dome. "They can't last long doing that."

"Who speaks of Feverfew?!" boomed a voice out of the undergrowth – a deep, powerful voice, trained to rise above the fiercest gale.

CHAPTER TWENTY-FIVE

"Who speaks of Feverfew?"

Arthur and Suzy leapt to their feet and drew their weapons. But there was no sign of the person who'd spoken. The rain forest around them was quiet and still.

"No one ever looks up," continued the voice. "Interesting, isn't it?"

Arthur looked up, his sword at the ready. There was a Denizen high up in the nearest tree, hanging on with the aid of hooked spurs in his boots and what looked like clawed gloves, though Arthur wasn't entirely sure if they were gloves or actually the Denizen's hands. He was wearing a shirt and breeches of light tan splattered with patches of green mould, effective camouflage for the rain forest, particularly since the mould looked like it had spread across the Denizen's skin as well.

"Now for the traditional questions," said the Denizen. "And the traditional warning. Answer correctly or you will die where you stand. Or, to tell a truth, die a bit later, because our arrows, while tipped with Nothing-contaminated mud, are not very effective."

Arthur looked around as the Denizen spoke. There were rustlings in the undergrowth around them and he spotted several other green-mould-and-tan-wearing Denizens moving up on them. These ones had short bows. Not crossbows, but the simple stave and bowstring kind.

"We're friends," called out Arthur. "We're looking for the Followers of the Carp."

"Can you just wait for the questions?" asked the Denizen up the tree. "Let's do this properly, please."

"Sure," said Arthur.

Suzy yawned and sat back down.

"Denizens," she muttered to herself.

"Are you now or have you ever been a pirate?" asked the Denizen.

"No," said Arthur.

"Do you serve the pirate Feverfew in any capacity?"

"No," said Arthur.

"Do you believe in the Carp?"

"Uh, I'm not sure what you mean. I want to meet it—"

"Is that a 'no'?" asked the Denizen.

Arthur took a sideways glance at the bow-wielding Denizens, who were nocking arrows and drawing bowstrings back.

"We do believe in the Carp, don't we, Suzy?"

"Sure," said Suzy. "I'll believe whatever you want."

"You must have faith in the Carp," said the Denizen. This statement was echoed in a whisper all around.

Arthur nodded vigorously several times, indicating that he had tons of faith in the Carp.

"Now, also for the record, state your names."

Arthur thought for a moment.

If the Carp is who I think it is, I can't go wrong. But if it isn't, then...

"This 'ere's Lord Arthur, Master of the Lower House, Lord of the Far Reaches, Hero of the House, Eater of the Biscuit and Rightful Heir of the whole lot," said Suzy, standing up again. "And I'm Suzanna Monday's Tierce, so you'd better act a bit more respectful, if you don't mind."

"Really?" asked the Denizen in the tree. "I mean, I have faith and all, but are you really the Rightful Heir?"

"Yes," said Arthur. "I am. Can you take us to the Carp?"

"And you're going to rescue us all from Feverfew's dominion?"

"What?"

"Rescue us, like the Carp says you will."

"Uh, I have to talk to the Carp first."

"How many of you are there?" asked Suzy. She was staring out between two of the trees, where more and more green-tinged Denizens were becoming visible as they moved out of cover.

"Seven hundred and seventy-nine, at last count," said the Denizen as he slid down the tree trunk, his boot-spikes shredding bark. He landed and bowed in one smooth motion.

"Allow me to present myself. I am Jebenezer, First Follower of the Carp and formerly Second Mate of the *Naiad*, may her wooden bones rot in peace."

Before Arthur could answer, a female Denizen pushed forward and bowed, declaring, "I am the Second Follower of the Carp, and my name is Pennina!"

"I am the Third Follower," shouted someone else, further back. "My name is Garam. I have faith in the Carp!"

A cacophony of voices followed, with Denizens shouting out their names, their numerical ranking as Followers and various protestations of faith in the Carp, belief that the Rightful Heir would come and other stuff that Arthur couldn't hear properly over the din.

As they shouted, the Denizens moved closer and closer. More and more of them appeared out of the undergrowth, till there was a great crowd advancing on Arthur.

"Uh, I think I'd like to see the Carp right now," said Arthur as he retreated back against a tree trunk. Many of the Denizens had forgotten to put away their Nothing-poisoned arrows, and there were lots of muddy, sharp arrowheads sticking out ahead of them, straight at Arthur.

"The Rightful Heir says everyone take three steps back!" shouted Suzy, but even her sharp voice was lost in the tumult.

"I'm the Ninety-Ninth Follower—"

"Hundred and Sixth—"

"I believe—"

"Faith in the—"

"The Carp! The Carp!"

"Three steps back!" roared Jebenezer, at a volume to match Sunscorch's best shout.

The Denizens halted, then – after some scuffling – stepped back. Arthur took a breath, found he couldn't get a full lungful and concentrated on staying calm.

"Lord Arthur wants to see the Carp," said Suzy.

"I'm in a bit of a hurry," Arthur added, a slight wheeze underlying his words. He looked at his watch. They'd been out of the submersible for two hours. Ten hours to go before the *Balaena* departed, and now he had nearly eight hundred Denizens thinking he was going to do something for them as well.

"Of course, sir! Follow me!" said Jebenezer. He pushed

two Denizens aside and gestured at the others to move to make Arthur a path through the crowd. "It's just natural high spirits, sir, most of us having been trapped on this island for so long and in fear of recapture. Feverfew always sinks captured slaves."

"Sinks?" asked Suzy.

"In the Hot Lake," Jebenezer continued. "If the mud doesn't drown you, or the heat burn you up, the patches of Nothing do the business. Nothing's quick, of course, or should be. But Feverfew don't let that happen. He's got a yardarm rigged up so he can lower you in a bit at a time, like a leg or whatever. A hand usually. He likes to start with the hands—"

"I get the idea!" interrupted Arthur. He felt very tense. Every minute wasted could mean disaster, and he had so many problems and so many decisions to make. And then there was the asthma, lurking...

"Where is the Carp?" asked Suzy. "Is it far from here?"

"Why, the Carp is under our feet, ma'am," said Jebenezer. "When the Carp first freed the slaves, that's the first twenty, which is me and Pennina and Garam and Obelin and Herush and Peppertoe and Thin Edric and—"

"Maybe save the names for later," said Arthur. "Just tell me the basic story."

"Well, when the Carp freed us from our shackles in the dead of night, we picked him up and carried him into these hills. He said if we had faith, and looked around, we'd find a place to shelter, a fortress safe from Feverfew. And sure enough, we soon found a mighty cave, and it has served us ever since as our home. And the Carp said that we must have faith that the Rightful Heir would one day come and bring us all back to the House, and blow me down if it isn't happening, and me still here without being dissolved into Nothing or my bones bleaching out in the Stomach! Here we are."

The Denizen stopped before what appeared to be a cliff face, a vertical section of pale yellow rock, liberally covered with the same green mould or lichen that grew on his clothes and skin.

"Just step through, sir. It looks solid, but if you believe it to be a door, as the Carp says, then it'll be a door."

"That Carp sounds like a right pain in the midsection," grumbled Suzy in a low voice to Arthur. "And a faker as well. I bet it just made the cavern entrance look like this and carried on with all that belief hocus-pocus."

"We won't get that mould growing on us, will we?" Arthur asked Jebenezer.

"Oh, no, sir!" the Denizen replied. "That's the Carp's special moss, that is, not mould. It takes cultivation to get that growing right, that does."

Arthur shut his eyes and stepped forward, holding his hands in front of his face, just in case he did run straight into a mossy cliff.

After four or five paces, when he didn't suddenly impact with rock, Arthur opened his eyes. He found himself in soft darkness, lit here and there by soft green lights. Some of the lights moved, including one close, bright clump of green lights above Arthur's head.

"The moss is luminous!" he said.

"Aye, it shines in the darkness, to illuminate our path," said Jebenezer. "As does the Carp."

"It doesn't shine very well," said Suzy. "And I can't see a path."

Arthur looked around, but he couldn't see anything more than a few feet away. But judging from the echo of Suzy's voice, and the patches of both moving and static green light, he knew he had to be standing inside a huge cavern, somewhere near the top. It looked like it extended downward for a few hundred feet and back for at least as far.

"The path to the Carp is a little difficult," admitted Jebenezer. "Even with the gift of our light. I'd better go first and you might care to hold the back of my belt, sir. Miss Suzy, please hold Lord Arthur's coat-tails."

Suzy muttered something that Arthur felt he was probably glad not to hear. He reached out and hooked two fingers through the back of Jebenezer's belt. With one leg not as nimble as it should be – though the crab armour did a great job – he didn't want to take any risks in the dark.

He felt Suzy grab hold of his coat-tails a moment later.

As a makeshift train it was a slow shuffle down. Most of the time Arthur couldn't see how narrow the path was, or how far he could fall, but every now and then they encountered a large patch of the glowing moss in exactly the right place to illuminate the danger.

Despite these momentary flashes of light and terror, they reached the cavern floor without incident. For the first time, Arthur looked back and was unnerved to see a long line of moving green light zigzagging back up behind them. It looked as if all eight hundred–odd Followers of the Carp were coming down the path. All very quiet now, in contrast to their shouting outside.

"We approach the Carp," whispered Jebenezer. He pointed ahead, indicating a straight way lit by regularly spaced clumps of luminous moss. At the far end, perhaps two hundred feet away, there was a soft, golden light that occasionally twinkled with a red glint, as if there was a distant fire caught by a mirror.

"The Carp's road is flat; there is no danger," said Jebenezer. "You should go ahead here, Lord Arthur, and we will follow."

Arthur let go of Jebenezer's belt and started walking slowly towards the gold-red light. He was having last-minute doubts with each step. Surely, the Carp had to be Part Three of the Will? But what if it wasn't? What if it was some other powerful entity, something like the Old One in the Coal Cellar? Something strange, strong and dangerous that was expecting some other kind of Rightful Heir, somebody else entirely.

As he drew closer, Arthur saw that the greenlit road ended and there was a band of darkness. Beyond that was a kind of sunken arena or theatre, a deep bowl with terraced sides where the Denizens could sit. The gold-red light came from inside the bowl, but it was deep enough that he could not quite see its source.

Arthur crossed the darkness and stepped down on to the first terrace. He paused there for a moment, looking down. The light came from a huge glass bowl about twenty feet in diameter, with a bronze lid that appeared to be riveted to the glass in some way. The bowl was full of sparkling clean water, and in the water was the biggest goldfish Arthur had ever seen. It was ten feet long and six feet high, with huge goggly eyes and long moustache-like tendrils hanging down from its mouth.

Arthur stepped down to the next terrace and the next. There were forty in all before he reached the lowest and stood in front of the glass bowl. The goldfish watched him approach, just bobbing up and down. It didn't look very intelligent.

Arthur cleared his throat, not without some difficulty, and spoke.

"Greetings! I am Arthur, chosen by Part One of the Will to be the Rightful Heir to the House!"

"I knew you were coming," said the Carp, its words mysteriously echoing all around the arena. Its voice was of a strange pitch and could have come from either a deep-voiced woman or a high-voiced man. "It is as I have told my Followers. Hold true to your faith that the Rightful Heir will come. The pirate Feverfew will be cast down and we shall return to the House!"

"You are Part Three of the Will, aren't you?" asked Arthur. It was hard to see through the curved glass, but he could see that the fish was actually composed of tiny shining letters, moving in lines. Its skin was like the detailed etching on a banknote. From a distance it looked like solid colour, but up really close you could see what it was made of.

"Indeed I am," replied the Carp. It did a circuit around the bowl and returned to face Arthur. "What was your name again?"

CHAPTER TWENTY-SIX

"Arthur!"

The Carp blew out a huge stream of bubbles and a strange chuckling, gargling sound filled the air. It took Arthur a moment to realise the goldfish was laughing.

"Only joking, Lord Arthur! I am not a goldfish, though I have that shape. While it is true I depend upon newly escaped slaves for news of the House and Realms beyond this island prison, I have heard of your heroic exploits!"

"You haven't read that book about me, have you?" asked Arthur. "Because it isn't true—"

"I have read no book," said the Carp. "I have merely heard stories. Now tell me of the ships waiting to enter this worldlet and the legions amassed to assault the vile Feverfew's fort!"

"Uh, there's just me and Suzy," said Arthur. "We had to sneak in through Wednesday's stomach. In the Raised Rats' submersible."

"Only the two of you?" asked the Carp. It did four rapid circles of its bowl, then calmed down and approached Arthur again. "And you dealt with the Raised Rats? You are very confident, Lord Arthur. But I expect that my Followers can defeat the pirates after you have slain Feverfew himself."

"I wasn't planning to run into Feverfew," said Arthur. "I just planned to sneak in here, find you – the Will – and sneak out again. The submersible is waiting to take us back out of Drowned Wednesday. Then Wednesday can release you and give me the Key. Once I have that, I can take on Feverfew. I have to rescue my friends in the slave huts – if they're still alive – as well as your Followers, but I can't do it straightaway."

"I have faith," muttered the Carp. "But there are limits. Why did you not bring the First and Second Keys with you? I cannot feel their presence."

"Because I want to stay human," said Arthur angrily. "I don't want to turn into a Denizen. This is all your stupid fault anyway. I mean, the Will's fault. I never wanted to get involved, but now I have to sort it all out and I wish I didn't have to but I do! So how about helping me instead of complaining?"

The Carp started doing circles again and did not respond, but Arthur heard a strange whooshing sound. He looked around and saw that the Followers of the Carp had begun to file into the amphitheatre and sit down on the terraces in numerical order. Suzy and Jebenezer were right behind him.

The strange whooshing sound came from the assembled Denizens all drawing in highly indignant breaths at the same time. But before they could say anything or start throwing things, which some of them looked like they wanted to do, the Carp stopped circling and came right up to the glass near Arthur.

"You are the Rightful Heir, proclaimed by the two parts of the Will that precede me. There is no doubt about that. So I must help you to help myself. It is a pity that things were not arranged otherwise, but I believe it will all turn out for the best. How do you intend to take me to this submersible?"

Good question, thought Arthur.

"Uh, I was hoping you'd be in a more... mobile... shape. Can you get out of that bowl?"

"My current shape has been fixed by the Third Key, as part of my imprisonment," said the Carp. "If you had the other Keys you could free me, but that is water under the bridge. The bowl is a later addition of Feverfew's. As the Rightful Heir, I suspect you could banish the bowl, but then I should only be able to flop around on the ground."

Arthur scratched his head with both hands and resisted the urge to pull his hair out or start smacking his forehead.

"How did the slaves carry you up here, then?" asked Suzy. "You and that bowl would be a mighty heavy load even for twenty Denizens."

"Both my person and my bowl were smaller then," said the Carp. "As my following has grown, so I have grown, reflecting the worship of my Followers."

"So you can shrink yourself and the bowl?" asked Arthur.

"I could," admitted the Carp. "But it would not befit my station to appear less than I am."

"Shrink," commanded Arthur. "I haven't got time to argue about it. Get as small and light as you can."

"That is no way to speak to the Carp!" protested someone back up a terrace or two.

"Arthur is the Rightful Heir," said the Carp. "It is my duty to obey his orders, however given. I shall dwindle to a transportable size."

"First time I've seen a part of the Will with a sensible attitude," muttered Suzy.

"We still have to get back to the water gate," said Arthur. He took the small case and checked the green bottle inside. It was intact, he was pleased to see. So the *Balaena* had not encountered trouble. Or not yet. "There's those four pirates to get past too."

"May I have my Followers sing as I shrink?" asked the Carp.

"Sure, whatever. They can dance too, if they like," said Arthur. "But please hurry."

"Song of Faith Number Eighty-One," instructed the Carp. "I shall diminish myself and my bowl as the song progresses, and at the end shall be positively minute."

"How long is the song?" asked Suzy.

"A mere hundred verses and the chorus repeated as often," said the Carp. "I shall set the key."

"No," said Arthur. He was feeling really agitated and tense, as if every second lost was vital. "You've got two minutes. Please just shrink. We'll also need some help to fight the gate guards, so maybe, Jebenezer, you can pick a dozen—"

The boy stopped in midsentence as he thought that through. The Denizens who came to fight the guards at the water gate would never be able to get back to the hills. They'd have to go with Arthur to the *Balaena*.

"No, say just four of your very best archers to come with... to help us get past the gate."

Arthur turned to look at all the luminous green Denizens sitting on the terraces and raised his voice.

"And I do promise that if I make it back out and get the Third Key, I will return! I will make sure you are all brought out to the House, even if I have to use the Improbable Stair to get here."

This speech did not evoke wild cheering, but the Denizens appeared slightly happier. Arthur sighed and twisted around to look at the Carp and was taken aback. There was no longer any huge fishbowl with a giant carp in it. There was only Suzy and Jebenezer.

"What?"

Jebenezer held up something that looked like a jam jar full of water, with a two-inch goldfish whizzing around and around in it.

"Small enough?" asked the Carp. Its voice was still as loud and omnidirectional.

"Thank you," said Arthur. It was a heartfelt expression of gratitude. "Jebenezer, can you carry the Will... I mean the Carp... and lead us out of here? And can you get those four archers?"

"I can," said Jebenezer. "But... but what is to happen to us when you leave with the Carp? It is only the Carp's powers that make this cavern safe from Feverfew. Once the pirate knows the Carp is gone, he will attack and his sorcery will invade our home."

Why is nothing straightforward? thought Arthur. *It's bad enough that I can't go and rescue Leaf and the crews from the*

Moth *and the* Mantis. *Now I have to worry about all these Denizens as well. I bet heroes who only had to beat up dragons or monsters never had to worry about whole populations and their friends, not to mention what might happen to their family back home...*

"I'll be back as soon as I can," said Arthur. "Perhaps you should split up and hide all over the hills."

"You must have faith," intoned the Carp.

"We must have faith," echoed back the Followers.

"I reckon splitting up and hiding might come in handy as well," said Suzy. "I mean, faith is fine and everything, but you got to be practical."

The Carp stopped circling and peered at Suzy for a moment.

"If you have faith, all will be well," said the Carp. "But to sharpen your faith, my Followers, I shall test it. When I have left, so must you disperse among the hills, in groups of no more than three, and meditate quietly. No singing and no loud praising of me. If you are true to your faith, Lord Arthur will return and save you. If not, doubtless Feverfew will capture you and end your doubting existences in the Hot Lake."

"The Carp is wise, long swim the Carp!" chanted the Denizens as Arthur, Suzy and Jebenezer started to climb back up through the terraces. As they passed through the crowd, Jebenezer held the jar up above his head and the

Carp's radiance lit up the faces of his Followers, while Jebenezer singled out the archers who were to accompany them to the water gate.

Ascending the path to the cavern exit was considerably easier with the Carp's light, though Arthur was slightly shocked to see some parts of the path that he'd blithely walked along were not only narrow but the rock was crumbling on the edges as well. This time he traversed these sections with his back against the rock wall, trying not to think about how easily he could have put a foot wrong and fallen to his death.

It was a relief to get back outside. The sun was still shining, though it was a little lower in the sky. Coming out of the darkness, Arthur thought that the sunlight was tinged a little pink, like a grapefruit skin, and so the island was probably not a piece of his Earth, pinched off to become Feverfew's worldlet, but was from one of the myriad other worlds in the Secondary Realms.

"So, do we head straight back the way we came?" asked Suzy. "Cos if we are, I hope you know the way we came. I need streets and buildings, personally. Can't find my own elbow in these woods."

"The quickest path down from here goes round the shores of the Hot Lake," said Jebenezer. "Then we can strike nor'-nor'-east to the peninsula and follow that to the water gate. Only the pirates'll probably see us coming, either from the water gate, the fort, or the *Shiver*. We'll have to run the length of the peninsula, burst through the guards and go into the Stomach."

"Is it a lack of faith to be thinking that we're all going to be slain or captured and sunk into the Hot Lake?" asked one of the four chosen archers.

"Yes," snapped the Carp. Its voice was more restrained now that it was out in the open. "Believe in Lord Arthur. Believe in your Carp. We shall prevail."

"Provided we get a move on," muttered Suzy.

I can't run the length of the peninsula, thought Arthur as panic began to make his stomach feel tight and his breathing shallower. *I just can't run that far without having an asthma attack...*

"Shall we take the quick path, Lord Arthur?" asked Jebenezer.

I can't run that far... I can't run that far... Arthur's thoughts were in a loop of fear and doubt. He felt like he was drowning in them, unable to think about anything else. Then all of a sudden, he felt, rather than heard, the Carp speak, inside his head. He couldn't describe it or see it, but he experienced the Carp's words as if he heard them and read them at the same time.

Have faith in yourself, Arthur. Take it one step at a time. Let us get to the peninsula. Then we shall take the next step. Perhaps we will not need to run. Perhaps you will run better than you think. One step at a time.

You can read my mind! Arthur thought back.

Not normally, replied Part Three of the Will silently, for Arthur alone. *But your fear was so great that it opened the doorways of your mind. They are closing now, and I will not*

"Arthur! The quick path or not?" asked Suzy.

"Sorry," said Arthur. He shook his head and found it clear of the paralysing fear he'd felt a moment before. "Yeah, let's take the quick path."

"Florenza and Padraic, take scout," ordered Jebenezer.

The two Denizens he'd named looked at each other nervously, then slowly advanced into the forest, bows ready.

CHAPTER TWENTY-SEVEN

The quick way down the hill would have been a very slow way if it had been up to Arthur or Suzy to find it, Arthur thought as they were led through seemingly impassable tangles of undergrowth, under arching tree roots and between rocks. But within forty minutes they were back down to the flat area, skirting the Hot Lake, keeping just within the border of the forest before it died back and was replaced by bare, sulphurous yellow earth.

"It does stink," said Suzy as she tied a torn-off flounce from her dress over her face.

Arthur took a deep breath and was surprised to find that it went all the way to the bottom of his lungs. The air did smell horrible, like rotten eggs, but he could actually breathe it more easily than the cool, wet air of the hills.

Across the Hot Lake, Arthur could see Feverfew's yardarm. The pirate had simply transferred a mast and its yards from a captured ship, and set it right on the lake's edge, with a block and tackle to swing prisoners out and dip them. There was a viewing platform nearby.

"I reckon we've done it," said Suzy a little later, as they passed the eastern shore of the lake. "Plenty of time to spare too."

"Let's not talk about it till we're actually out of here and out of Drowned Wednesday's stomach," said Arthur. "Or, better still, getting served tea by Sneezer back in Monday's Dayroom."

"If you believe, all will be well," intoned the Carp.

Its words were punctuated for the worse by the thud of two things hitting the ground just ahead of Jebenezer. For a moment Arthur thought they were coconuts or large round fruit. Then he saw that they were decapitated heads.

The green-mottled heads of Florenza and Padraic.

"Feverfew!" croaked Florenza's head.

"Sorry!" whispered Padraic's.

"Don't forget to—"

"Stick our heads back on if—"

"You win."

"Give me to Arthur!" snapped the Carp. Jebenezer just

managed to thrust the jam jar into Arthur's hands before a whirl of yellow dust swept around his feet and he froze like a statue. Another gust of yellow particles wound around Suzy as she drew her knife, and she froze too, as did the two archers who were bringing up the rear.

"I can oppose Feverfew's powers to some degree," said the Carp hurriedly. "But it is up to you, Arthur!"

Arthur stuffed the jam jar in his pocket and drew his sword. The dust-laden breeze kept whipping around him, but it had no effect, other than to make it hard to see.

There was no other sign of Feverfew.

Arthur turned in a circle, his eyes darting from side to side. Everyone else was frozen around him. He could see no movement. The lakeshore, only twenty paces away, was bare and empty. The sick-looking trees and undergrowth would hide someone, but only if they stayed still.

Where was Feverfew?

No one ever looks up...

Arthur jumped back and looked up, just as a shadow fell across him and a blade whistled through the air. The boy raised his own sword to block, felt a shock all along his arm and sprang away, his back up against the rough, vine-covered trunk of a large tree.

Feverfew closed his wings and dropped to the ground, the sound of both wings and footfall clouded by the whine of the yellow wind.

He looked just like Arthur imagined a pirate captain would. Tall and dashing, his long black hair flowing, his black beard braided with jewels and smoking match-cord. He was handsome, as handsome as a superior Denizen, and his clothes were bright scarlet, trimmed with gold lace and had golden death's heads as buttons. He carried a cutlass with a blade of black iron that smoked as much as the matches in his beard.

He looked nothing like the horrid visitation Arthur had seen in the mirror. Until Arthur looked at him out of the corner of his eye.

Seen that way, Feverfew was a horrid, barely human thing. His skin was the red of severe sunburn and shrunken against his bones. His eyes were like olive pits, black in red sockets.

He was not dressed in fine clothes, but covered in hundreds of pieces of paper. Papers of all different sizes and colours, all of them written on in a flowing, glowing script, all of them reeking of Nothing and sorcery.

"You bear the Red Hand," said Feverfew. Arthur heard the pirate's voice twice, the two voices just a little out of sync with each other. One was deep, melodious and commanding. The other was high-pitched, whiny and horribly penetrating. "You have stolen from me."

Arthur licked his lips and took a stronger grip on his

sword. He only had one chance, he knew. A clean cut to the neck...

"Yet that is not all you are," continued Feverfew. "Not just a thief. But also the chosen instrument of the Architect's Will. I know who you are, Arthur."

Feverfew took a step forward. Arthur tensed, ready to step forward and swing.

"I know who you are. I know all about you. Don't I, young Leaf?"

Feverfew smiled, his cracked, too-thin lips curling back from yellow teeth.

Arthur didn't take his eyes off Feverfew, but in the corner of his vision, he saw a line of pirates slowly walk into view. Right at the front, wearing the same clothes he'd seen her in on the *Mantis*, but now with a black cap, was Leaf.

"Yes, Captain," said Leaf.

"So I know you haven't got the first two Keys with you," said Feverfew. "Of course, if you had, I'd hardly be given the time to speak, would I? And I suppose that old fish is around somewhere, talking too much about how everything is going to work out. For it, of course."

Just one step closer, thought Arthur.

"I expect you'd like to chop off my head," said Feverfew. "Now, as I'm a sporting gentleman, I thought I'd give you that chance. I have a proposition for you, Arthur. A wager, between two folk who once were mortals, as equals. What do you say?"

Arthur kept his sword up and ready. He would not blink or look away.

"What proposition?" he asked.

"Why, an exchange of blows," said Feverfew. "One each and you can go first. If you slay me, then you and yours go free. If I slay you, then I inherit all that is yours. I become the Rightful Heir to the House!"

"I don't know if it would work like that," said Arthur. "Even if I did agree."

There has to be a catch, he thought. *Like in the story with the knight and the green giant. I know Feverfew can reattach his head, even more than most Denizens. But Sunscorch said that if I can get grit on his neck-stump or lay the flat of my blade there...*

"That's my concern," said Feverfew. "There's that old fish to witness. Set it out of your pocket, so it can see the goings-on. Now, I shall give you one minute by my watch to decide. A friendly wager or a free-for-all against me and my pirate crew."

He smiled and took a jewel-encrusted watch the size of an orange out of his pocket. At the same time, he casually stepped back, so there was no chance Arthur could reach him before his own pirates came forward.

Arthur flicked his gaze to Leaf, just for a second. She

looked normal enough, but she wasn't looking at him. She was staring at Feverfew.

"I get the first blow?" asked Arthur. "There'll be no interference from your crew?"

"They shall stand as trees on a windless day," replied Feverfew.

"Can you be cut by steel?" asked Arthur.

"Steel or silver, iron or bronze, all blades sunder my flesh. It is an honest wager, as I said, between two mortals, as transformed by time, the House, sorcery and Nothing."

Arthur turned his head sideways a little and looked at Feverfew out of the corner of his eye again. The scrawny, inhuman thing clad in tattered papers would be much easier to strike than someone human-looking. His neck seemed thinner too.

"I want to talk to the Carp first," he said. "Give me another minute."

"One more minute," said Feverfew coldly. "Since it is you who asks."

Arthur kept his position against the tree and his sword in his right hand. With his left, he pulled out the jam jar and raised it close to his head.

I'm plenty afraid now, he thought. *Can you hear me, Carp?*

I can, responded the Carp silently. *You must have faith, Arthur—*

Stop! Just tell me, as far as you know, can Feverfew be killed by having his head cut off if I lay the blade flat on his neck-stump?

Perhaps, the Carp replied. *That would work even with most superior Denizens. But Feverfew is devious.*

Perhaps!! What kind of answer... never mind. Is there anything you can do to free Suzy and Jebenezer and the others? Or my friend Leaf? She must be under a spell. There's no way she'd be with the pirates otherwise—

I have kept you free of Feverfew's spell. Perhaps I could free one more...

There was that word again. Arthur couldn't stand it.

Perhaps! he repeated in his mind. *You're the one who needs to have some faith—*

Indeed, Arthur. I have never claimed otherwise—

"Time!" interrupted Feverfew. "Or close enough. What is your decision, Arthur?"

"I accept," said Arthur. As he spoke, he felt suddenly sick, but he willed the nausea away.

"Excellent," said Feverfew. "I shall kneel here then and you may strike when you will. Please do ensure the fish has a good view of the proceedings."

Arthur nodded. He started to set the jar down near his feet, but changed his mind and put it down right up against Suzy's right foot. At the same time, he scooped up a handful of earth.

"I haven't got all day," said Feverfew. He had already removed his wings and put them aside as he knelt down. His illusory self was winding back his long black hair to bare his neck. In reality, he had almost no hair and was just going through the motions.

Arthur stepped close to him, his mind racing.

Strike fast, throw the earth on the stump, lay the flat of the blade there, to be sure.

"Oh, hurry up!"

Arthur raised his sword. It felt much heavier than it had before. He lifted it as high as he could, then brought it down with all the strength of his shoulder and the weight of his upper body.

I must keep looking, Arthur thought. *Don't be distracted. Throw the earth and lay the flat of the blade.*

It felt surprisingly like hitting a six in cricket. There was a sudden shock through his arm, then the sword was free again.

Arthur had kept his eye on the target. He threw the earth and laid the blade firmly against the neck-stump, which was dry and bloodless. Feverfew's head rolled on the dirt for only a moment, then with frightening speed, it hurtled into the air. At the same time, his body jerked back and stood up. Arthur had to jump too, to keep the flat of the blade on the neck.

The head dropped like a hawk, landing true where

Arthur's blade lay on the neck-stump. But neither earth nor blade inconvenienced it at all. Arthur watched in horror as the flesh spread up from the body's part of the neck, and down from the head's share, meeting in the middle.

Feverfew reached up and pulled Arthur's sword free of his almost totally healed neck. The point of the blade came out with a pop as the boy staggered back.

"My turn, I think," said Feverfew with a smile that was as horrible in both his true and illusory forms.

Arthur had failed.

CHAPTER TWENTY-EIGHT

"Just kneel down where you are," said Feverfew. He ran his thumb down the black blade of his cutlass and flicked away a single drop of blood that was so tainted with Nothing it sizzled as it hit the earth. "I'm hoping you haven't the trick of reattachment. Many centuries it took me to learn the way of it. And twice as many to do it with complications. Young Leaf tells me you've had no such time. Kneel, I said!"

Arthur found himself kneeling, his body moving independently of his mind, which was furiously trying to think of some way out of his predicament.

We agreed to exchange blows... exchange blows... I went first...

"You won't feel a thing," said Feverfew. "Which is a pity. I shall enjoy sinking your companions in the Hot Lake."

I only agreed to exchange blows... I didn't say I wouldn't dodge or duck... I didn't even say I'd be still...

Arthur tried to move, but found his muscles would not obey him. The yellow wind was winding round his wrists and ankles, holding him in place. He turned his head and saw Feverfew raising the black cutlass.

Carp! Carp! Help me move! Help me!

Have faith in yourself.

Blinding anger filled Arthur. He couldn't believe the Carp couldn't do anything except carry on about faith!

Fury coursed through his blood and muscle, and the yellow wind flinched before it. Arthur sprang back, just as the black cutlass swept down – into the dirt.

"What!" roared Feverfew. He twisted around, his cutlass sweeping at Arthur's knees.

Arthur sprang over the black blade, cutting back with his own two-handed stroke, his sword once again severing the pirate's neck. This time, as the pirate's head bounced on the ground, Arthur tried to kick Feverfew in the chest, only to find his foot suddenly wrapped in paper and deflected towards a tree.

Arthur hit the tree and staggered back, badly off balance made worse because his crab armour was trying to keep his leg straight.

The boy teetered backwards as Feverfew's head shrieked into the air and then plummeted once again towards the stump of his neck.

It never got there. Suzy suddenly leapt across and smashed Feverfew's head to the ground with a broken branch. As it started to rise again, Leaf darted out of the ranks of pirates and, in true soccer striker–style, kicked the head as hard as she could out towards the bubbling, Nothing-laden waters of the Hot Lake.

Everyone, including the pirates, watched as Feverfew's head splashed down. Ripples spread around its impact point, but still everyone kept watching to see if it would rise again.

Arthur was staring too, when he was suddenly gripped from behind by two paper-shrouded, slithery hands that began to tighten around his neck. He just managed to get three of his fingers under those grasping hands, but he couldn't get them off, or stop them from slowly strangling him to death.

To make things even worse, Feverfew's head rose back out of the boiling mud. All the flesh, illusory and real, had been stripped from it and it was now just a yellow-tinged skull, its teeth chattering, a sorcerous tongue of blue smoke flickering as Feverfew shouted his last words before tumbling back down into the muddy depths, to be totally destroyed by Nothing.

"Let Nothing remain!"

The hands around Arthur's neck suddenly fell away. The boy staggered forward, his crab-armoured leg failing to bend at the knee, and was caught by Jebenezer, who twirled him into a sudden and unwelcome dance.

"You did it! You slew Feverfew! And I saw it happen!"

"Stop! The pirates!"

Jebenezer paused in midtwirl, sending Arthur cannoning into Suzy and Leaf, who were shaking hands. They caught Arthur and turned him so that he could see Feverfew's pirates running into the trees, throwing away their weapons as they ran.

"You don't have to worry about the pirates," said Leaf. "They're a gutless bunch. Feverfew could make them brave, but without him, they're hopeless."

"I just about had heart failure when I saw you with them," said Arthur. "What were you doing?"

"How about 'thanks for the great kick'?" said Leaf crossly. "I was staying alive, what do you think? Feverfew said he only enslaved Denizens. Or Piper's children at a pinch, because they're as hardy as Denizens and a sight cleverer. First off he was going to throw me over the side, till I told him he could get a ransom for me."

"From who?"

"From you, of course," said Leaf. "When he heard that, he got all interested."

"And you told him whatever he wanted to know!"

"Duh! I didn't have any choice! He could read my mind for starters."

"Sorry! Sorry!" said Arthur. "Let's start again. Thank you for that wonderful kick. Thank you, Suzy, for an equally fantastic smash with the stick."

"That's better," said Leaf. "You can make the thanks official by getting me out of here and back home where I now fully realise I belong!"

"Good idea," said Suzy. She pointed up at the sky. "If we can get out."

Arthur looked up. The sun was wobbling in the sky and there were strange, streaky black clouds spreading out from it.

"Uh-oh. They're cracks!"

"This worldlet is collapsing," said the Carp, once more being carried by Jebenezer. "But we must believe in a way out, for then we shall find one."

"The augury puzzle," snapped Arthur. He turned around to look for Feverfew's body. "It must be on Feverfew somewhere. We grab that, find someone who can use it among the slaves, take a ship—"

He stopped talking. Where Feverfew's body had been there was just a big dark stain on the ground and long, thin, useless strips of curling paper.

The ground rumbled under Arthur's feet. Branches

dropped from the trees and the Hot Lake bubbled more ominously. Mud began to spread beyond its shores, oozing oilily across the yellow earth.

"How long have we got?" Arthur asked the Carp. "And can you do anything to stop it or slow it down?"

"I have no power over such structures as this. I estimate the worldlet will last between six and twelve hours. Perhaps a little less, perhaps a little more. It depends on the nature of the eventual demise. Slow dissolution by intruding Nothing or cataclysmic rupture into the Void."

"How were you going to get out, Arthur?" asked Leaf.

"By submersible," said Arthur. "One run by the Raised Rats. But it can only fit half a dozen Denizens and—"

As he spoke, he got out the box and opened it to check the bottle. But the bottle was gone, in its place a pile of green glass dust and a tiny fragment of cork.

"—they're not going to be picking anyone up anyway. They've already left. Or been destroyed."

"So we're stuck here, which means we're dead," said Leaf.

"How about the Improbable Stair?" asked Suzy. "We did it before, Arthur. It ain't so bad. You lead the way and we all troop along behind."

"I can't get on to the Stair without a Key," said Arthur. "But maybe the Will can—"

"Not in this form," said the Carp.

"At least we destroyed Feverfew," said Suzy philosophically. "Even if it's one of those whatchamacallit victories where you win and croak before you get all the loot and everything."

"A pyrrhic victory," said Leaf. "Great. There has to be some other way out of here. We need to try and think outside the box. Or laterally. Or with different hats. Beyond the normal... only I guess that *is* normal here..."

"There might be a way out," said Arthur slowly. "We have to get everyone to the harbour. On to the *Moth*."

"But it's an old tub," protested Leaf. "If you think you can get a ship out, we should take the *Mantis*!"

Arthur shook his head.

"We can't get a ship out. The Rats were sure Feverfew's Gore-Draken augury puzzle was the only way to find a gate in or out, and I bet that's true. But there might be a way out using the *Moth*, because part of the *Moth*'s insides are actually somewhere else, inside the House."

"What?" asked Leaf and Suzy at the same time.

"I'll explain when we get there," said Arthur. "Jebenezer, you'd better send someone back to the cavern and order the Followers to the harbour before they start spreading out everywhere. Oh, and did anyone stick those two Denizens' heads back... oh, good... will they be all right?"

"They will survive," said the Carp. "But they will suffer

for many months and they will not be able to drink for a year."

"Good," said Arthur absently. "Let's go! Carp, I presume you can free the slaves held down at the town?"

"Now that Feverfew is gone, I can loose their shackles even from here," said the Carp. It swelled up like a blowfish, flared as bright as the sun for a instant, then flashed around its jar in its usual shape at immense speed for several seconds. "There, it is done!"

By the time they reached the town, it was a shambles. The suddenly freed slaves had turned on any pirates still left. The most recent slaves, the crews of the *Moth* and the *Flying Mantis*, had re-formed under their officers and mates and were busy restocking their ships with supplies and the choicest pieces of salvage from the vast selection in Feverfew's warehouses. The slaves who had been there longer mainly sat around, waiting to be told what to do by somebody.

When Arthur arrived he first had a brief but very welcome reunion with Sunscorch, who was overseeing the resupply of the *Moth*. But long explanations had to wait, so after a little back-slapping that left his shoulders sore, Arthur had the Carp use its ability to make its voice heard everywhere around the harbour, to tell the former slaves that the worldlet was doomed and that if they wanted to live and return to the House, they must gather aboard the

Moth, bringing only one small item of salvage each.

Naturally this caused a panic, only quelled by the Carp using its voice more forcefully, and Jebenezer, Sunscorch, Pannikin and various others using their voices and belaying pins to bring order to the mass of Denizens that was trying to get on any of the four small boats that could take them from the harbour wall to the *Moth*.

Leaf also had an important role to play, convincing Captain Swell that he must abandon the *Flying Mantis*, and that even such a practised Navigator-Sorcerer as he would not be able to find a way to sail it out. As he had already tried every augury puzzle he could find, the logic of it was clear, but it was still very hard for him to leave a ship he had commanded for nigh on ten thousand years.

Captain Catapillow presented a different problem, for he did not want to let anyone into his quarters, for fear that they would destroy his stamp collection. But when Arthur lost his temper and spoke sharply to him, he caved in and withdrew to his bed, Ichabod calmly drawing the curtains after him.

Arthur had been worried about how many Denizens would fit in the strange chamber within the *Moth*, particularly since he had promised the Followers of the Carp that he would try to save them, and as they would be last to arrive, they would be the most likely to be left behind. But the chamber was even larger than he remembered and Ichabod moved the display cases around to create even more space, while telling him that his coat needed to be cleaned, his boots washed and that the creation of vastly more space within a room was merely a matter of correctly arranging the furniture.

At last, five hours after they'd begun, the room was entirely packed with at least three thousand Denizens, Arthur, Suzy and Leaf. There was no room to move at all for most of the Denizens, with everyone pressed together like standing sardines.

As far as anyone could tell, no one had been left behind.

Outside, the cracks in the sky almost stretched from the sun to the ground, and the Carp now predicted a catastrophic implosion, with the worldlet suddenly collapsing and being sucked into the Void of Nothing.

"Then, if this worldlet has been properly constructed, the breach in the Void will seal over and cause no more trouble," the Carp pronounced. "Or if shoddily made, it will spread Nothing everywhere around it and cause many more problems to the locality."

"You mean Wednesday's stomach," said Arthur.

"Yes," said the Carp. "Now, as to the matter of our survival – I do not think this room would survive such a catastrophe, as it is linked to the ship that will be sucked into the maelstrom of Nothing."

"I know we have to get out of here too," said Arthur.

"But as this room is actually somewhere else within the House, all we have to do is find a way from inside here to outside there. As I asked you to look into several hours ago."

"Indeed," said the Carp. "Unfortunately while I have found out where this room actually is, I can't find a way to get out. And even if I could, I'm not sure how much use it would be."

"Great," said Leaf. "Excellent work, Arthur."

CHAPTER TWENTY-NINE

"Why won't it help to get out of the room?" Arthur asked the Carp. "We have to!"

"This room is still where it was," said the Carp. "In the old Port Wednesday. Underwater. I don't know how far. Besides, I can find no way from here to the outside of the room."

"Because there isn't one, or because of something else?" asked Arthur.

"There may be an exit," said the Carp. "But this room is strangely twisted and I simply have not had time to work out its exact place within the fabric of the House. I doubt anybody could, save the Architect herself."

"The Atlas!" cried Arthur. He reached down into his boot and pulled out the green book. "Can you use the *Compleat Atlas of the House*?"

"No," said the Carp.

As it spoke, there was a commotion near the door out to the *Moth*. Arthur jumped up on to Catapillow's blanket box to see over the heads of the Denizens. Sunscorch, who had been handling the last few stragglers, was just inside the door.

"A piece of the sky's fallen in!" he roared over the hubbub. "And the sea is starting to turn like water going down a plughole!"

"There has to be a way out!" said Arthur. He held the Atlas and focused all his attention on it.

"Arthur—" said the Carp.

"Not now!" hissed Arthur. His knuckles were stark and white against the green book, he was gripping it so hard. "I'm concentrating!"

"Arthur—"

Arthur ignored the Carp and concentrated on his question.

Where is the way out of this room back into the House?

The Atlas stubbornly failed to open. Without a Key, it just would not respond.

"Arthur!" roared the Carp, so loud that Arthur's ears rang. "I cannot use the Atlas, but I can help you use it!

Place your right hand against the glass of my jar!"

Jebenezer held up the jar and Arthur slapped his palm against the glass. The Carp came right up against it, puckered up and kissed the side of the jar against Arthur's fingers three times. Each time it did, it shone more brightly, some of the light travelling through to bathe Arthur's fingers.

"Ask your question!"

Arthur took his hand away and gripped the Atlas again, repeating his question, willing the book to open with a determination that shut out everything else around him.

Nothing happened for three seconds, just long enough for the Carp to start to say, "We must have—"

Then the Atlas exploded open. Arthur fell off the blanket box, but was so hemmed in by Jebenezer, Suzy, Leaf and other Denizens that his feet didn't even touch the floor.

Arthur didn't notice. He was watching the perfect, though rapid, penmanship of the invisible writer in the Atlas. Words spread across the page, Arthur shrieking them aloud as he read.

"*The chief clerk's office of the Blue Moon Company's Second Counting House has been twisted seven turns sideways and inclined twelve degrees to the impossible, due to incompetent renovation. There are three means of egress from within the office. One is to the ship* Moth, *through the former front door. The second opens on the Void of Nothing and has been sealed under the floor ten paces to the left of the front door. The third opens in the ship telegraph turret of the Blue Moon Company in old Port Wednesday, and is located through the mirrored back of the former records safe, now in use as a wardrobe—"*

"No!" yelped Ichabod, but his voice was drowned out by the surge of Denizens towards the wardrobe.

"Hold!" roared the Carp. "Followers, link arms!"

"Moths, stand still!" roared Sunscorch.

"Mantises, hold yer ground!" shouted Pannikin.

"And may be activated by peeling off the wallpaper backing," finished Arthur. He slapped the Atlas shut, jumped down and wormed his way between the Denizens to the wardrobe. It was a huge oak-panelled affair, easily ten feet high and fifteen feet wide.

"Ichabod!" called Arthur. "Is there any trick to going in?"

"No, sir," said Ichabod stiffly. He had managed to appear at Arthur's elbow, unruffled and calm once more. "Simply walk through. But if I may remove the Captain's clothes before they are trampled—"

He was interrupted by a very loud cracking sound and the floor shivered under Arthur's feet. He didn't wait to hear any more from Ichabod, but strode straight at the mirror.

The inside of the wardrobe was bigger than the outside. There were racks of clothes against the side walls, and shelves of boots, shoes and accessories. The rear wall was wallpapered with a simple blue flower pattern and had a chaise longue against it, next to a small table with an open book of fashion plates on it.

Arthur hurried over, shoved the table and book aside and pulled the chaise longue away from the wall. Then he reached up and pulled a loose corner of wallpaper. It came away easily, revealing a mirrored surface underneath. Arthur ripped some more, and then Suzy and Leaf and Jebenezer and even Ichabod were there pulling at the paper as well.

"What if it's really deep on the other side?" asked Leaf. "Will we get the bends going up? Can you get the bends in the House?"

"I don't know!" snapped Arthur. "We haven't got a choice, have we? Go through as soon as the paper's off."

"What about you?" asked Suzy.

"I've got to make sure everyone gets out," said Arthur. "You guys go or you'll get trampled."

As the paper was almost all off, he took the Carp's jar from Jebenezer and stepped back out of the wardrobe, hitting a solid wall of waiting Denizens, who were barely kept in check by the combined efforts of the Mates, some of the Carp's Followers and the more dependable crew.

Arthur managed to squeeze through back to the blanket box. He stepped up on that, ignoring the fact that it was vibrating, along with the floor, like a badly tuned car.

"OK, Carp, maximum volume," said Arthur. "Repeat what I say."

"I shall do so," replied the Carp.

"Quiet down!"

"Quiet down!"

"Don't push and wait your turn!"

"Don't push and wait your turn!"

"Everyone will get out!"

"Everyone will get out!"

"Listen carefully but don't move till I tell you to."

"Listen carefully but don't move till I tell you to."

"There are two walls of mirrors to go through."

"There are two walls of mirrors to go through."

"Walk slowly and carefully through the wardrobe mirrors and keep going through the next set of mirrors. You will come out underwater. Swim up and try to help anyone who needs it."

"Walk slowly and carefully through the wardrobe mirrors and keep going through the next set of mirrors. You will come out underwater. Swim up and try to help anyone who needs it."

"Everyone at the back stay still. If you're in front of the wardrobe, start walking slowly forward!"

"Everyone at the back stay still. If you're in front of the

wardrobe, start walking slowly forward!"

"As space opens in front of you, walk slowly forward! Steady! Everyone will get through!"

"As space opens in front of you, walk slowly forward! Steady! Everyone will get through!"

Arthur kept giving instructions as the Denizens shuffled forward into the mirrored doors of the wardrobe. Every now and then one would panic and Arthur would stop breathing as it looked like the fear would spread, only for everything to come back under control as calmer Denizens wrestled the panicked one back into line.

But it's all taking too long, Arthur thought as he was forced to step down from the blanket box, which was shaking itself to pieces. The floor under his feet was starting to glow a nasty, dull red – if it wasn't for his Immaterial Boots, Arthur was sure he would feel the heat.

"Let's move a bit faster!" he called out, the Carp repeating his words. Perhaps half the Denizens had gone through, so there was more room and less likelihood of a terrible crush.

Five minutes later, the walls started to weep black, tarlike tears the size of Arthur's head, and the floor was twisting and tilting by as much as six inches up and down.

"Come on, faster now!" called Arthur. "Jogging on the spot and then forward when space opens up!"

He demonstrated jogging as best he could with his

crab-armoured leg on a moving surface. Perhaps two hundred Denizens remained, but the room was clearly under enormous stress and that meant that the *Moth* and the worldlet outside must be close to final destruction.

"Can you tell what's happening outside?" whispered Arthur to the Carp as he moved to the back, smiling and waving on jogging Denizens. "I mean the *Moth* side, Feverfew's worldlet."

"It's still there because we're still here," said the Carp. "Hold on a moment. I'll check."

It whizzed around its jar several times, then stopped.

"The underlying structure is holding, though the cosmetic features, like the hills and so forth have all gone. Remarkable, really. Grim Tuesday lacked true flair, but his work was always very solid."

"How long have we got?"

"Minutes, not hours," said the Carp. "I can't say closer than that."

"Right," said Arthur grimly. There was some sort of holdup near the rear ranks of Denizens. He threaded his way over to it, to find Sunscorch, Pannikin and Captain Swell trying to pry Captain Catapillow from a display cabinet. Arthur was only mildly surprised not to see Concort, who must have already fled through the wardrobe.

"I can't go without at least the heart of my collection,"

sobbed Catapillow. "Just one cabinet. You can help me carry it! If it can't go, I won't go!"

"Lord Arthur, please tell the Captain he has to leave the stamps behind," said Sunscorch.

"You do have to leave them," said Arthur. "Look around! This place isn't going to last much longer. We have to hurry everyone through and you need to set an example."

"No," said Catapillow mulishly. He hugged the cabinet. "If my collection is to be destroyed, then I'll go with it."

"I guess let him stay, then," said Arthur. He glanced over the remaining Denizens. There were perhaps fifty left, all gathered near the wardrobe, which was becoming harder to get into as the floor bucked up and down. "Everyone else, let's get through the mirrors!"

The boy turned and joined the back of the relatively orderly queue that was steadily streaming into the wardrobe. He was glad to be able to grab hold of Denizens around him, because he would have fallen over otherwise, the floor was so unstable.

"The ceiling's slanting down, isn't it?" Arthur asked as they got down to the last twenty Denizens. "From that corner. Really quickly!"

In the far left corner, the distance from the floor to the ceiling had been cut in half, and the ceiling was still steadily moving down, like some kind of industrial crusher. It hit some of the display stands, which resisted the downward pressure for a moment, then buckled in a spray of glass and metal.

"Catapillow! This is it! Come now or you'll die!" shouted Arthur as he edged closer to the wardrobe. There were only a dozen Denizens in front of him now – and Suzy and Leaf! Arthur's head snapped around, Catapillow forgotten for a second.

"I told you to go through! We might not make it now!"

The floor broke in half as he spoke, a crevasse opening up in the middle of the room. Yellow mud boiled up out of it, preceded by clouds of stinking gas. Catapillow was on the wrong side, still clutching his display case.

Arthur held his breath and grabbed Leaf and Suzy, or they grabbed him, and the three of them jumped through the wardrobe mirrors, only just making it as the crevasse split the floor even further, toppling the wardrobe over.

Inside, the wardrobe was a tangled mess of trampled clothes and broken furniture. But even worse, it had toppled forward, so that the mirrored back wall was now the ceiling, twelve feet above the three children and impossibly out of reach.

"Stand on my shoulders—" Arthur started to say, but he hadn't seen Sunscorch, who had wedged himself in a corner. Without wasting a word, the Second Mate picked up Leaf and threw her straight up and through the mirror gate. As he turned to pick up Suzy, she jumped, got one foot on his shoulder, and leapt up without assistance.

Arthur stumbled, his crab-armoured leg caught in discarded coats.

"Go!" he shouted to Sunscorch as he desperately tried to untangle himself and only made it worse. "Go!"

CHAPTER THIRTY

Sunscorch went, but he grabbed Arthur under one burly arm, jumped on the exposed springs of the wrecked chaise longue and used their bounce to propel himself, Arthur and the tangle of coats up through the gate.

It happened so quickly that Arthur barely had time to get a breath, and he didn't have time to make sure the Carp's jar was securely in his pocket. He saw it hurtle past, and then he was through the mirror and completely surrounded by water.

Arthur kicked the coats free, but Sunscorch didn't let him go. He struck out in a direction that Arthur hoped was the surface, because he couldn't see anything except dark blue and tons of bubbles.

We could be hundreds of feet down, he thought. *I've got through so much and then to drown at the end... I'll never make it... the Denizens will, but I won't... and Leaf won't... It's all my fault, I should have made her leave the hospital... how am I ever going to explain to her parents... I have to take a breath, I have to take a—*

The dark blue water suddenly became lighter, interrupting Arthur's panicky thoughts. He saw Denizens all around, some doing powerful strokes and kicks, some barely dog-paddling, a few just floating.

Then, before he could begin to think that the light must mean the surface was close, he was suddenly there. His head broke through, light and air welcoming him, and he gasped and laughed and water ran out of his nose all at the same time.

Denizens bobbed everywhere, as far as he could see, gently lifted by the small swell. Arthur's gaze moved across each survivor superfast, looking for the faces he most wanted to see – and there they were. Suzy, about ten yards away. Leaf somewhat closer. And there was a jam jar moving mysteriously across the water, into Arthur's hand.

"You can let me go now, Sunscorch," said Arthur. "Thanks."

"I might have lost the ship, but I still ain't lost a passenger," said Sunscorch. He released Arthur, who promptly sank and had to be hauled up again till he got his treading-water action going properly.

"I have summoned Drowned Wednesday," said the Carp. "She is on her way and will be here shortly."

"You what? She'll eat us! I thought we'd get on some dry land first!"

"I am sure she won't eat us," said the Carp. "Have faith, Arthur..."

Arthur wasn't listening. He craned his head out of the water to look around, hoping to see some sign of solid ground, or a ship, or something. But all he could see were thousands of floating Denizen snacks looking tempting for one crazily hungry Leviathan.

"How did you communicate with her?"

"I am the Will. She is the Trustee. Now that I am back in the House, I am able to speak into her mind, much as I did into yours, Arthur."

"Well, tell her to transform into her human shape," said Arthur. "And tell her to order her Dawn to get here with as many ships as she can. Can you do that?"

"I can speak the message into her mind," said the Carp. "Whether it will totally penetrate is unclear. It is done."

"Can you speak with your mind to anyone else?" asked Arthur. "The Raised Rats, for example?"

The Carp shook its moustachelike growths back and forth.

"No. I am connected to you as the Rightful Heir and to Wednesday as the Trustee."

"Land ho!"

The cry came from some Denizens to Arthur's right. He paddled himself around, but even before he looked, he was pretty sure what he would see.

It wasn't land, though it looked like it.

It was Drowned Wednesday, bearing down on them. Still vast and almost certainly still hungry.

"We made it!"

That was Suzy, splashing over backstroke.

"Stop saying that!" said Arthur. "We haven't made it. We're probably going to get eaten. Wednesday won't be able to help herself if she sees all these Denizens floating about. It'll be like three thousand crisps waiting to get munched."

"Is that her?" asked Leaf, whose swimming style was very economical and practised. She leaned back and floated easily, making circular motions with her hands. "Wow! Talk about huge!"

"If anyone has any bright ideas, now is the time to spit them out," said Arthur, spitting out some sea water himself as his mouth was splashed midsentence.

"Pity the Captain's not here," said Suzy. "It'd be really

interesting to see what his harpoon could do to a whale that big."

"No way!" said Leaf. "I'm not letting anyone harpoon any whale. I'm a member of Greenpeace—"

"She doesn't mean it, Leaf," said Arthur. "And the Mariner wouldn't do it anyway. I think. I wish he was here. In a ship."

"The Mariner?" asked the Carp. "That would be the Architect's adopted son? The middle one?"

"Yes," said Arthur and Suzy together.

"I might be able to talk to his mind," mused the Carp. "Seeing as he is of the Architect's kin. I suppose I could talk to the Piper for that matter too, or Lord Sunday."

"Lord Sunday!" exclaimed Arthur. "What? Is he—"

"The eldest child of the Architect and the Old One. Their first experiment together, when the Architect inhabited a mortal woman—"

"OK, we don't need a history lesson now!" interrupted Arthur. Drowned Wednesday was looming larger and larger, and the glad cries of "land ho" among the Denizens had been replaced by cries of fear. "See if you can communicate with the Mariner! Maybe he can get here with a ship and pick us up before Wednesday—"

"It's not as simple as that," said the Carp. "I haven't seen him for millennia, and it's not as if I'm charged with making him do anything. I'll have to try and recall what he looked like to begin with. Besides, I'm sure that Wednesday won't eat us up—"

"Why not use the Mariner's charm you wear?" Sunscorch asked Arthur. "Or is it worn out?"

"The Mariner's charm?" Arthur asked. He pulled it out, sank below the surface yet again and came spluttering back out. "You mean it can actually do something?"

"So legend has it," replied Sunscorch. "Dr Scamandros would know, but he is gone now, like our late Captain Catapillow."

"I hope Scamandros is still alive," said Arthur. "The *Balaena* probably just had to leave for some reason... oh! You don't know. The doctor survived the battle with Feverfew. He escaped to me and... I'll tell you later. How exactly does legend say this disc worked?"

"You speak into it and the Mariner hears you," said Sunscorch.

"I've already done that!" protested Arthur. "Heaps of times when I first got swept up! Carp, you have to contact the Mariner!"

"Did he have grey hair or was it more white?" asked the Carp.

"I reckon that whale *is* shrinking," said Suzy.

Everyone swam around to look.

"I don't know," said Arthur. "She looks just as big to me."

"Keep watching," said Suzy. "She's getting smaller."

"Aye, she's shrinking," confirmed Sunscorch. "But will she shrink enough?"

"OK," said Arthur. "Even if she is shrinking, we don't want to tempt her with lots of Denizens to eat up. So I'm going to take the Carp and swim towards her, and everyone else can swim off at a right angle. OK?"

"No way," said Leaf. "I'm sticking with you, Arthur. You're my ticket home."

"I want to see what happens," said Suzy. "Besides, if she's normal size we might be able to help fight her, if we have to."

"Sunscorch, can you at least start organising all the Denizens to swim away?" pleaded Arthur. "I really do think Wednesday might not be able to resist temptation."

"Aye, aye, sir," said Sunscorch. He touched a knuckle to his head in salute and dived under.

"That's what you two are supposed to do," said Arthur. "Say 'aye, aye' and swim away."

"Yeah, as if we would," said Leaf. "You don't have to do everything by yourself, Arthur."

Arthur didn't answer. He just started swimming towards the approaching Leviathan. But secretly he was glad not to be alone. And Wednesday was getting smaller, so perhaps it would all be straightforward after all.

"Does this mean I don't need to try to reach the mind

of the Mariner?" asked the Carp. "Have you regained your faith in me?"

Arthur spat out some water and said, "Yes. You could say that."

He paused to tread water for a while and rest, and looked behind. The Denizens were very slowly beginning to swim away in the other direction. But that wasn't all that caught Arthur's eye.

"Is that a ship on the horizon?"

"A three-masted brigantine, under full sail," said Leaf, shading her eyes with one hand. "See, I didn't waste my time on the *Mantis*. Albert... Albert was a good teacher too."

"The ship's boy," said Arthur, suddenly horror-struck. "I haven't seen him! We couldn't have left him behind, could we?"

"No," said Leaf in a very small voice. Her eyes grew red, though Arthur could see no tears on her sea-washed face. "He... Albert got... Albert got killed when Feverfew attacked the ship. I've been trying not to think about... that's why I want to go home... I... I don't want any more adventures."

Arthur was silent. He didn't know what to do or say.

"He lived a long time," said Suzy. "I reckon he would have had a lot of good times, even if he couldn't remember a tenth of 'em, cos of the washing between the ears. And like all of us Piper's children, he would've died long ago if he'd been back on the old Earth. Remember what he taught you and he'll always be with you. That's what we say, when one of us goes."

"Drowned Wednesday is almost upon us," boomed the Carp suddenly. "The time has come to release me from my bowl! Lord Arthur, please unscrew the cap."

Arthur wiped his eyes, kicked hard with his legs and picked up the jar.

"Feverfew is dead and his bindings with him," said the Carp. "I have grown used to the bowl, but no more shall I be imprisoned in any way!"

Arthur unscrewed the lid as he sank, getting it off just as Leaf and Suzy helped him back up. They could kick much more efficiently than he could and he appreciated their help, even if every now and then one of their kicks connected with him rather than a vacant patch of sea water.

The Carp swam free. A tiny goldfish that turned to face the onrushing whale.

"Wednesday!" roared the Carp. "I, Part Three of the Will of Our Supreme Creator, the Ultimate Architect of All, do summon thee to fulfill thy duty as Trustee of the said Will!"

Drowned Wednesday slowed and shrank faster, though she still came forward. When she was thirty feet away, she was the size of a misshapen dolphin. It leapt into the air – and when it came down, it was a woman who stood upon the sea as if it were land.

She was not the misshapen, lumpy thing Arthur had seen before. She was beautiful, impeccably dressed in a gown of shimmering mother-of-pearl, the trident of the Third Key glowing in her hand. Only the uncontrollable trembling of that hand and the blue blood flowing down from her bitten lip indicated the difficulty she had keeping such a presentable shape.

"I, Wednesday, Trustee of the Ultimate Architect of All, do acknowledge the Third Part of the Will and ask into whose hands shall I place that which was entrusted to me?"

Arthur knew what came next. Without prompting from the Carp, and held up by Leaf and Suzy, he spoke quickly but clearly.

"I, Arthur, anointed Heir to the Kingdom, claim this Key and with it Mastery of the Border Sea. I claim it by blood and bone and contest, out of truth, in testament and against all trouble."

The trident flew from Wednesday's hand to Arthur's. As his fingers closed around it, he felt himself rise out of the sea, Suzy and Leaf letting go.

At the same time, Drowned Wednesday cried out in pain and doubled over, sinking into the water. She clutched her stomach and rolled, her arms and legs ballooning.

"Be as you were," commanded Arthur, pointing the Third Key at her. "When you were never hungry, when the Architect was still here."

The puffiness retreated, but Wednesday remained hunched over, still sinking.

"Float!" commanded Arthur. He felt the trident hum in his grasp and the sea around Wednesday momentarily shone a deep, rich blue. Wednesday bobbed to the surface, clawing at her stomach.

"Too late, Lord Arthur," croaked the Denizen. "I am poisoned within. Nothing eats at my flesh and bone, and soon I shall be no more. But I thank you, for I did not wish to end as I was, a vast thing, near mindless in hunger. Rule my Border Sea well, Lord Arthur!"

Something small and jewel-like sparkled in her mouth as she spoke. It trembled on her lip long enough for Arthur to see what it was, and in the instant that it fell, he directed the power of the Third Key upon it.

"*Balaena*," he said, naming it so his directions would not go astray. "Float over there and stay small until you do."

He waved the trident and the tiny metal cigar-shape that was the *Balaena* floated through the air and over to a clear patch of sea. Arthur dipped his trident and it slowly fell. As it hit the sea, there was a huge eruption of water, from which the full-sized submersible emerged, looking battered but intact.

Arthur looked back at Drowned Wednesday, but all that was left was a horrid, oily slick of Nothing that was moving against the wind towards Leaf and Suzy.

Arthur pointed the trident at it, relishing the feel of power flowing through it and into him.

"Return to the Void!" he ordered. The sea flashed gold in answer and all that had been Drowned Wednesday vanished.

CHAPTER THIRTY-ONE

Arthur hardly moved for at least a minute after he'd banished the Nothing. He felt stunned. It had happened so quickly, and now one of the seven Trustees of the Architect was not only defeated, but dead.

And the Third Key to the Kingdom was in Arthur's hand.

"How about helping us all walk on water?" asked Suzy finally, when Arthur continued to just stand there staring at the trident in his hand.

"Sorry," he mumbled. He waved the trident and visualised Suzy and Leaf rising out of the waves. This happened, but they shot up about twenty feet, then splashed down again up to their waists, before getting a proper footing.

"What happens now?" asked Leaf.

"We must commandeer that ship and get swiftly to Port Wednesday," said the Carp, who had suddenly grown up to a similar size it had been when they first met. "There will be a tremendous amount of work to see to. Ha-ha. Pardon me. There will be a great deal of work. A new Noon and Dusk will need to be appointed. I shall have to meet with Dame Primus, with a view to... ahem... consolidating my paragraphs into the greater whole. I believe the Border Sea has spread where it should not, so the bounds will need to be reestablished. Judging from Feverfew's loot, considerable unauthorised and dangerous trading has been going on between the House and the Secondary Realms and this must be regulated..."

The Carp continued, but Arthur wasn't listening. There was a whole lot of stuff popping to the surface just near the bow of the *Balaena*. Salvage, floating up from the depths. One item had caught his attention. Something small and round, in a particular shade of yellow. He walked over to it, ignoring the Carp's indignant call.

The object was a fluffy yellow elephant. A sleeping elephant, curled into a ball. Its head and trunk were bare, the yellow fluff worn down to the cloth underneath.

Arthur picked it up. It was his elephant. The one toy his

birth parents had been able to give him before they died. He'd had it for years and years, but had lost it on his fifth birthday when he took it to a picnic that had been suddenly abandoned due to rain. Bob and Emily had hunted for it the next day, and his older brothers and sisters had as well, several times, but Elephant had never been found.

Arthur slowly put Elephant in his pocket and turned back to where the others were waiting. As he did so, the hatch in the conning tower of the *Balaena* sprang open behind him. A Rat, his head swathed in bloodied bandages, climbed out, then reached back in and helped Dr Scamandros emerge.

"Lord Arthur! You did it! You defeated Drowned Wednesday!" the doctor called.

"She helped me," said Arthur. "I'm glad you're OK. What happened?"

"Uh, the full story may have to wait," said Scamandros hurriedly. He climbed down on to the hull as more Rats came out of the conning tower and deployed an inflatable raft. "I fear this vessel is held together merely by my own poor sorcery, and that is rather coming adrift as well. In fact, if you wouldn't mind, Lord Arthur?"

Arthur pointed the Key at the submersible.

"Don't sink!"

His hand trembled as he gave that directive, and Arthur

was surprised to find that it took an effort to hold the trident up. It began to shake in his hand and grow unpleasantly warm.

"Nothing contamination," gasped Scamandros as he was helped into the raft. "As soon as everyone's out you'd best let it go."

Arthur nodded. He had to grab the Key with his other hand – it took all his strength to hold it level. It felt like the Key was some kind of lever, propping up a very heavy weight.

There was no movement at the conning tower. The Key began to slip down, then when Arthur thought he couldn't hold it up any longer, Longtayle popped out. The Rat jumped from the conning tower straight into the sea, as the raft pushed off. As it did so, Scamandros fell back in a faint. Large parts of the *Balaena* crumpled or fell off as he did.

"Go," said Arthur. "Return to the Void."

The submersible collapsed in on itself, becoming a small, dark star for just a second. Then it too was gone.

Arthur put his left hand in his pocket and felt the soft synthetic fur of Elephant, weighing it up against the heft of the Key in his right hand. He could feel the power of the Key still, flowing gently through his arm. Changing him, making him into a Denizen. Making it impossible for him to be human.

If he kept using it.

"Ho, Arthur!"

The hail was not from the Carp. It was as loud or louder, but far deeper in tone. Arthur jumped and looked around.

The three-masted brigantine was heaving-to only a hundred yards away and its Captain was calling from the quarterdeck, without the aid of a speaking trumpet. He was tall and craggy, and cradled a harpoon that glittered and shone with unearthly light.

"I came as fast as the winds could carry me across a dozen worlds," shouted the Mariner. "Yet it seems you do not need my help at all, for now you walk where others must swim or stand upon a wooden deck!"

Arthur shook his head. All that fearful time pleading for help, hoping the Mariner's disc would do something, and *now* he came!

"I'm not walking on water for long," shouted Arthur. He put the Third Key through his belt. As it left his hand, he started to sink into the sea once again, as did Suzy and Leaf.

"So," called Arthur, just before he got a mouthful of sea water, "we do need someone to take us – and three thousand Denizens – to Port Wednesday, as soon as it can be done."

"We'll take you," answered the Mariner. "As for your

three thousand Denizens, there are five vessels manned by fine Rats following not far behind. They'll take on passengers, for a fee."

"Wednesday's Noon will arrange payment," Arthur answered, the brigantine drifting closer, so he didn't have to shout so loud.

"There is no Wednesday's Noon," objected the Carp.

"He used to be called Sunscorch," said Arthur. "We'll fix up the formalities when we get ashore, provided he wants the job. There'll be a new Dusk too, if he wants the job when he regains consciousness. A Denizen called Dr Scamandros."

"This is most irregular," said the Carp. "I believe you're supposed to consult me about such matters."

"Believe away," said Arthur. He put his head down and swam a few strokes to the net the brigantine's crew had flung over the side. "I'll see you in Port Wednesday, if you're quick."

"What? What?" asked the Carp. "What are you going to do?"

"I'm going to go home," said Arthur. "Just to make sure everything's all right. Then I'm going to come back and take on Sir Thursday. And I'm keeping the Third Key for now. I just won't use it too much."

"But you're needed here!" protested the Carp. It was goggling at him as only a goggle-eyed fish could do. "The

Key is needed here! Without it the balance between the Border Sea, the Realms and Nothing may go all awry!"

Arthur had started climbing the net, with Suzy and Leaf close behind. He stopped and hung there, looking back down at the Carp.

"I need it!" he shouted. "I'm tired of being powerless when the Morrow Days come and attack my family and my world, or drag me back here straight into trouble. Like I said, I'm only going to zip home and make sure everything's OK, then I'll come back. I don't want to, but I know I have to."

He started climbing again, but as he reached the deck he stopped and looked down at the Carp once more.

"So just leave me alone!"

"It won't," said Leaf. "Just like the Morrow Days."

"I know!" snapped Arthur. "I know—"

"Please excuse me," interrupted Suzy in a very prim and proper voice. "I must immediately find something suitable to change into. Miss Leaf, I daresay I could find a dress for you too."

"A dress!?" asked Leaf. "Why would I want to wear *a dress*?"

"She promised Dame Primus to behave properly on the Border Sea," said Arthur hastily. "So that's another good reason for all of us to get out of here."

"Indeed, I am most eager to return to more civilised

regions," said Suzy. She nodded slightly to Arthur and Leaf, then hurried across the deck, pausing only to offer a curtsey to the Mariner, who tipped his cap and chuckled before striding over to offer his hand to Arthur, who shook it firmly.

"Where away, Lord Arthur?" asked the Mariner. "I've a mind to take a cruise around the Border Sea, for it's long since I sailed these waters, but I'll land you wherever you please."

"Like back on Earth?" asked Leaf.

The Mariner bent his piercing blue gaze on her.

"A ship's boy should generally include 'sir' in their questions," he said. "Yes, I could sail this ship to Earth, for wherever the Border Sea's waters have lapped a shore, so they may touch again. But I do not think it would be wise. The Border Sea has already spread too far and that fish was right. The shores and bounds of this Sea need to be fixed once more by the Third Key."

"I said I'll be back with the Key," protested Arthur. "But for now, can you take us to Port Wednesday so we can get an elevator to the Lower House?"

"Aye," said the Mariner. "Port Wednesday it is."

"Where do we go from the Lower House?" asked Leaf.

"Through the Front Door," said Arthur wearily. He bent his left leg and looked down at the crab armour. The Third Key could remove that, but he thought he'd leave it on till the last moment. It was going to be hard to explain what had happened to the original cast. "Straight back to the hospital, I hope, a few seconds after we left."

"So it'll still be Wednesday?"

"Yep."

"Longest Wednesday I've ever had," said Leaf. "I'll be happy to get home."

"Me too," said Arthur.

CHAPTER THIRTY-TWO

"Arthur, are you sure you're OK?" asked Emily. She was hovering over his bed again.

The boy looked at her, but did not speak or meet her gaze.

Emily turned away to check the readouts on the diagnostic equipment next to the bed.

"Come on, son," said Bob from the other side. "Just tell us you're OK. I know it must have been a terrible shock to have that water main exploding like that, but you're all checked out now. No injuries."

The boy rolled over and buried his face in the pillow. Emily and Bob exchanged glances over his back.

"We're just going outside for a little while," said Emily. She gestured at the door. "But we'll be close."

"There's no water main here, either," added Bob. "I've checked. Nothing can go wrong."

Arthur's parents tiptoed out and closed the door. In the corridor, they both took deep breaths.

"He's never been like this before," said Emily. "Never, even when he's been barely conscious with a whole team working to re-establish his breathing."

"It was a weird accident though," said Bob. "Must have been a huge shock. That sudden over-pressure in the firefighting riser. No one's been able to explain it to me."

"Budget cuts," said Emily wearily. "The hospital hasn't been properly maintained for years. I just don't understand why Arthur won't talk. He just... I don't know... he just doesn't seem himself."

Inside the room, the Skinless Boy grinned and let the illusory flesh that covered half his body slide away to reveal the red ochre bones of the skeleton beneath.

THE KEYS TO THE KINGDOM

will be continued in

SIR
THURSDAY

For a sneak preview,
please read on...

On the fourth day, there was War!

Following their adventures in the Border Sea, Arthur and Leaf head for home. But only Leaf gets through the Front Door. Arthur is blocked because someone – or something – has assumed his identity and is taking over his life.

Before Arthur can take action, he is drafted by Sir Thursday and forced to join the Glorious Army of the Architect. The Army has its headquarters in the Great Maze, a defensive area of the House. Half of the Maze has already been dissolved by Nothing, and hordes of Nithlings emerge regularly to attack the rest. If the Nithling invasion can overcome the Army and the Great Maze, the House will be lost and the whole universe with it.

While Leaf tries to banish Arthur's doppelgänger on earth, Arthur must survive his basic training, avoid getting posted to the Front and work out how he can free Part Four of the Will and gain the Fourth Key from Sir Thursday. If the latest, strongest and most dangerous Nithling offensive doesn't break through first...

About the Author

Garth Nix was born on a Saturday in Melbourne, Australia, and got married on a Saturday, to his publisher wife, Anna. So Saturday is a good day. Garth used to write every Sunday afternoon because he has had a number of day jobs over the years that nearly always started on a Monday, usually far too early. These jobs have included being a bookseller, an editor, a PR consultant and a literary agent. Tuesday has always been a lucky day for Garth, when he receives good news, like the telegram (a long time ago, in the days of telegrams) that told him he had sold his first short story, or when he heard his novel *Abhorsen* had hit *The New York Times* bestseller list.

Wednesday can be a letdown after Tuesday, but it was important when Garth served as a part-time soldier in the

Australian Army Reserve, because that was a training night. Thursday is now particularly memorable because Garth and Anna's son, Thomas, was born on a Thursday afternoon. Friday is a very popular day for most people, but since Garth has become a full-time writer it has no longer marked the end of the work week, however Garth and Anna's second son, Edward, was born on a Friday morning so it is now a special day too. On any day, Garth may generally be found around the beach suburb of Sydney where he and his family live.

GARTH NIX

THE KEYS TO THE KINGDOM

MISTER MONDAY

"Mister Monday slowly reached inside the left sleeve of his silk robe and pulled out a slender metal spike... He spoke too quickly for Arthur to make out what he was saying. He didn't slow down until he reached the final few words. 'And so let the will be done.'"

Arthur Penhaligon is not supposed to be a hero. He is supposed to die. But then he meets sinister Mister Monday and everything changes.

Seven days. Seven keys. One mysterious book. One strange house filled with secrets.

Dare Arthur enter and accept the fate that awaits him within?

HarperCollins *Children's Books*

www.garthnix.com

GARTH
NIX

THE KEYS TO THE KINGDOM
GRIM TUESDAY

"Grim Tuesday had hidden the Second Clause of the Will, and had once been sure that no one else would ever reach it. But now the first part had escaped and found itself a Rightful Heir. That meant Grim Tuesday would be next..."

When Arthur left the strange house that had almost killed him on Monday, he didn't expect to be called back there the very next day. But with his family and friends in danger, he has no choice.

The stakes are high. And time is ticking.

HarperCollins *Children's Books*

www.garthnix.com

GARTH NIX

The Ragwitch

*The person in front of Paul was a hideous mixture of
girl and doll: half flesh, half cloth, and the eyes and face had
nothing of Julia left at all, only the evil features of the doll.*

When Julia finds the ugly doll in the strange ball of feathers
on the beach, Paul instinctively knows his sister has meddled
with something that is going to cause trouble. But already it's
too late – the power behind the doll has his sister in its thrall
and, later that night, the Ragwitch claims Julia for its own.

Fighting against his natural urge to run from this hideous
being, Paul is drawn into the creature's own world. Can he
save his sister or even himself?

HarperCollins *Children's Books*

www.garthnix.com